Do you like dinosaurs
and other
forms
of
prehistoric life?

If so, be sure to check out
PREHISTORIC MAGAZINE
www.PrehistoricMagazine.com

PREHISTORIC

Michael Esola

CRANE CANYON PUBLISHING

ISBN: 0692375856
eBook ISBN:
ISBN 13: 9780692375853
Library of Congress Control Number: 2015931932
Crane Canyon Publishing
Pittsburg Ca.

Cover design copyright ©2015 by Michael Esola

Printed in the United States of America

Visit Michael Esola on the world wide web at:
www.MikeEsola.com

To my Aunt Karen (Ganghi) who first introduced me to Jurassic Park all those years ago, and to whom I credit with starting me on this journey into prehistory and all the mysteries of the world. I love you very much, and this book is dedicated to you.

"I do not rise each morning to do the simple, mundane tasks of the common man; rather I rise each morning to follow myself each and every day. Always have and always will."

--John Corstine, Creator of the Boardwalk

PROLOGUE

The boardwalk sprung to life as the Indonesian man fled for his life. He flew across the boards as fast as his legs would allow for, sucking in huge breaths of the warm and humid jungle air as he pushed himself onward, past the point of complete exhaustion, past the point of knowing the difference between pain and sheer suffering. Whatever it was that was on his tail could smell him, and was closing the gap on him. An urge dating back eons drove it forward in its relentless pursuit of the man.

Fire. The man's lungs registered an intense burning sensation as he pushed himself far beyond what he ever had known before. Time seemed to stand still for him in a strange out-of-body experience, as he tripped over his own feet, his body sailing rhythmically through the air before gravity stepped in and gripped him tightly in its clutches. He fell to the boardwalk with a loud and resounding thud, rolling and skidding several feet before finally coming to a complete stop. For a moment he just lay there, completely senseless and dazed by the short but intense fall from grace.

The tingling vibration rippling through the boardwalk sprung him back to his feet as the will to live had not left him. His feet quickly began running down the boardwalk once again, limping somewhat but still carrying him nonetheless. Whatever it was that continued to pursue him, did not slow, rarely ever tired, and just continued to keep up its relenting pace, seeming to stop at nothing before it got what it wanted.

Little by little the man's tireless pace had taken its toll on his damaged leg, and he slowed somewhat. He could not believe the sight as his eyes struggled to take it all in. For up ahead some fifty yards or so was what appeared to be the end of the boardwalk, and like a train without train tracks to run on, he was about to become derailed.

The end to the incomplete boardwalk high in the rainforest canopy, dropped off some one hundred feet or so to the forest floor below. The man recoiled in horror at what his eyes were showing him.

Slowing himself he came to the edge of the boardwalk, the end resembling a massive sinkhole of sorts in the way it seemingly fell away from all that was familiar. He peered over the edge, and quickly at that, his eyes making their way all the way down to the forest floor below, the very bottom of this dense and steamy Southeast Asian rainforest ecosystem.

Looking over his shoulder frantically, he could hear what was pounding his way. As if a crazed serial killer were on his tail, his options were few and far between. Jump and face certain death, or face whatever it was that was rapidly thundering toward him.

His feet suddenly gave way from beneath him, as he fell backwards in the most sickening of contorted manners. Landing on his back with his legs bent underneath his body, he flailed his right arm back and tried to pull himself away from the edge, his bloody stump on the left was nothing more than a little reminder of the limb that used to be, and what had been taken from him in one clean bite only moments ago.

It had all happened so quickly for him. He had been busy doing survey work for John Corstine, the creator of the boardwalk, in what was essentially an area known as quadrant seven, meaning the last five miles of the boardwalk. Corstine himself had broken the thirty-five mile boardwalk project into seven quadrants, primarily for their own convenience as well as being able to accurately send out workers to various areas in order to address problems and difficulties as they arose. The man had been busy testing the structural integrity of quadrant seven when out from behind the foliage peeked something from his worst nightmares. Before he could even comprehend what was happening, that something opened up and chomped down, taking his left arm clean off.

The moments that followed were a dizzying mixture of blood-filled terror as the man ran for his life away from the foliage.

Bringing himself back to the present, inch by bloody inch, he dragged his body back away from the edge with only the power from his right arm. Exhausted from both the blood loss and the exertion necessary to pull himself backwards, he lay flat until he was looking up at the sky.

The white clouds, interspersed with what branches from the canopy extended and grew above the boardwalk, greeted his view. The clouds had formed swirl formations high above him, and for a moment he lost himself completely. His mind drifted towards freedom and the wide open spaces of the world. How he longed to simply let his body float to the safety of those soft and fluffy clouds high above, away from the world, and most importantly John Corstine's boardwalk.

He cursed to himself the day he ever first encountered both John Corstine and his vision to construct the boardwalk. It was to be a massive structure offering guests a once-in-a-lifetime opportunity to walk at the very top of the rainforest canopy on a scale never before seen while still preserving huge swaths of intact rainforest ecosystems. He cursed all of it, as well as the decent sized advance that Corstine had happily offered him for his assistance in the initial phase of the project.

Money, he managed to think to himself as he continued to bleed out. *The root of all evil.*

A tiny tingling sensation beneath him had now given way to small but noticeable vibrations in the boardwalk. With a steady stream of tears now running down his face, he heroically managed to hoist himself back to his feet, though weakly at that. He now stood inches from the edge staring down at the forest floor below.

Go out on my own terms, he thought. *Die by my own sword.*

And with that thought he stepped off the boardwalk and out into the open air.

No sooner than he had begun to fall towards the forest floor, something reached out from above and pierced him violently, and began to pull him in. Immediately he was overwhelmed with a hot stinking breath, and his last credible thought before darkness took him was that he was being eaten alive.

CHAPTER ONE

M ulti-millionaire real estate developer John Corstine stood as still as a statue and poised deep in thought. Corstine was sixty years old, average height and build, with a salt and pepper beard to go along with his gray hair up top. He was wearing dress slacks and a dress shirt. Corstine had been standing in his office at the corner for nearly ten minutes looking out at the magnificent lush view of the pristine green Indonesian rainforest that greeted his eyes. He had hardly moved as much as a muscle before finally deciding to stride to the other side of the large window pane. Corstine's office was in quadrant one of the boardwalk, high atop it, and made of light-weight materials, the same type of material one would expect to find with a portable classroom or modular unit in a school setting.

Corstine was looking at his baby, his creation, his dream. The boardwalk stood strong and covered nearly thirty-five miles of lush virgin Indonesian rainforest, and was an impressive seventy-five feet in width, give or take a few feet here or there where the architects had chosen to weave the boardwalk in and between what the rainforest trees gave them. The boardwalk stood approximately one hundred feet above the forest floor. It had been created with two goals in mind: the first being to protect a huge track of rainforest that was near and dear to Corstine's heart, and, second, to offer tourists and guests the chance of a lifetime to walk near the very top of the forest canopy on a wide stable flat platform, while paying top dollar to do so, something that was also very near and dear to Corstine's heart. Corstine planned to brand the image in the adventurer's mind of a walking path in the sky, made only for human foot traffic, and vastly different from what most rainforest canopy experiences offered up in terms of an unstable swaying base that shifted and moved as people walked about. Corstine wanted it to be as familiar as walking on solid ground.

Corstine let out a long and drawn out sigh. He was close, oh so very close, to his dream becoming a reality. His mind drifted back, way back, to his first business venture when he was in his early twenties. Corstine even at a very early age, had shown great promise as an entrepreneur as well as a keen interest in television. When he was fresh out of college, he decided he was going to start his own television channel. So he did what all entrepreneurs were supposed to do. He gathered all his notes and constructed a twenty-five page business plan, complete with a mission statement, financials, and five-year growth projections.

He could remember vividly gathering up the only suit and tie he owned, getting in his beat-up old Volkswagen, and driving to Los Angeles from San Francisco. He presented his business plan to a well-known businessman who had successfully launched two television channels. The memories were flooding back as Corstine now strode towards the middle of the room and sat at the head of the conference table. He sat down and rather than stop or fight the flood of memories, he dove right in and let them take him wherever they did.

He remembered standing at the office building of the man from whom he was seeking the initial startup capital investment. His heart beat wildly as he waited patiently and knocked on the open door of the office.

Standing there he slowly brought himself in front of the entrance, the man behind the desk motioning for him to have a seat while he finished his phone call. Corstine could still see himself bouncing his legs nervously as he waited to enter the office. By the time he finally entered, he had many an opportunity to make himself even more nervous.

The two sat down on a pair of plush leather couches, and before Corstine had another opportunity to talk himself into being nervous, he was asked to pitch his idea straight up. And quickly he did just that, blazing through his business plan like it were a homework assignment completed last minute the night before, talking way too fast and even getting tripped up on his own words from time to time. When it was all over, the television executive sat with his back straightened to the couch and promptly asked him a question while folding his arms.

"How old are you?"

Corstine cleared his throat before he replied, somewhat stunned at the harsh tone and abrupt nature of the question. "Twenty-six."

"Twenty-six," the T.V. executive repeated to himself, as if pondering the thought. "Twenty-six."

Corstine could feel a knot forming in his stomach.

The T.V. executive adjusted himself just before he spoke once again. "Look, no one is going to give millions of dollars to a kid to launch an idea. What you have here is simply an idea and not a full-fledged business. Nothing more, nothing less."

A knock at the door broke John Corstine from his thoughts and brought him back to the present day. He could see that he had failed to close his office door as his assistant Collin Fairbanks stood before him. Collin was in his late twenties, Caucasian, with dark brown slicked back hair, dressed in his usual attire of a suit and tie. Always a suit and tie everyday despite being in the middle of "bleeping nowhere," as Collin often referred to it as.

"Sir, all is squared away," Collin reported, still standing in the entranceway.

Corstine smiled. "Well done. Well done, indeed."

And with that Collin left Corstine to return to his thoughts. Corstine reclined in his seat with his hands behind his head and thought if that television executive could only see him now, if he could only see him now.

CHAPTER TWO

B ick Downs stood with his feet firmly planted on the west end of the boardwalk, quadrant one to be exact. He was only one hundred yards from John Corstine's corner office and where future patrons would hopefully pay top dollar and congregate before their rainforest canopy experience would begin. His hands were still feeling the effects somewhat, having just climbed down the black rope ladder that unfurled from the helicopter, blowing the tops of the trees back and forth in its powerful wake, and then slowly, but steadily, rose off into the blue Indonesian sky.

Downs was somewhat agitated and jittery from the drop, and this surprised him despite his love of all things extreme. He looked down at his large and calloused hands, the same hands that had taken him rock climbing in Yosemite National Park and trekking in the wilds of the Himalayas. Downs could see that his hands were still shaking somewhat. He wondered what was going on.

Maybe I'm getting too old for this, he thought, despite having just been minted as a new thirty year old. And then he shook his head and smiled, as if answering that very question himself.

In fact the way Downs saw it in his mind, he was now at the bottom of the social hierarchy of thirty year olds, the youngest of that batch of people. He felt he had been getting old when he was twenty-nine, at the top of that barrel, and now that he had entered a new age bracket, he was just starting off once again, clean slate and all.

Downs was both Italian and Austrian, and his workout regimen was what allowed him to stay in such amazing shape. Still though, his 6'3" 205 pound body was feeling the lingering effects from his arrival via the ladder down from the chopper. His lower back ached somewhat, followed by a deep and resonating burn in the back of his hamstrings. He reached up and rubbed his buzz cut with his hand, doing his best to sop up the sweat that was now dripping down the sides of his face, fully happy with his decision to buzz his brown hair to half an inch only days prior. He had by his own estimates about a week's worth of beard growth on his face. He knew that his beard had entered what many often referred to as the "itchy phase," and the humid conditions were only making things worse, far worse. He would just have to deal with it though.

Sweat continued to trickle down from his head to both sides of his face in a seemingly never-ending stream.

Downs checked his Nike wrist watch, wondering when the others would be touching down, and how? He did a 360 degree turn, wondering once again if they were here? Would their entrance be as grand as his, or would they use a more civilized approach like a huge grand staircase.

Downs moved forward a bit, and as he did so noticed for the first time the magnificent grand staircase that appeared to make its way down to the forest floor below. It seemed oddly out of place as he moved closer. He had been privy to a certain set of documents via the offices of John Corstine. These were quick to point out this grand staircase in all its beauty, showing how it started wide and formal at the bottom of the forest floor, gradually narrowing in the middle, and then beginning to widen once again until finally reaching its full width at the top of the boardwalk for all to marvel in as they ascended the last stair. He followed the sweeping staircase with his eyes for about forty feet before dense green foliage seemed to swallow it completely from visibility. Downs knew from the aerial photos from Corstine's office that it did continue on though. He also knew that Corstine was no fool, and wouldn't build staircases that led to nowhere, a la what Sarah Winchster had done in the early 1900's with the Winchester Mystery House.

"They should be here by now," he muttered to himself, once again glancing down at his Nike wrist watch for a quick time check.

Downs made his way forward until he was at the edge of the siding to the boardwalk and peered down over the railing. It was a long, long way down to the forest floor. He saw crisscrossing branches, vines, limbs, and a host of rainforest creepy crawlies that inhabited the canopy and the emergent layers of the rainforest.

As he continued to peer over the railing, he let his mind roam to casual science for a brief moment. He remembered from adolescence that rainforests are divided into different layers of vegetation. The top of the rainforest layer being the emergent layer, followed by the canopy layer, next the understory layer, and lastly the forest floor. Downs assumed that the boardwalk itself fell somewhere in between the emergent layer and canopy layer.

He continued to peer through the green leaves and branches, in some spots the interweaving and crisscrossing of the jungle itself was so dense that even the air itself seemed to be feeling the pinch. Downs could not see the forest floor below despite repeated attempts. Then something strange happened to him. It was a feeling from inside, and from where it came he did not know. As he stared down as far as his eyes would allow, a certain uneasiness washed over him. He suddenly felt flush and hot and had become quite dizzy to top it all off. He pulled away from the railing, sucking in deep breaths of the warm humid air.

He tilted his head back, looking up at the blue sky above. He felt nauseous, yet he forced himself once more to peer over the side.

Gripping the railing tightly he pulled himself closer to it, and then he closed his eyes as he continued to breathe in.

Slowly he opened his eyes, the dense jungle below him was still in clear focus, but the feeling of uneasiness remained. He held on until he could take no more and pulled back quickly from the railing.

Breathing hard, he hunched over and rested his hands on his knees.

"Mr. Downs, I presume," a voice suddenly rang out from behind.

Downs turned around instantly, somewhat shaken and more than likely with the unmistakable look of someone who was becoming sicker by the minute.

The man, in his late twenties, extended his hand towards him, and Downs managed a weak yet clammy handshake.

"Forgive me for disturbing you. I am Collin Fairbanks, Mr. Corstine's personal assistant. I look after Mr. Corstine's personal and corporate investments as well as his overall well being. I have been tasked with overseeing the boardwalk project through to its completion."

Downs took a big gulp, mustering all the strength he could as he took a good look at the well-dressed man in a suit and tie who stood before him. Collin's stunning dark suit was capped off by an equally bright and floor-stopping red tie. His hair was slicked back and his command of the English language was impeccable.

Collin once again spoke. "Forgive me, sir, but you look terribly ill. Can I please get you something?"

The manly side of Downs wanted to shake it off, dispelling what he was experiencing as nothing more than a minor inconvenience, but he knew deep down that his body was telling him something. Downs had never been the type of person to take free hand outs. He was always the kid in sports who never needed water in time-outs, proving to everyone else that he was both mentally and physically stronger than all. However, today was different. He wasn't quite certain what it was that was different. He just didn't feel himself. He wasn't up to his usual over-the-top adventuresome self.

What he did next surprised even himself, as he turned and nodded affirmatively to Collin Fairbanks' question.

CHAPTER THREE

Downs was seated on a plush leather sofa bordering a huge glass window with a view of the rainforest that only someone without the ability to see would not have been enamored by. Collin had gone off to fetch him some sort of libation, most assuredly water. Downs continued to just sit there, staring and taking in his surroundings. He felt like he was in a portable unit that was decorated far too fancy, trying to be something it was not, made to feel as if one were in a real office building. In the dead center of the room was a desk that most likely would be for a future office secretary, but for now the small area had only a flat screen computer and a chair to accompany it.

Downs' stomach had settled and his body was feeling closer to normal than not normal. He was still shocked at the whole height and uneasiness feeling that had crept over him. How in the world could he be feeling a fear of heights? He had never been afraid of heights before, and then, all of a sudden, something like the incident earlier hit him full bore. He wondered if it was just the boardwalk in general that had him feeling jittery and off his game.

His eyes began to gravitate towards his surroundings once more. The office space, although plain and rather unassuming by its outward appearance, was rather quaint and spectacular on the inside. The sweeping views of the rainforest were provided by several large windows. For a second Downs couldn't get over the fact that he was in a comfortable office setting, high atop the canopy of an immense rainforest ecosystem. It was all so very surreal.

Downs stood to his feet and made his way towards the window that was nearly the entire wall length itself. He looked out at the rainforest, wondering how in the hell someone could even plow and cut a track through the seemingly impenetrable walls and walls of thick vegetation. Even with all the money in the world this seemed almost impossible. The growth was dense, and he knew that space for new plants to grow and compete with the older plants of the forest was at a premium on the forest floor. Jutting up and towering high above the rainforest canopy were huge trees that upon first glance looked like massive eucalyptus trees, but Downs knew better. Taking in these towering behemoths, he shrugged his shoulders knowing that he would most likely learn more about them once the tour began.

His eyes gravitated towards the hallway to which Collin had retreated and wandered down. In dark bold lettering on the wall printed:

CORSTINE HOLDINGS, INC.

Downs smiled to himself, knowing full well the type of financial backing that John Corstine brought to his fanatical pursuit of bringing life to this huge boardwalk endeavor. He knew that Corstine himself had, undoubtedly, brought a large portion of the investment needed to bring the boardwalk to fruition. Yet Downs also knew that Corstine was a shrewd businessman who most likely brought on other investors to fund the building of the boardwalk to its completion. However, the death of the Indonesian worker only a few weeks ago had scared off several of his foreign overseas investors, leaving the creator of the boardwalk scrambling to find other investors to fill in the missing pieces to the puzzle. Most importantly, this left him with an incomplete boardwalk.

Already his mind was beginning to take it all in, weighing the options as to whether or not this was the type of investment in which his dad would have wanted to participate in. More importantly, would his dad have wanted to and have been patient enough to wait the five years that Corstine said it would take before the boardwalk was indeed profitable and could offer significant returns for its investors.

Downs' head focused on his dad. It had been seventeen years since his father had gone missing in a remote part of the world, much like the one Downs found himself in at the current moment. He lowered his head before finally coming back to the present.

One investor from Australia openly expressed that he simply could not wait the proposed five years for the venture to become profitable, and he backed out rather late in the game. The back out of the Australian investor more than likely created a ripple effect, because following his departure from the project an English investor followed suit, and lastly a Chinese woman in her late twenties living in Hong Kong, worth slightly North of one billion, backed out as well.

Patience, Downs thought to himself. *All good things take time, and any good investor or business man knows this.*

Downs continued to gaze out the window, his thoughts leaving the world of investing and company profitability behind. His eyes took in the outside surroundings. He marveled at how the green landscape before him rippled up and down with differing elevations at different points, stemming from the fact that the trees themselves were all various heights. The never ending blanket of green flowed out in all directions and captured his full attention as he pressed himself up against the glass, just as he used to do back when he was but a wee child at the San Francisco Academy of Sciences.

"I trust you're enjoying the view," Collin suddenly said, interrupting Down's walk down memory lane.

Downs spun around to see the assistant walking towards him with a cold drink in hand. Collin promptly handed him an ice cold glass full of what appeared to be Sprite.

"I trust this will aid in the settling of your stomach," Collin said.

"Thanks," Downs replied and gulped it down in a few aggressive mouthfuls.

"Walk with me," Collin said.

Downs did just that, placing the glass down on the future secretary's desk and following the assistant down a hallway until the two of them entered a conference room. Collin motioned for him to have a seat, and he sat down in the middle of the long conference table. As Downs waited for Collin to have a seat at the head of the table, he could see what looked like a series of various financial projections on the walls.

Downs didn't look too closely, his eyes darting back to Collin as the assistant scooted his chair towards the table, but he knew that they had to be the five year projections about which Corstine had previously mentioned to investors.

Five years to turn a profit, Downs thought. *Dad would still be interested in it despite the length of time.*

"As you may know," Collin said, "Mr. Corstine has assembled really an exquisite group of investors for this venture. Very nice and wonderfully diverse, if I do say so myself."

Downs nodded his head as his eyes darted one last time towards the wall.

Yep, he thought to himself. *The five-year projections.*

"But a venture such as this one," Collin continued, "needs vast amounts of capital. Capital for when things are going good, and capital for when the monsoon rains drench this part of the world. I trust you catch my drift."

"Hence the guided tour this weekend," Downs said.

Collin smiled with his hands clasped atop the table. "Precisely. Let me cut straight to the chase Mr. Downs. Your father's respectable fortune could potentially represent some of the last and final pieces to the investor conundrum currently plaguing Mr. Corstine's project. Think wisely this weekend as you are on the tour Mr. Downs. Think wisely."

Downs didn't reply, rather he let out an uncomfortable chuckle.

"Well," Collin said looking down at his watch. "Time to gather with the others. Your rainforest canopy experience is about to begin."

CHAPTER FOUR

Downs was escorted out of the conference room and past the financial projections for the boardwalk. The assistant led him out via the hallway through which they entered and politely showed him to the door, before returning back to his own small and cluttered office to handle more of John Corstine's personal affairs.

Do you trust him? Downs thought to himself.

Downs felt as though his gut had already told him the answer, yet he was fighting in an effort to not jump to conclusions so quickly. One thing he did know with certainty was there was something deceiving and deceitful in the eyes of Collin Fairbanks. He couldn't quite place it, and he hated the idea of rushing to judgment so soon, but there was something in his eyes that had caught Downs' attention. The thought itself was quickly flushed from his mind as the sight of a small gathering of people could be seen just outside on the boardwalk. Downs exited the building and was instantly greeted with the thick and sweltering air that hit him like a punch to the face. His skin and hair seemed to perspire almost instantaneously, and there was that annoying beard itch again, or at least his brain was busy convincing him so.

All eyes were on Downs the minute he came into visibility. Calmly though he made his way towards them, being sure not to walk too fast. Rather he stuck his chest out and held his head up high. He did his best walk as if he were striding down the eighteenth fairway of a golf tournament about to close out and defeat the finest professional golfers in the world.

"The famous Bick Downs," a cocky and arrogant voice said, though it took Downs a moment before he could put two and two together and put a name to a face. "Did Daddy's estate send ya on a little overseas excursion to do some potential investment speculation for the old portfolio?"

The rude comment drew a snicker from the others.

Downs knew the man, though he had never met him before in his entire life. William Jamison was his name, and Downs had spent the better part of his childhood watching him as he raced up and down the NBA basketball courts for sixteen seasons for the New York Knicks, before eventually old age sent him into retirement.

Downs looked at the overwhelmingly large man. At the age of fifty, William Jamison was still quite the specimen at 6'9", 265 pounds. He had arms that made him look like he could still go toe-to-toe with any NBA big man. He was in a type of physical condition those half his age would give their left arm for.

"Well, all of you are in good hands with Ms. Kingsworth," Collin interrupted from somewhere behind the group. "But before I go, Mr. Corstine has one simple last request of all of you."

Out of his back pocket Collin pulled a black hefty garbage bag and opened it up. Downs cocked his head to the side ever so slightly, wondering what in the hell the assistant was getting at.

Collin then made his way to the circle with the garbage bag wide open. "If you will. Mr. Corstine has requested that he have your utmost attention out there and that you, therefore, remove yourself literally from the world for the duration of this weekend. Your cooperation would be most appreciated in regards to his wishes."

Like little children who had just been caught red-handed with candy and toys and been told to give them back, each member of the group reached into his or her pockets and dropped all iPhone's, tablets, kindles, and any other worldly connections into the garbage bag. Some even had multiple phones that were dropped inside the bag. As the bag made its way around to Downs, he, too, did the same, pulling his Samsung Galaxy phone out from his back pocket and dropping it into the bag. He never was one to fully buy into the iPhone mass market craze.

The liberation was almost instantaneous as Downs felt the connection to the technological twenty-first century go straight down to the bottom of that black garbage bag. Although Downs felt a sense of liberation, and to him it was almost an intoxicating, wonderfully warm spreading feeling that radiated to all parts of his body, he could see that the looks on the faces of the others did not hold the same joy. After all, they had companies to run, stocks and portfolios to check, and income property to manage and oversee.

Downs too had his own small business, an extreme action sports store located beneath a six unit apartment building that was willed to him upon his father's disappearance. Although the business had been in a steady state of decline, he had ideas about how to bring it to profitability. In the mean time though, he was somewhat looking forward to the mental break away from the world of cell phones and constant distractions.

"It'll do you all some good to get out and disconnect a bit," a voice said.

Downs looked up to see a very attractive brunette standing about ten feet or so from the group, dressed in khaki shorts and tan hiking boots. Downs had been so preoccupied by the small gathering of people that he had failed to realize her presence.

"That's the spirit, and on behalf of Mr. Corstine, he and I would like to formally welcome you to the Rainforest Canopy Experience,"

Collin said as he wrapped the bag up and slung it over his shoulder. With that he made his way, garbage bag and all back to his office.

"My name is Nat Kingsworth, and I'll be your weekend guide."

Downs' eyes bulged forward a bit, looking at her. She must have been 5'9" and possibly in her late twenties, with brunette hair and a pistol holstered at her side. Downs was busy pondering the need for the pistol in the first place, when suddenly an elbow nudged him from behind. He turned to see a familiar face, a very familiar face to put it bluntly.

"Holy crap," Downs blurted out. "They told me you weren't coming," he said with a big high five to the man.

Standing before Downs was what he had considered for the better part of his life to be his best friend, Josiah Young. At thirty two years of age, Josiah was slightly older than Downs, but the two had grown up together and spent many a day enjoying the San Francisco Bay Area and all that it had to offer. At six feet tall and mixed with African and Irish heritages, Josiah possessed the most striking of good looks. He had a light beard and sported shoulder length dread locks.

"You know me," Josiah said, "I always like to make that great big entrance."

Downs smiled and turned to see the entire group staring their way, the reunion of the two good friends on display for all to see. Quickly though both of them made their way towards the circle.

"Where was I then?" Nat asked. "Right, introductions."

CHAPTER FIVE

"I'll go first," Nat said. "My name is Nat Kingsworth, and I'll be your interprctive guide for the duration of this weekend trip. Previously I worked at O'Reilly Rainforest reserve in Queensland, Australia as an interpretive guide, where I spent my days hiking up and down the jungle hillside situated next to the resort giving beautiful little rainforest tours. Quite an exquisite place if you ever happen to find yourself in that part of the world."

Nat turned to her left, looking at a white male, late forties who stood about six feet in height and was slightly overweight.

"Ridley Bells here," the man said with a low yet surprisingly sophisticated tone. "Previously the Founder of two television channels with a third in the works." That's all he said, keeping it sweet and to the point with a slight smile.

"Great, I like the brevity," Nat said. "Continuing on."

"Hi, everyone, I'm Frederick Douglass," the overweight average height Caucasian man said in a deep and booming voice. "I founded what is currently the largest online magazine dedicated to raising capital on the internet. And no direct relation to the famous historical figure Frederick Douglass, and yes I've had to answer that question my entire life."

William Jamison spoke up next. "Maybe we oughta get you to do a feature of Corstine's little pet project here in your magazine."

"We'll get to you in a second, William," Nat said. "Okay, Frederick, anything else you'd like to add?"

He paused for a moment looking up at the sky. "Avid reader and each year make the annual pilgrimage to Comic-Con where I'm usually reduced to a giddy school boy waiting in line for autographs with the rest of the hordes of fans."

"Might want to leave that last Comic-Con part off the old online dating profile there, Big Guy. It might scare the chicks away," Jamison cracked. "Chicks dig athlete's, man."

Downs looked over at Nat as the interpretive guide simply rolled her eyes. "Okay, William. Give your brief, and I do want to emphasize brief background."

Jamison chuckled and stepped forward a few paces. "Where do I begin? After a stellar three sport career in high school, I made my way to Ohio State where I headlined the basketball team there. We woulda cut down the nets my senior year but the lure of the NBA eventually drew me in."

Guess you didn't headline four years then, Downs sarcastically thought to himself.

Jamison continued on. "Woulda, coulda, shoulda turned into a sixteen year career in the NBA. Following that I formed my own consulting company working with young NBA players helping them transition into multi-millionaire status. And just last year I penned my first novel which recently hit the bestseller list and is currently under option by New Line Cinema for big screen movie status. I divide my time between Los Angeles and Martha's Vineyard."

"Well," Nat began, her voice not seeming impressed in the least bit. "Thank you, William, that's quite a bio. Moving on, next."

"Um hello everyone, Max Caldwell here," the young looking man in his mid-twenties said, straightening out his glasses. "Zoologist by degree, adventurer in my heart. Um, looking to possibly get into crocodile relocation work, and I'll be your resident zoologist for the next two days or forty-eight hours pointing out anything that catches your eye as well as mine."

"Cute," Jamison muttered quietly. "Real cute. Would you like fries with that happy meal?"

"Josiah Young, everyone. Personal guest of Bick over here."

Jamison snickered to the others. "You're a poet and you don't even know it."

"William, please," Nat said. "I must insist you let everyone finish so we can get on with it. Our precious time on this tour has already begun to tick."

Jamison did not reply and hardly said anything, not even acknowledging Nat's comment.

"As I was saying, Josiah Young here. Wished I could have played sixteen years in the NBA. Big fan of yours over the years by the way. Instead, currently have taken my passion for dinosaurs as an adolescent and trying to turn it into my career. Working in the education department at my local museum and in year one of earning my doctorate in vertebrae paleontology. Trying to follow my dreams, but most importantly not allowing anyone to tell me what I can and can't do."

"Nice," Nat said. "Very nice indeed. Especially love the motivational part at the end."

"A brotha, diggin' up dinosaurs bones," Jamison said with a shake of the head. "I just don't get it. I simply just don't get it. Out of all the fields out there, you want to do that."

Downs was baffled by what he was hearing, and by the sound of it, so was everyone else. Not a word was said regarding Jamison's comment.

Nat looked over at Downs, smiled once again and nodded for him to proceed.

"Bick Downs here," Downs said, looking at everyone except William Jamison. "Here on behalf of my father's estate and currently looking to invest in this project. A lover of all things extreme as well as outdoors. Currently own and run a small action sports store in the Potrero Hill neighborhood of San Francisco. Ecstatic to be here in what is my favorite habitat on earth, the rainforest."

Nat gave Downs one last look and then nodded, signaling all was done. And with that she applauded. "Well, very nice to meet all of you, and without further adieu, let's head out and begin our experience."

CHAPTER SIX

C ollin Fairbanks dialed the first contact that came up on his smart phone and waited several seconds as the phone continued to ring on the other end.

"Corstine," the voice said.

"All done, sir, and as you call it, the twenty-first century consumer of time, aka the cell phone, has been removed from each individual. And without using excessive force, I might add. All complied without a struggle. Nice, neat, and orderly," Collin said proudly.

"Excellent," Corstine replied. The real-estate tycoon had within the last hour left the boardwalk and retreated to his small rainforest bungalow only a short distance from the ground entrance to the boardwalk. "Make sure you stay in constant radio contact with her and keep me updated should a problem arise."

Corstine hung up before Collin even had a chance to reply.

John Corstine reclined in his outdoor lawn chair on the small and somewhat confined patio in the back of his bungalow. From his chair he had a very up close and personal view of the rainforest as the thick and dense impenetrable jungle budded right up to the small slab of cement. The patio served as nothing more than possibly an area to relax with a drink and entertain a guest or two while taking in the sights and sounds of the rainforest.

Corstine sipped gingerly at the beer he had been nursing for quite some time. He was tired and needed the rest. Corstine was already feeling the lingering effects that the boardwalk was having upon him. For the past forty days and forty nights, Corstine had been acting as a scavenger, sleeping sometimes only an hour or two and being up at all hours of the day searching for capital, the very capital that the boardwalk not only needed to survive but to get completed and up and running in a timely manner.

Corstine took another sip and savored the flavors blending together in his mouth as he continued to stare at the dense vegetation that pinched tightly around his small patio on all sides. He breathed in the warm and humid air, and although it provided little relief from the humidity, simply being out in the open and away from the eight hundred pound gorilla that was raising capital felt good, only if it was for an hour or so.

Corstine decided to take the rest of the evening off, to sit back and wait, and to see if there were any takers in the form of investors responding to all the feelers he had sent out. He wondered hard about that, because if not, it would be back to the drawing board for him, and that was not a route he wanted to traverse down again. Corstine pondered about the idea of putting up the remaining amount of capital himself, but he as well as his financial advisors knew that an overwhelming amount of his money was tied up in various investments around the world. It would not be an ideal situation for him to front the last amount of money that the boardwalk needed. For now his Kindle e-reader was quietly and politely calling his name.

CHAPTER SEVEN

Downs had rather unassumingly slid into the dead last position of the group, not that he had to, but for some reason or other that was the way it worked out. Josiah was in front of him with Max positioned more towards the front next to Nat. Downs figured that if he had any pressing scientific questions lingering at the tip of his tongue, he would pass them Josiah's way for the time being.

The entire group was wired to Nat Kingsworth at the front via wireless headsets as well as wired to one another. If he or she had something to chime in with, they could simply do so over the radio. The same went for Max Caldwell, who would be pointing out various interesting biological flora and fauna as the team made its way across John Corstine's boardwalk.

"Not much up this high in terms of ancient life," Downs said, tapping Josiah on the shoulder from behind.

"Wrong," Josiah replied back as he slowed his pace, giving the others room to go ahead while ensuring some privacy for an exchange of words.

"There is and was prehistoric life in these rainforests," Josiah continued. "Dinosaur fossils have been found in certain rainforest ecosystems around the world. Despite this, the prospect of a fossil is still a rare thing."

"Why?" Downs asked.

"Plant cover, man," Josiah said.

Downs felt he knew where Josiah was headed, but decided to let his friend speak.

Josiah continued. "In these rainforests that we're talking about, plants cover the majority of the outcrops that could house fossils. The outcrops that are exposed often suffer from being too weathered or they are buried deep underneath the soil of the rainforest."

Downs smiled. "Fascinating."

"Yeah it is," Josiah said. "No dinosaur fossils come to mind that have been found in Indonesia per se, but I know for a fact that there was a spinosaurid tooth located in Malaysia, but the thing could indeed turn out to be crocodilian instead. Anyway, I could go on for days about this stuff man. Point is these rainforests could harbor spectacular fossils waiting to be unearthed."

Downs was about to speak but Josiah cut him off.

"Remember, dinosaurs inhabited every continent on Earth. The possibilities are out there. One just has to keep an open mind."

Downs nodded his head in agreement.

"Never gave much thought to that idea," Downs said. "One always pictures a dusty windswept desert as the place to find fossils."

"That's the branded traditional image," Josiah replied. "Paleontologists as well as television channels have made the wind out to be the best friend of the paleontologist, stating that with the passing of each year, the wind brings and exposes more fossils to the surface. And while that is true, I also like to keep an open mind and think about the possibility of what a place like this might hold."

Ever since a very young age, Downs had held an interest in prehistory and all the wonders that it entailed. The idea that there were worlds long since gone and buried by the sands of time, waiting to be discovered by some fledgling scientist, was enough to keep him turning the pages of books deep into the wee hours of the night. He always had the desire to want to keep learning more, and he never wanted to stop. Only when sheer exhaustion would take over would he meander off to the world of sleep.

As as a youngster, Downs was most intrigued by the idea that in the age of disease, war, and famine, there were places that existed in the geological timeline of life on Earth that knew none of the above. Life at its purest and rawest form, he would always think to himself, and as a child there would have been nothing greater than being given the ability to be transported back to see a sauropod dinosaur as big as a blue whale moving about on land or watch one of the massive carnivores stalk a primeval jungle. Downs would have given his left arm or the last few years off the tail end of his life, but poor grades in high school chemistry coupled with his weak understanding of math prohibited him from moving forward in the field of paleontology.

"You two slow pokes need to hurry up," Nat's voice pinged in over the headset, bringing them back to the tour.

"Will do," Josiah replied. "We're on it."

The two of them looked at one another and then towards the intended path where the rest of the group had gone.

"Guess we've been moving at a snail's pace," Downs casually joked.

Josiah nodded, "But look at the view. Just look at it."

The sea of green that they saw was amazing, absolutely breathtaking and stunning in ways that neither of them had ever seen before. It extended out and away in all directions from where they stood and was all encompassing. It offered up a sense of a surreal green enchantment.

There must be an ungodly number of undocumented species up in those treetops, Downs thought.

"I know what you're thinking," Josiah said. "Just like when we were kids, I know exactly what you're thinking. Just reach out, find a branch, and pluck whatever it is that's crawling around out there and introduce it to the world as a brand new species."

Downs smiled and folded his arms. "That'd be nice. Man, that'd be nice to name a new species and get to publish an article on that topic. Won't ever happen for me, man, but there's hope for you."

"Yeah," Josiah replied, continuing to hold his gaze on the rainforest. "I can see it in the magazine Scientific American already. Well, we probably should get goin'."

And with that the two of them took off at a light jog back towards the rest of the group. Both Downs and Josiah were good athletes and kept a good pace for a while. Not good enough to win the New York Marathon anytime soon, but good enough to hopefully get back to the rest of the group in a timely and efficient manner.

The conditions were still suffocating as they continued to move across and snake their way through Corstine's highway in the sky. Josiah had pulled away from Downs a bit and the thirty year old high tailed it even faster in an attempt to catch him when suddenly he saw Josiah slowing down, and his pace slowed until finally it turned into walking and then a complete stop. Downs could see that Josiah had made his way towards the side of the boardwalk and appeared to be examining some of the foliage as it hung over the boardwalk in no particular order.

"What's up?" Downs asked, fighting to catch his breath.

Josiah didn't reply, rather he reached out and pulled one of the branches closer to him. Downs moved in until he was right next to his good friend.

It became apparent that the answer to Downs' very question had been answered the minute his eyes began to take in and register the green surroundings.

"Is that-"

Josiah cut him off mid-sentence before he could even finish. "It is."

Josiah had what looked like blood on the tips of his fingers. Once again as Downs' eyes began to take it all in, he could see the smattering of blood that covered the leaves of the vegetation.

Josiah's brain was working things out. Despite his background in the paleontological field, he had spent several summers aiding and helping many of his professors with their research expeditions to the Amazon and other tropical places of the world.

"Any idea what happened here?" Downs asked as he leaned in further.

Josiah bent over the railing as far as he could. "It's possible some type of bird was severely injured and flew through here, blooding the foliage in the process. My guess is just your everyday bird of paradise homicide."

Downs managed a laugh as both of them continued to stare at the bloody foliage.

CHAPTER EIGHT

"We don't leave anyone behind," Nat Kingsworth said as her voice once again pinged over the radio to the others. "And where are they? I've been calling them over the radio for several minutes now."

She had wanted to give the investors space to make their own decisions about the place, but this was downright ridiculous. But worst of all, it was her fault the two were missing.

Jamison was right behind her, his strong and muscular NBA legs still doing the trick despite his half a century in age. He had sprinted until he had caught up with Nat, who was jogging back towards Downs and Josiah.

"Television guy is painfully behind," Jamison said.

"Television guy?" Nat asked, with a raised eyebrow.

"Yeah television guy. Mr. I'm-on-to-my-third-network-launch right now," Jamison replied. "Just look at him. His body is the reason he's behind."

From the minute that Jamison had opened his mouth, Nat Kingsworth had formed the opinion that she did not like him. She did not like his arrogance, his tone of voice, or the downright belief he portrayed that he was better than everyone else. She simply did not care for him, but she could tolerate his supreme fitness level looking over at his massive neck and arms, hardly having even broken a sweat.

Nat glanced down at her watch. The others were taking forever. She looked at Jamison who had a look of serious frustration on his face. Nat wanted this to go well. She wanted to wow the investors and get them to sign on to the project. After all, Corstine was offering her a slight minuscule stake in the boardwalk if she could successfully get all four of them to invest in the project. So to say that she had fully invested herself in the boardwalk was quite the understatement.

"I'm going back for them," she said. "Wait here."

And with that she headed back to Josiah and Downs.

CHAPTER NINE

Ridley Bells had somehow managed to find himself isolated and momentarily separated from the group, having taken a slight detour on the boardwalk a while back while no one was looking. At 5'10" and 220 pounds, his out-of-shape frame was struggling with the humidity and literally bringing him to his knees. It weighed so heavily upon him that he felt as if he was at the bottom of the ocean with the full weight of the water itself bearing down upon him.

He had perspired right through his brown colored Patagonia shirt and paused for a moment to take off his green Augusta National golf hat, wiping his hair with the sleeve of his shirt. However, it was no use. He was absolutely drenched from head to toe. For a moment it felt good, like he might be moving towards his goal of losing weight. Surely as he now found himself bathed in sweat, he had to have lost a few pounds of water weight. Yet that feeling was quickly replaced with one of sheer discomfort.

Pausing for a moment and struggling to regain his breath, for the first time on the trip he felt the sheer isolation of the boardwalk. Ridley knew they were in the middle of nowhere, but it took him being all alone, completely isolated, to truly appreciate just how isolated they were. They may as well have been on an alien planet for all Ridley was concerned, but what was killing him was the sheer brutality of the humidity, which, by the minute, was sapping every last ounce of energy from his body.

Several unidentifiable calls from out in the canopy caught him off guard and put him on high alert.

Just birds, Ridley, he thought to himself. *Just birds. Get a grip on yourself.*

Life had been going well for him, and had been going well now for quite some time. When his first successful creation and launch of a television channel was sold and bought by a much larger international network, Ridley did what most entrepreneurs do who are suddenly thrust into his position and flush with cash: he went back to the drawing board and started yet another television channel. Armed with cash from his first sale, he set off with his nose to the wind, hell bent on conquering the world of media and television.

The sale of his second television channel put Ridley Bell's net worth just slightly north of twenty million, and he went from being someone considered well-off to instant multi-millionaire status. It was also around the time of the sale of his second channel that Ridley first encountered John Corstine, and the two hit it off instantly, drinking late into the night and spilling their guts to one another of past, present, and future business endeavors.

Corstine spoke of his initial architectural blueprints for the boardwalk and instantly peaked Ridley's interest both in the environmental protection of huge swaths of land as well as his passion for all things architectural. This divulging of secrets on Corstine's part prompted the light bulb in Ridley's brain to go off, and in the wee hours of the morning both of them conceived the plans for a new and innovative television network.

Ecological Television was hashed out on the back of several napkins that they were able to piece together from the bar top. For several hours they tentatively worked out the mission statement, a multitude of logistical issues, and the suggested amount of capital that they would either need to raise or pump in via their own deep pockets. For Ridley it would be channel number three, but for Corstine Ecological Television would be both scratching and satisfying an itch to plunge himself as well as part of his fortune into the media industry.

The overwhelming urge to urinate brought Ridley back to the boardwalk and away from his thoughts.

Gotta go, he thought. *Can't wait any freaking longer.*

He looked behind him, realizing that he was all alone and quite isolated.

It's now or never.

Ridley headed towards the railing of the boardwalk and unzipped himself, forgoing the idea of peeing and hanging himself out in all its glory smack dab in the center of Corstine's boardwalk. He looked down for a brief moment, realizing that they had reached somewhat of a clearing. The foliage at this part was not as dense, and he could make out the jungle floor below. Not that he was an adrenaline junkie or a high flying x-game acrobat, but he didn't mind the heights, actually he was downright enjoying them.

Even though so far they had seen next to nothing in terms of wildlife, and once again his mind roamed to a trip he had taken in his late twenties to Costa Rica in which he and his college buddies rode an aerial tram up into and through the rainforest. The only wildlife they saw was a lone anteater rummaging through the garbage in back of the restaurant where they dined following their day's outing in the rainforest.

Ridley knew that nature and wildlife were often elusive things, to say the least, being seen only when they wanted to be seen, and heard only when they wanted to be heard. Already Ridley was beginning to address this as an issue of concern for Corstine.

Like having an open zoo full of paying patrons, and all the animals are nowhere to be seen.

Ridley pondered the dilemma for a moment, wondering how Corstine would make sure that patrons got to see and experience all that the rainforest had to offer in terms of wildlife. He shrugged his shoulders. Future Corstine's problems. But then again he knew if he were to officially invest in the project, those same issues would become his problems as well.

Ridley was just about to relieve himself when something caught his attention from below, ground level to be exact, a streak of something here and there, and then nothing. His eyes wanted more, but nothing was granted. After searching for several more seconds with his eyes he gave up.

He shrugged his shoulders once more and began to pee, immediately relieved of the growing burden that had been bothering him since they embarked on their tour of the boardwalk. As he finished and began to tuck himself in, another overwhelming feeling suddenly came over him. But this time instead of his annoying bladder it was the unmistakable feeling of being watched. It was as if he felt eyes on him.

He peered out with his eyes, but saw nothing. And then he felt it from behind and immediately shot around, turning himself to face the other direction, as several distant birds called out, seemingly almost mocking him. Beads of sweat continued to pour down his face, but he just let them run, his senses on factory overload telling him that he was indeed being watched. But from where and what was watching him remained the great unknown? He spun around again and could swear that he heard something breathing, way out in the vegetation, a deep and low resonating sound. He listened closer with his ears, and there it was again, the sound of breathing mixed with a chewing and grinding sound.

That was all it took. He had heard, felt, and experienced enough. With his fly still down, Ridley Bells took off running back towards the others.

CHAPTER TEN

Downs bent over to tie his shoe lace and thought he noticed just the tiniest of vibrations coming from the boardwalk. As if checking for an oncoming train, he crouched low to the ground and listened with his ear. He wasn't certain if he had imagined it or not, but he continued to listen, touching his ear to the surface ever so gently.

Meanwhile Josiah was still busy checking the leaves of the branches as Downs resurrected to his feet.

"What are you two doing?" the voice of Nat rang out from behind. Her panting breath evident she had been running. "I've been calling you over the radio for quite some time. And you shouldn't have fallen back in the first place. With all that said, good to see the two of you."

"We got sidetracked by something. Plain and simple," Downs said, realizing that his and Josiah's headsets were both not where they should have been.

Nat looked at him for a moment, as if trying to decipher his words. She then fixed her glance on Josiah.

"We found something," Josiah said. "You should come have a look."

The three made their way towards the branches that Josiah had originally spotted.

"Is that…?" Nat asked, already noticing it from a dozen or so feet away.

Josiah had managed to break off a slender branch and sniffed at it. "It is. Blood, and by the looks of it rather fresh."

Nat moved in for a closer look. "Well, this is a living, breathing rainforest, and living breathing rainforests bleed from time to time. All part of the live, breathe, bleed, and die cycle."

Downs looked over at Josiah, who didn't seem to be buying it; the paleontologist shook his head and sniffed the blood once more from the branch, before finally discarding it and tossing it over the side. Josiah moved away from the two, peeking out and over the railing to see if he could see any more of the trail of blood.

"Well," Nat said, "We really should get back to the others. Like I said earlier and I'll say again, our forty-eight hours up here is ticking."

Noise could be heard once again as Downs' ears registered the familiar yet cocky voice of William Jamison, with Frederick and Max close behind. "This better be worth it. We have a forty-eight hour window, and time is money to everyone on this boardwalk in the sky, especially to me."

None of the group replied as Jamison crept up from behind and peered in at what the three of them were concentrating their efforts on.

"This is what all the fuss is about," Jamison said.

Downs looked at Jamison, and over his shoulder he could see Frederick coming as well. The two of them looked as if they had just run a marathon, but they had arrived back nonetheless.

"Where's Ridley?" Downs asked Jamison.

Jamison chuckled. "His out-a-shape ass was far too heavy even for someone in superior shape such as I to carry him. The poor mofo took one of those damn detours that we passed by. I believe he took the first, or it might have been the second detour. Hell, he took a detour and that's all I know."

Nat silently cursed herself for being so stupid as to not notice he was gone in the first place. "You saw him wander off and you said nothing?"

Jamison shrugged his shoulders and flashed her one of his trademark cocky ass innocent smiles, all smile mixed with some teeth. "He took that detour a ways back, the part where the boardwalk momentarily split in two. Figured he was doing some due diligence so I just let him be."

Nat let out a sigh. Her disappointment in herself was evident, but realized that getting into a full fledged argument with Jamison was a useless effort, and an absolutely futile one at that. As the tour's official guide, she was breaking John Corstine's first rule on this weekend excursion, which was to never leave anyone alone. Her mind instantly began running rabid with worst case scenarios, and she knew instantly that she was at fault, and they needed to get back to him immediately.

Downs felt Nat's hand on the back of his shoulder as she began to try and pull them away from the dried blood. "We must be going."

"Cool by me," Jamison said. "Never been into the dried blood thing anyway. You know how it is."

Josiah immediately pulled back from the vegetation, made eye contact with Jamison, and continued on passed the towering big man, the tension between the two already seeming to be as thick as the humidity itself. With each encounter Jamison appeared to be egging on the paleontologist, and oddly enough there seemed to be a bit of racial tension mixed in with it as well.

The group left the bloody vegetation behind and began where Jamison said Ridley had rather quietly and unassumingly split off from the tour. Downs had decided to give Josiah some space, knowing full well that the former NBA player was wearing on his last paleontological nerve, so he decided it best to let his friend air out some steam at the back of the group.

Downs pulled into the middle of the line, with Nat and Max once again up towards the front. This time, with every hundred yards or so that passed, Nat Kingsworth would look back to ensure that her tour, and Corstine's potential investors, were all accounted for. She wanted to give proper space while still maintaining a sense of order. It was a delicate balance to say the least.

About a quarter of a mile or so after spotting the blood on the hanging vegetation, the group happened upon a still-moving Ridley Bells, but the out-of-shape television entrepreneur looked as though his goose had been cooked.

"Ridley," Nat shouted. "Thank God you're okay. We were worried. Please don't ever do anything like that again."

"Oh, I'm alive," Ridley joked, sucking on the water straw that was hooked up to his backpack, and pausing to catch his breath. "Just got sidetracked on a little detour. One thing led to another and before I knew it, I was out on my own."

"Well, you're not the only one," Nat said, looking back in the direction of Josiah and Downs. "Let's get going. We need to retrace our steps quickly. Time to continue the tour."

"Oh and one more thing, Ridley," Nat said jokingly while covering her mouth. "Your fly is down."

CHAPTER ELEVEN

The group was officially back in unison, single file as Downs made his way behind Josiah and occupied his usual position at the end, with Max just a little bit up ahead of Josiah. The three men had put a small distance in between them and Jamison, Frederick, and Ridley, essentially breaking the rainforest tour up into two small groupings. This time, however, Nat, the leader in the front, was keeping a tighter watch on the group. Already she was feeling the pressure mounting. She saw it as a tight balance whereas she wanted to give the investors space to spread out and talk amongst themselves. Yet she still needed to point out little tidbits of information here and there, and how much space was too much? She certainly didn't want another Ridley Bells' incident making its way back to Corstine or his personal assistant Collin.

Nat sighed quietly to herself, not fully knowing the answer to the very questions swirling and circulating in her head.

"You all need to hurry up and see this," Max pinged in over the radio.

Quickly the group made their way to where Max was standing and looking out into the canopy.

"What's up?" Downs asked patting Max on the back playfully.

"Interesting grouping of birds out yonder," he said. "Thought everyone might be interested."

Max began to explain just exactly what they were looking at. "Um before we begin with the wildlife, if you all look out in that direction, you can see a tree called a dipterocarp. Dipterocarps top off at about 120 feet and this one looks like it has a combination of vines, lianas, and strangler figs growing up it. Make a ninety degree turn with your eyes and you can see a tualang tree, and these guys can grow to a staggering height of 280 feet, making it the third tallest trees species in the world. Lucky for the rainforest it is almost never cut down as a result of its hard wood and massive buttresses down on the forest floor. If you folks also take a look out there, you can clearly see a small gathering of punai, whose more common name is the 'green wood pigeon.'"

The bird that Max was pointing out had green feathers, and a forest green breast to match. Its tail was spotted red, blue, and black. The head itself was a light purple in coloration.

"These birds," Max continued, "are close relatives of the pigeon."

"Rats with wings in the jungle," Frederick joked. "If there was a parking structure up here, they most likely would be in it."

"Yeah and if there was a parking structure up on this here boardwalk, they'd be shittin' on your car," Jamison fired back with a smile.

Nat shook her head ever so slightly. She knew the investor type. After all, her ex-boyfriend had been an investment banker. But more importantly she also knew that if there was a parking structure way out here in the jungle, they'd be hell bent on monetizing it to the fullest.

Jamison looked back to Josiah who was no more than a few feet from the ex-athlete. "Relax there, big fella. I heard these birds stay clear of brotha's cars. Then again on second thought in your case."

Josiah had enough and moved away from the group, as Jamison's comments had reached a very personal level once again. Downs glared over at Jamison and decided it was about time to speak up and say something. "Hey man, what's your problem?"

Jamison seemed startled by the harshness of Downs' tone, but the big man said nothing as Downs made his way past him and headed out towards Josiah. Josiah was moving quickly, but Downs was moving quicker and immediately caught up to him.

"Forget about Jamison," Downs said as he finally caught up to Josiah. "The guy is out of his mind, and he's obviously trying to get you all riled up. Probably been doing it his entire life to those around him. He was a bully in the NBA, and most likely a bully in his schooling days. And now he's just some shit-talking multi-millionaire in his retired days."

Josiah shook his head and looked off into the distance. "How can I when that guy's bustin' my chops every chance he gets."

Downs nodded. "I know. The guy is a jackass who has a bigger ego than Corstine's boardwalk spans."

The look of frustration on Josiah's face turned into a grin as he smiled at the comment. "Damn right," he said. "Never in all my life have I met such an egotistical you know what."

Downs grabbed Josiah by the shoulders. "Look, we all know that Jamison is a real piece of art, one of those pieces of crap that is highly valued by society, but I need you to stay with me mentally. And just know that I greatly appreciate you being here."

"I know," Josiah said. "Been way too long since we've seen each other man.

"Now, do me a favor. Don't pay any attention to a word that jackass says from here on out," Downs said.

Josiah nodded and smiled. "Will do, man. Will do."

CHAPTER TWELVE

"You two missed an amazing display," Frederick said as Downs and Josiah returned to the group.

"Yeah damn near knocked me off my feet," Jamison fired back sarcastically.

Downs would have rolled his eyes in scornful distaste but Jamison's eyes were focused on him, with what seemed like one eye on that of Josiah as well. Jamison seemed to have it out for the paleontologist, though Downs wasn't quite certain what the reason or internal motives exactly were.

The two of them had taken two completely different routes in life. Jamison entered college as an avenue to master his skills and make the jump to the NBA. Josiah had entered the university system to hone and develop his paleontological skills and to earn a PhD in the subject, hopefully one day returning to the university setting as a professor, hoping that, in turn he would receive grants and the ability to fund his digs in the remote far flung corners of the world.

Whatever the reason was, there was obvious tension between the two, and Downs had already made it his mission to keep the two of them apart, but, most importantly, to keep the peace.

"As we were saying," Max continued. "The small gathering got flushed from their perch and flew up and into the air. Something must have spooked them."

Downs shrugged his shoulders. "Next time. Next time we'll catch it."

Jamison intercepted Frederick and Ridley and pushed them a few feet away from the others.

"I'm just not seein' the potential of this place," Jamison said into the ear of Ridley. "Sparse wildlife here and there, hit or miss opportunities to see things. Just not seein' it."

Frederick nodded. "Me too. I side with your concerns."

"Now wait a second, you two. We haven't even seen the rest of the boardwalk yet. Let's not jump to rash conclusions here," Ridley said.

Jamison stood tall and stepped directly in front of the television entrepreneur, looking him square in the eyes. "When it's my upfront capital, I'll be damned if I'm not going to jump to conclusions, no matter how early in the ball game it may be. Question everything. Trust little to no one."

Ridley stepped back. Although he was a large man himself, he was never one for confrontations, and he seemed like half a man compared to the 6'9" Jamison.

Frederick didn't like Jamison, at least that was what he was starting to feel as he had observed the whole encounter from the side of them, but he did see where the big man was coming from. "I just don't see how you monetize such a place."

"Mona what?" Jamison asked.

"Monetize," Frederick continued. "You know when you own a website and decide it's time to monetize it by placing advertisements on the site in return for payment, or when you have a successful video up on YouTube, you can place advertisements on the video. Monetize is the key word here."

Jamison raised his hands and began to press them downward, as if he was trying to squash Fredericks's thoughts. Frederick didn't let Jamison see the look of disgust on his face but thought to himself the idea of Jamison becoming insanely wealthy off the idea of guaranteed contracts.

There are no guarantees in the business world, Frederick thought to himself. *Would be nice if all you had to do was incorporate a company and there would be a guaranteed contract waiting for you to sign like that of professional athletes.*

Frederick knew damn well that athletes were spoiled, some spoiled to the tune of Fortune 500 CEO executive compensation plans, and salaries that no man or woman should receive, but one could make the exact same argument for the business world at large. Nonetheless, William Jamison had made a small fortune off of a talent and trade that the world deemed worthy of multi-millions.

Frederick kept his mouth shut though. He didn't question Jamison's ability to back his word up with cash, but what he did question was his business acumen. The due diligence that he had already pulled on Jamison raised several red flags in his opinion. There were a string of restaurants following his successful career in the NBA that went belly up for some reason or another. From the public records that Frederick was able to pull on Jamison, it showed that his chain of restaurants were up and running for only sixteen months, just a little over a year before citing "lack of funds" as the main reason for each of their ultimate demise.

Frederick didn't stop there though, and discovered that Jamison had come up with another idea of opening a string of Vegan restaurants, and being that he also maintained a residence in Berkeley, California, he believed they would thrive under such conditions. They did not though, and as Frederick once again investigated more into the public records, it appeared that Jamison had run into several logistical issues surrounding the functionality of the restaurants, the main one revolving around parking issues, or lack thereof.

Frederick wondered if Jamison was the kind of athlete who watched out for his own funds and personal interests, or if he had someone doing it for him, a handler who watched out for his own financial well-being. Someone who people like Jamison could call in the wee hours of the morning after they had gotten a DUI, and who would work diligently to make it all better.

Frederick wondered a lot of things as the humidity continued to suck the everlasting life out of them. It was hot, uncomfortably hot to say the least.

CHAPTER THIRTEEN

"I need you two to do me a big favor," Nat said as she came walking over to Downs and Josiah.

Josiah just looked at her. "Pretty tough when we're hanging with 'the most interesting man in the world.'"

She laughed. "I know, right. What hasn't the jackass done?"

"We were just talking about that very subject," Downs added.

Nat now stood in front of both of them but focused mainly on Josiah. "I need you two to just grin and bear it. Let that guy say whatever he wants, process it, and then discard it like the utter trash that it is."

"I'm assuming you're referring to none other than Mr. Jamison," Downs jokingly said.

"How'd you guess that," Nat joked. "But in all seriousness, as you guys can already see, he's a real jackass. A real big one to put it bluntly, and I'm no happier than the two of you probably are for having him here, but he is, and he represents a sizable investor to John Corstine."

Downs folded his arms. "We know."

Nat let out a sigh. "I need you two to just get along with him for the duration of the trip and then that's it."

"And then plunk down a sizable amount of cash with him and invest in the project," Downs countered.

"Correct," Nat replied. "And never have to see his ass again, except at maybe a general meeting once or twice a year. Can you two do that for me?"

Downs looked over at Josiah and then back up at Nat. Both of them nodded in accordance.

"Good," she said, "because, here he comes."

Downs took a deep gulp as he could clearly see Jamison heading towards all of them, with Ridley and Frederick not too far behind.

Here comes trouble, Downs thought.

"You ladies done with your little tea party," Jamison announced, striding in like he was trying to barge into a private party or something.

"We were just talking about you," Nat said with as genuine a smile plastered across her face as she could muster.

Jamison grinned at her. "I bet it was something nice then."

"Check this," Jamison said. "The three of us were talkin' about just doing our own thing for the rest of the day. You know takin' our time round this little invention of Corstine's, walkin', talkin', checking under the boards to make sure all the nuts and bolts are nice and tight. You know that kind of thing. Do some of our own due diligence round here and meet up with you all a little bit later."

It was quite apparent that Nat was taken aback by the oddity of the request.

"But we're supposed to be a team for the next two days man," Josiah countered. "Don't you understand the team concept here? I pass the ball to you, you pass to someone else, the end result is we score a basket. Don't you understand that?"

The minute the words flew out of his mouth, Downs really wished they hadn't, but to his surprise Jamison did not comment back. Rather his full attention was focused solely on Nat.

"Look," Jamison said. "The three of us want to be our own team for the rest of the weekend, a team of potential investors doing the necessary due diligence of this place by our own eyes and account. Not all the birds and the bee's crap that might have been planned. No offense"

Jamison looked over to Downs. "You're more than welcome to join us if you want."

Downs nodded as he folded his arms. "Thanks but I'm fine right where I am."

Jamison didn't even so much as bat an eye at Downs' response.

"But that was the agreement," Nat replied. "The plan was to give you all the tour as if you were actual paying customers. Then you could come to your own conclusions about this place. That was the agreement."

"Well, plans change," Jamison said, folding his massive arms, the thickness in them resembling that of a python.

Downs suspected it was highly plausible that Frederick and Ridley were just going along with what Jamison was saying, but it was believable that they weren't entirely on board with his plan, but for some reason or another had decided to go along with it.

"Is this what you all want?" Nat asked, looking past Jamison and in the direction of Frederick and Ridley.

Both of them gave a quick nod of the head, although from where Downs was standing, it appeared to be a half-ass nod at best. Just as Nat was about to speak, something slammed down hard onto the boardwalk.

CHAPTER FOURTEEN

Collin Fairbanks sat in front of the computer screen and pressed a few buttons, examining the different security cameras as they came up on the screen in front of him. Behind him John Corstine strode back and forth nervously, having decided to forego his evening with his Kindle in favor of returning to the boardwalk. Anxiety, tension, and an impending sense of overwhelming doom were the issues currently plaguing Corstine as he continued to pace.

There were roughly a dozen or so security cameras that had been set in place all along the boardwalk, in one mile intervals, to monitor and make sure things were functioning smoothly. More security cameras were in the works but for now the number sat at twelve. Another thing to add to Corstine's "to do" list. Collin was busy looking at security camera number six. Something off in the trees had caught his attention and he adjusted the camera to have a better look. He yawned quietly and wiped his eyes, looking over at his empty coffee mug which was in desperate need of a refill. For the past two nights he had little to no sleep, making sure everything was in place for this investor weekend. He planned to sleep for a solid week once he returned to civilization. However, for now he continued to focus all his might and energy on the computer screen in front of him.

Collin looked once again at security camera number six and shook his head, dismissing what he thought he saw earlier as nothing more than a figment of his imagination.

Corstine, meanwhile, had walked to the corner of the office, gazing out at the rainforest as he had been known to do from time to time. It had always done him good and he considered it to be his safeguard, and it was one of the main inspirations for, in fact, creating a thirty-five mile track of boardwalk high in the sky in the first place. Corstine believed that the world would flock to see it, experience it, and get the same type of metaphorical high that he felt every time he gazed out into the treetop landscape. The boardwalk would be as solid and familiar as if one were walking on the deck in his or her own backyard.

Collin toggled back and forth between a few more buttons, and brought up security cameras seven through twelve.

"Any update?" Corstine asked from the far corner, still staring out at the green.

Collin took a closer look, zooming in with camera seven and then quickly zooming out. Corstine was now hovering over his assistant's back once more, literally breathing onto the hairs of his neck.

Collin could feel John Corstine's presence behind him. He could always feel his looming presence in his life. He had worked for Corstine for the better part of three years now, starting simply as an assistant doing clerical work and making the occasional coffee or dry cleaning run to eventually working his way into Corstine's financial life, both personal and business.

Not that Collin minded. He had been looking for an opportunity like this for a long time, an opportunity to grow and nurture a venture into something far greater. Many of his friends had taken safe and sound corporate jobs, but not Collin. It wasn't his cup of tea.

Collin felt as though he had been slowly infiltrating his way into Corstine's life, gaining his trust week in and week out, until he had finally reached the level of trust where he was responsible for a small yet growing wing of Corstine's vast fortune. He had assigned Collin with a wing that promptly was referred to as "new and emerging markets." Currently under this new wing was the boardwalk project as well as the potential for Ecological Television, which hinged strongly on the involvement of investor Ridley Bells.

Bells, as Corstine would often fondly refer to him, was the main component in the idea behind Ecological Television. Corstine knew that he could look elsewhere for capital, and he had, over the years, developed close ties with angel investors and several different venture capital companies around the world. However, the first-hand expertise as well as the connections and contacts within the cable and satellite communities were what Ridley Bells brought to the equation. Corstine knew that this was something which would be very hard to match with any other person he might bring on board.

Corstine knew that he needed Bells' expertise, having created and built from scratch two successful television networks. He would be hard pressed to find someone more suited to launching a new television channel in an already crowded and difficult industry. Corstine had been through the rigors of pitching the concept for the channel to a select group of people, and he had already been told "no" more times than was good for the human spirit. Bells told Corstine not to worry about the capital part, that he would leverage his twenty plus years in the television industry to help them secure the necessary financial backers to get them up and running in a timely manner.

Corstine enjoyed the idea as well as the logistical challenges that Ecological Television would present, but, for the moment, his thoughts were entirely focused on both getting the boardwalk officially up and running and on the security camera at which his assistant was still currently staring.

CHAPTER FIFTEEN

The creature's mouth hung slightly agape as it adjusted itself from its perch high atop one of the towering trees. It had climbed and forced itself more than three quarters of the way up into the canopy. With its two back limbs holding the majority of its weight from below, and providing a stable and sturdy base, its two front limbs still served a purpose as they held on to a nearby branch above it while the rest of its body clung tightly to the tree. Suction cups like that of tree frogs was what made the unachievable achievable, thus allowing a creature of this size to move about between the trees. Its four three-toed feet looked and felt like those of a tree frog, just on a much larger, more robust scale. Each of the feet spanned the size of a manhole, with the actual suction cups on par with a basketball in terms of size. Its feet were tinged a forest green, and they were lined with three enormous talons on each foot. The talons were there to puncture through both prey and tree bark if needed, an added luxury to something that was already a fully capable and adept predator.

Despite its large size, it was surprisingly nimble, moving from tree to tree as if it were a fraction of what it truly was, its long limbs allowing it to move in and about its rainforest habitat like some type of overgrown predatory tree frog.

The creature tilted its head to the side and stared at the small humans. It was processing information, thinking, working out logistics, all while in the background a raw and growing hunger rumbled inside its stomach. This feeling was something for the moment that it was containing, but it knew somewhere inside its brain that there would be a breaking point where it could contain itself no longer.

The humans looked tiny and insignificant to the onlooker despite the fact that it had only encountered a handful of them over the years. Tilting its head to the other side, it had three memories regarding them. The first was when it first laid eyes on them from the secrecy that only its dense rainforest habitat could provide. The second memory was the way it remembered how it loved smelling their fear. The fear seemed to exude and ooze out of their very pores. It took delight in the way they panicked, the way they attempted to power themselves away from it with their small and often powerless legs.

It loved every second of the chase. It hunted out of the need to feed, but also to quench the desire to hunt. It enjoyed the pursuit, and, most importantly, the conquest of its victims. Lastly, the creature remembered how they tasted. The first remembrance of bones breaking and cracking under the immense power of its jaws mixed with the pleasant warm taste of human blood drove it almost to the point of insanity.

It reached out with one of its powerful front limbs and pulled itself with ease to one of the nearby tualang trees, the basketball-sized suction cups making it all possible. It had hunted and patrolled these forests for years now, with very little, if any, human contact whatsoever. Keeping mostly to the treetops, it descended only to the forest floor to hunt and drink, and the prey consisted of, reticulated pythons, Komodo dragons, and whatever else it could seemingly get its hands on. Anything was fair game. It was comfortable and adept on the forest floor as well as up high in the canopy. As it continued to look on, it appeared that a new and growing food source was brewing before its very eyes as the creature once again cocked its head to the side and adjusted itself.

A gnawing and growing hunger had been tugging in its stomach for quite some time now. With its jaws slightly agape and possessing a mouth full of sharp serrated teeth, saliva dripped from the opening and onto one of the nearby lower branches. The creature's mouth opened more, further displaying an arsenal of deadly serrated teeth several inches in length which harbored bits and pieces of stringy decaying meat between them, making for the most foul of smells. It pulled itself back to the original tree via the same way as before.

Its brain was twisted at the moment into a state of confusion, as it wondered if it should return to feed on its previous kill or focus on this new and intriguing meal, new victims to not only attack, but to track and hunt down. Despite the urge to hunt, it retreated and pulled itself backwards, disappearing out of view and into the dense jungle.

CHAPTER SIXTEEN

A lifeless, tanned, leathery brown blob of an object was up ahead as the group carefully moved towards it. Instantly they were overwhelmed with the smell of decaying meat mixed with the unmistakable hint of death.

"What the hell," Downs mumbled to himself as the group closed in.

"No way," Max called out. "Absolutely no freaking way."

Downs could see that it was the upper torso of something, but he couldn't tell what yet. The smell was absolutely nauseating, and the entire group was forced to pull their shirts over their noses, just to keep their stomachs composed and in check. Surprisingly, everyone except Max did this. He was moving full steam ahead towards the object, breathing in the air almost as if he enjoyed it, like a mad scientist possessed he seemingly floated towards it.

"Damn psycho," Downs heard Jamison remark from somewhere close behind.

Downs thought he was imagining things, that the thick humidity was playing tricks on his fragile and vulnerable mind. It was as if they were all moving towards a mirage, a pristine water source in the middle of a barren desert. His mind took a moment to run through its mental catalog like Google performing an image search, with countless images flashing here and there before one finally stuck out and took hold above all the others.

Komodo dragon. The thought registered like a bolt of lightening to his head. It sounded so strange and completely out of place, but there it was before him, lying before all of them for that matter.

"Can you believe this," Max said with the wide eyed excitement of a child as he bent down to have a better look.

The beady black eyes of the Komodo dragon stared back at the group from the ground, with a cold almost evil remorse still evident, devoid of all feelings, everything except an ancient and primeval look like it was ripped straight from the age of the dinosaurs.

"But from where?" Downs asked, spinning around. "And where the hell's the rest of it?"

Max reached into his back pocket, pulling out his bright red Swiss Army Knife and opened it up. Carefully, he began plodding around with it in what was left of the severed dragon. Downs bent down as well. The smell was still horrific, and the flies had begun to take notice as they buzzed in and around the crouching humans.

The Komodo dragon had been ripped in two by something, severed about the midway point as guts and entrails lay splayed out across the boardwalk. The scene looked like a butcher shop gone awry.

Max continued to prod at it with his knife. Meanwhile Josiah had come up from behind and bent down as well. Downs was just about to reach out and stop Josiah when a large barrel-like figure came in from behind.

"Out of the way, you pussies," Jamison demanded as he forced his way between the three and extracted an object with his bare hands, not giving a damn about rhyme or reason, cleanliness, or proper protocols.

"What the hell," Jamison said, as he pulled himself upright and to his feet. The object he held in his hands was rather long, blood encrusted, and identifiable.

Max pulled the object out of Jamison's hands, to the surprise of the big man who had so rudely and aggressively barged in. "What in God's name?"

"What in evolution's name," Josiah muttered to himself.

The tooth was somewhere between two to three inches in length, pyramid shaped, and possessed serrated edges which ran down both sides. It not only looked like an instrument for killing, but one which drew a striking similarity to that of the modern day Great White Shark.

"Let me see that," Nat said. Max happily handed the tooth over to her.

Each member of the group now stood hovering and gazing down at the white object.

"I'm no scientist," Jamison remarked, "but that's an instrument designed for one purpose and one purpose only, killing."

No shit, Downs thought to himself.

This time it was Josiah who grabbed hold of the tooth. He ran his finger over the fine serrations. Over the years Josiah had the opportunity to spend enormous amounts of time at the prep lab on the campus of UC Berkeley. During that time he was fortunate enough to see the teeth of several large predatory dinosaurs. One was of the monstrous and elusive late Jurassic predator Saurophaganax and the other of the famous Tyrannosaurus Rex. Both were equally impressive but what the young doctoral student took away from that encounter was the robustness of the tyrannosaur's tooth compared to that of the saurophaganax. The tyrannosaur's tooth was made for crushing bone and inflicting a deadly bite right off the bat, while the tooth of the saurophaganax was meant for biting and slashing at prey.

Josiah allowed the remembrance of both of those teeth to fully soak in before moving on in his mental images. Suddenly, Josiah's thoughts went to the catalogue of various extinct prehistoric sharks' teeth that he had come across in the lab over the years as well, teeth that were meant to tear into prey and bite off large pieces of flesh. He had seen teeth like this before, teeth designed to cut through flesh and bone.

As Josiah stared down at the tooth, he knew exactly that this was that same type of tooth he had in front of him. It was designed to act like a steak knife. Josiah believed and had already worked out the details in his head. In his hand he held a tooth that was designed solely for the purpose of inflicting massive damage to its unfortunate victims.

But on land what in the hell could produce such a tooth, he thought to himself, especially this high up? *What could produce such a tooth?*

CHAPTER SEVENTEEN

Downs slapped at the back of his neck once, then twice, and before he realized it they were totally engulfed in a thick black hovering mass. Biting insects of every kind imaginable flew in from all angles. The black hovering mass had come in, like death itself, inundating the group like a rising tide, and seemingly threatening to engulf everything in its way.

Downs saw something land on Jamison's neck and plunge the biting part of it into him as the big man slapped wildly at it, before flicking the thing to the ground, and then stomping down on it with his size sixteen's.

All out panic ensued as the dark masses moved in towards the rotting severed carcass. Downs continued to slap every which way as any part of open skin was being threatened with an attack. Mean, nasty things with an equally aggressive nature about them were fluttering and flying about everywhere.

As Downs ran out and away from the carcass, he noticed that there was a slew of other biting insects mixed in with the flies. Everything was happening so quickly that his mind was having a hard time registering it all. People were running in all directions. No order. No plan whatsoever. Just all out chaos.

Downs was back peddling, his eyes on the carcass, while he could still see Jamison who was repeatedly being stung. Frederick and Ridley were retreating with him, in the same direction from where Ridley had originally gotten lost, but it looked as though they, too, were being aggressively sought out by the biting insects.

"Come on," Nat shouted. "This way."

Downs took up chase after her, quickly locating Josiah and Max in the process. All three of them were now running full steam behind the expedition guide. Her foot speed was astonishing and surprised the rest of them with just how quickly she pulled away from them like a high-performance vehicle. From time to time she looked back, just to make sure they were still there, but for the most part she maintained a considerable distance between them and her.

Downs slowed his pace just a bit, to allow for Josiah and Max to catch up with him. They had been running hard for a full five minutes when the swarm of insects was finally becoming less and less and things were starting to thin out, until only a few random flies could be seen fluttering about.

Up ahead Downs could see Nat, pacing back and forth as if she'd just polished off a good half marathon, and was past the finish line waiting to collect first prize money.

"Where'd you get speed like that?" Downs asked as he came to a stop.

Despite her blistering speed, she was still breathing hard and took a moment to reply as she put her hands above her head. In between breaths she spoke though, "Ran track at Dartmouth. Not what I used to be but still better than most."

Instantly Downs thought two things to himself. The first was that he was impressed she ran collegiate track, and the second was that she attended Dartmouth. Both seemed quite impressive to him to say the least.

Josiah looked behind him. "I think we're in the clear."

His statement brought Downs back to the present and away from the world of competitive collegiate track filled with its long legged participants. Downs felt around on his body, and surprisingly it appeared as though he had gotten out relatively unscathed, although Nat seemed to have a few bites on the back of her neck and on the back of her hands.

"What the hell could have dragged a full grown Komodo dragon and dropped it off up here?" Josiah said, scratching at his beard growth that was creeping in more and more each day.

"Um, I think the more plausible question that needs to be addressed here is what the hell could have ripped a full grown adult Komodo dragon in half like a ragdoll?" Max chimed back. "As well as the question of tossing it up here."

"Then that means the other half might still be up in the trees somewhere. Just stowed away like luggage or something," Downs said. "This is all too weird. Been that way literally since my feet touched down on this damn boardwalk."

The others nodded as well, siding with both the confusion and frustration that Downs was exhibiting.

Nat had wandered a few feet from the group, pondering something as if she had the weight of the world atop her shoulders. Quickly Downs made his way over to her.

"You okay?" he asked.

"Yeah," she replied. "Been better though. A few of those nasty buggers got me on the neck."

"Do you mind?"

She shook her head, and Downs made his way behind her. It felt slightly uncomfortable at first as he pulled her brunette hair back and had a look at the bites. They were tiny and looked harmless, but he knew that tiny and harmless in the rainforest could turn into big and deadly very quickly. Rainforests and jungles had that theme about them, often capitalizing on and turning even minor cuts and scrapes into serious issues and infections that needed to be dealt with immediately.

She dropped her backpack to the ground.

"What do we have in terms of a medical kit?"

"Very little," she replied, not looking up as she rummaged through her bag.

She did, however, manage to pull out a small white box with a red cross on it. Downs laughed.

"Wow, is that all we have?"

Nat looked up and smiled. "Yep. Corstine spares no expense."

Downs shook his head in dismay. "You can say that again. Looks like the first aid kit to a kid's soccer team."

Both of them chuckled at the joke. Nat removed a small bottle of rubbing alcohol and poured a bit out onto a tiny cotton swab that she had retrieved from the kit.

"Would you mind?" she asked.

"It'd be my pleasure," Downs said with a grin.

Downs rubbed the cotton swab with the alcohol on it over the small bites, working on her neck before finally dabbing at the back of both of her hands.

"That should just about do it," he said.

Nat was about to put the kit back in her bag when Max and Josiah appeared with outstretched hands of their own. They had bites on them as well and wanted the same attention. She handed them the small medical kit.

"You boys are on your own," Downs joked, as they skirted off to address their medical needs. He pushed in closer to Nat.

"What are we going to do about Jamison's crew?" Downs asked.

Nat finished rearranging things in her bag before finally standing to her feet. She slung the backpack over her shoulders. "Thanks for the medical attention."

Downs smiled. "Anytime."

Nat looked up at the sky for a brief moment and then put her headset back on. "Do you guys read me? Over."

There was a long silence that lasted for a minute or so.

Nat spoke over the radio once more. "Are you guys out there? Do you read me? Even if you're deciding to go at it alone, at least give us a thumbs up via the radio that you're okay."

Another minute passed as Nat shook her head in frustration and pulled the headset off, wiring it so it was intertwined in the loops of her backpack, just in case there was a transmission back. However, she knew wholeheartedly that they had lost communication with them.

"Jamison and the others will be fine," she said. "That's what they wanted all along, so I guess they got their wish."

Max and Josiah had come over to where the two were standing.

"We've got big problems," Max said.

"We're going to continue with the tour as planned," Nat fired back. "This tour needs to be completed. Seemed doomed since the start, but I refuse to let that happen. We will continue on, even if it's with only one potential investor."

Max shook his head in defiance. It wasn't until he was a considerable distance closer that it was clear to the others.

In his right hand, Max Caldwell was holding an eyeball.

CHAPTER EIGHTEEN

"Now what," Frederick announced as he swatted at the last of the flies that were still in hot pursuit, almost defiantly fighting on long after the rest of their biting comrades had abandoned ship and called it a day.

"Well," Jamison said. "For one thing, we're out of the loser pack and off on our own, which is a good thing."

Frederick chuckled. "But seriously though, now what?"

Ridley looked at Jamison for a reply.

"You guys want me to do all the thinkin'," Jamison said. "Well, I say now we can have a good look at this boardwalk thing, on our own, free and clear of outside opinions."

"Sounds like a damn fine plan," Frederick replied, rubbing at the smattering of bites he had acquired.

Jamison smiled. "Okay then. We investigate and explore the hell outta this place, and then get the hell outta here. Maybe even earlier than expected. I'm sure you two have other things to do. As for me I've got my growing empire back home which needs my attention."

Jamison turned around towards them one last time. "Oh, and one more thing. By investigate I don't mean turn over every board of this thirty-five mile track. That would be foolish and idiotic. Auditors don't go over every transaction, rather they choose a few random samples and go from there. We will do the same here. Investigate the hell outta this little wing on which we find ourselves and draw much bigger conclusions from this one random sample point. Ya'll dig that?"

Frederick and Ridley both looked at one another and nodded. Then something caught Frederick's eye, and he wandered past Jamison and towards the railing part of the boardwalk.

"What the hell," Frederick muttered to himself.

Stuck in part of the railing in the most rudimentary of fashions was a small sign that read: AUTHORIZED PERSONNEL ONLY BEYOND THIS POINT.

"Guys, come here and look at this," Frederick yelled.

Jamison and Ridley followed suit.

"Saw this sign earlier," Ridley said.

Jamison turned and looked at the television mogul.

Ridley nodded. "This is where I wandered off to."

"And?" Jamison inquired. "Did you check this part out?"

Ridley shook his head. "Not much. Just needed to piss real bad. Heard some strange noises and then decided to hightail it back."

Jamison laughed sarcastically. "Well, that was useless. All the more reason to see this section now closely with our own eyes, fellas."

Meanwhile, Frederick pulled the metal sign out of the railing. "What gives?"

Jamison was thinking, processing all of the information that was being given to him at the moment. "Seems Corstine's been up to other things. Authorized personnel type of things. Things he probably doesn't want us knowing about."

"But what though?" Frederick replied. "Maybe this is just some random maintenance sign. All attractions need and have maintenance roads."

Jamison gave him a rank look. "Don't think so. You don't get to Corstine's financial status without a little foul play every now and then. I'm sure you fellas know all about foul play with your respected businesses."

"Oh, yeah," Frederick said with a big smile. "There was this one time-"

Jamison cut him off midsentence. "Let's keep focused, fellas. We can get into corporate shenanigans later, once the due diligence part of this weekend is over."

Jamison motioned with his hand for them to continue on. They did just that.

CHAPTER NINETEEN

Downs stumbled like a drunk towards Max's open outstretched hand. The detached eyeball stared ominously up at him, stared ominously at all of them for that matter.

"Is that human?" Josiah muttered.

"I-I-I believe so," Max stuttered back.

Max had managed to pluck hold of a leaf from the surrounding vegetation and calmly placed the eyeball down on top of it, not that it mattered, but he did so anyways, placing the eyeball atop the leaf and laying it down on the boardwalk. Everyone bent down around the thing, as if they were searching for a contact lens or something minute.

"We should get rid of it. The thing's creeping me the hell out," Josiah remarked.

Downs moved closer to Max and whispered ever so gently in his ear. "What do you think is going on here?"

"I think we've got a real problem," Max muttered back, his words barely audible.

"Do you guys get the odd feeling we're being watched?" Josiah asked as he sat up and craned his neck looking at the surrounding foliage.

Max turned and looked him dead in the eyes. "I do."

Josiah stood up and exhaled a deep breath. "Geez, because I've been thinking the same thing since we arrived. Either way you slice it, it's been an overwhelming feeling I've been harboring in my gut the minute that my feet touched down on these boards."

The other three rose up from the ground, leaving the eyeball still sitting neatly atop the leaf.

"Guys," Max said. "Um, let's not rush to any rash judgments here, but I think it's becoming increasingly evident and highly plausible that something is indeed watching us."

"Toying with us is more like it," Josiah said. "Having fun at our expense, like monkeys in a zoo flinging bits and pieces of their food and feces at the unsuspecting tourists."

"Um, well, call it what you want, but I now believe there's something out there in those trees," Max said. "All this stuff is just too random and chaotic for something greater not to be at work here."

His words hung in the air for a few tense moments.

The odd thing was that Downs had been experiencing the same gut feeling of which Josiah was speaking. It had been tugging annoyingly at him since he arrived via the rope ladder down from the chopper. Downs felt and had been feeling the same cold and foreign presence of eyes on the group, eyes other than the myriad of insect and reptilian creatures that called this part of the world home.

Downs looked over to Nat. She seemed as though something was eating at and bothering her.

"You okay?" he asked.

She shrugged her shoulders. It was clear to the eye that something was on her mind.

"Is everything okay?" he once again asked.

"Before we left," Nat began, "in fact, it must have been the morning of our departure, I accidentally came across a few documents on Corstine's desk. By mistake, I might add and not intentionally."

Downs frowned. "What kind of documents?"

Nat looked over at the others and then quickly back toward Downs. "Documents that spoke of something."

By now Josiah and Max had gathered round them. Downs continued to keep his voice low, but Nat shook her head in defiance.

"No, it's okay. They need to hear this," she said. "As I was saying, prior to our departure, I came across documents in Corstine's office. There was a ten page write up regarding the death of an Indonesian worker several weeks ago."

Max instinctively looked back to the eyeball, still lying atop the leaf.

The four of them scrambled back towards the eyeball and bent down once more to have a look.

"Do you really think?" Josiah asked.

Max looked up at him. "How many random eyeballs do you see floating around the rainforest?"

Max once again pulled out his red Swiss Army Knife and began to poke and prod at the thing. The eyeball sure as hell looked like it could have come from someone of Indonesian descent. The iris was dark brown in coloration, a commonality found among people of East Asia and Southeast Asia.

Suddenly, Downs was hit by an overwhelming amount of sadness and grief at what they were looking. Someone or something had ripped the eyeball straight from the socket. Downs' couldn't have imagined a worse fate, and for a moment he was completely lost in how the struggle must have ensued. Downs gently placed his hand atop Max's, and pulled back his right arm that was prodding at the eyeball back. For a second the zoologist seemed to look confusingly at him, but shook his head and retracted the knife.

Max stood to his feet. "I-I-I think it is definitive we're looking at the eyeball of that worker."

A deep and cold shudder ran through Downs, causing the hairs on his body to stand on end as the reality of the discovery became apparent. The cold, bloody reality of the situation was very much coming to life high up in the rainforest canopy.

"Did they ever retrieve the body?" Josiah asked.

Nat shook her head. "For the most part, no. The dental report that I had a chance to scan briefly, and I do stress briefly, stated two back molars were retrieved, but that was it. There is currently a one million dollar lawsuit against Corstine and his company by the family of the man, and the family has also enlisted the help of a local medicine man in these parts to, hopefully, retrieve the body."

"One million," Josiah said. "Seems quite small given someone lost their life."

"Not to these people," Nat replied. "One million is more than they could make in ten thousand lifetimes."

Downs nodded. She was right. One dollar was a lot to the locals. One million was a dream, something that most of them could barely even fathom, let alone ever achieve.

"The report," Nat continued, "spoke of sightings of a creature of sorts, a creature high up in the canopy, that has the ability to take to the trees or linger on the forest floor."

"To say that rainforest canopies are not very well documented is quite the understatement," Max said. "I mean, rainforest species on the ground are still being discovered routinely. So the canopy can be viewed as an alien landscape. One could contemplate and even hypothesize that a large bodied creature could potentially conceal itself up in the trees, or the canopy for that matter, assuming it has the tools necessary to achieve such a feat."

"What else do you know about this so-called creature?" Downs asked. "No better time than now to spill all of it."

Nat shook her head. "Nada. Nothing. That's it. The remaining files were mainly about the pending lawsuit. Besides, it would be speculative at that."

"She's right," Josiah added. "All that matters now is what is, not what's been written about or what should be."

He's right, Downs thought as he turned and stared back at the eyeball.

CHAPTER TWENTY

William Jamison strode out towards what seemed to be an ampitheatre, his long and powerful legs moving him effortlessly forward. Ridley and Frederick were close behind, their eyes wide with amazement at the sight they were beholding.

"Well fellas," Jamison said. "Looks like old Corstine's been up to some other stuff as well. Good old Corstine for ya."

"Yeah, tell me about it," Ridley said facetiously.

Jamison did not reply, rather just kept moving forward. He, too, was somewhat shocked at what his eyes were taking in.

The boardwalk came to a giant open circle that had a hollowed out middle and descended all the way to the forest floor below. Popping up through the middle of the circle was vegetation, with trees and branches rising high above the boardwalk while crisscrossing and splaying in all directions. As Jamison moved closer, he could see bleachers that went up eight, possibly twelve rows up, enclosing the whole thing as if it were some type of miniature stadium.

"What the hell's going on here?" Frederick asked as he continued to move forward. "There was no mention in the business plan of this. Did you guys ever get wind of this?"

"Progress," Ridley replied. "Outward expansion if you ask me. And to answer your second part, no, no, I never got wind of this?"

Jamison moved closer to the television mogul and folded his massive arms, making them appear even larger. "Don't fool us, Riddles. I'll drop your ass in two seconds flat if I think you're playing games or withholding valuable info from us. You dig?"

Ridley had worked closer with John Corstine than both Jamison and Frederick combined. He had gone over both Corstine's financials as well as virtually every other part of Corstine's business plan for the construction of the boardwalk.

Unless this is part of some unknown appendage in the business plan, Ridley thought quietly to himself.

"Well," Jamison said, arms still folded. "Was this ever mentioned?"

Ridley shook his head. "No. I'm seeing what you guys are seeing for the first time. That's the honest truth."

Jamison did not reply as he lowered his arms.

The three of them stood there, entranced by the entire scene that lay before them. In the middle of the circle, the trees still protruded upward, but as Jamison began to make his way around the circle, and towards the opposite side, he could clearly see what appeared to be the beginning of netting or some type of wiring. This is what separated the vegetation from the boardwalk.

Jamison walked up to the makeshift wiring and inspected it from the same angle that the bleachers were faced. Experience as well as his keen senses told him not to touch it. It could be razor sharp to the touch, and by its all-encompassing outward appearance, it was. He looked back towards the other two.

"Meant to keep something in, and by the looks of it, something big?"

"Like feeding time at the zoo or something," Frederick joked.

Jamison took the joke as just that, a joke, but he knew there was something more than simply what he was seeing. He knew there was truth in Frederick's statement. He allowed his eyes to gaze upward, following the netting all the way up fifteen feet or so, until it abruptly came to an end. He could see the scaffolding or supports on both sides. It seemed as though there were plans to take the netting even higher. Jamison stepped back a few paces, until the back of his legs touched the first row of the bleachers, and he envisioned what he was looking at. Eventually, he could see netting completely surrounding the sprawling vegetation, climbing past the top of the trees in the middle of the circle, and eventually closing off to form a roof on top.

Jamison's mind flashed back to the severed Komodo dragon. What in the hell could have done that? Unless it was just a bunch of locals having a bit of fun with them, toying around with the civilized world.

It wasn't that Jamison viewed himself that much better than everyone else. However, he did support the notion that the world had social hierarchies, places that people had and needed to occupy. Certain people belonged and needed to be at the bottom. He had always supported that notion. Jamison viewed himself on top of that hierarchy, both in terms of physical strength as well as social status. He viewed the Indonesians on the bottom of that hierarchical ladder.

Once again folding his arms, he smiled at the notion of a few jungle boys toying with them, the wealthy elite, the ones who had, the ones who never went without, the privileged few that Corstine was so desperately seeking out to finance the completion of his boardwalk. A few jungle boys finding the remains of a Komodo dragon more than likely, severing it with some type of primitive cutting instrument, and then finding a way to hoist it up and over the boardwalk itself by use of pullies.

Yet it just didn't make sense. It didn't seem plausible at that. As William Jamison continued to stare at the netting in front of him, he couldn't help but feel that something else was at work, something other than just a remote or obscure appendage in John Corstine's business plan.

CHAPTER TWENTY-ONE

The sun had almost made its way down, creating a burnt orange that hung and lingered for some time above the endless green tree line. For a moment the result was long and dark drawn out shadows in the jungle. Before darkness slowly overtook everything for good, the only available light came from the moon above and the portable headlamps that were strapped to each of their foreheads. Dinner for all four of them came in the form of premade sandwiches and a handful of protein and energy bars.

Downs knew that when darkness befell the rainforest the place truly came alive in all its grandeur! It was as if all the creatures waited patiently throughout the day until darkness settled. He thought of how Europeans come alive at night, embracing the restaurant scene and nightlife after their day at work. Downs smiled to himself with the thought, realizing full well that it had been ages since he last visited his good friend in Lisbon. He decided that as soon as he opened the doors to his small action sports store and got settled back home in San Francisco, he would make the plane flight across the pond to have a visit.

Downs swiveled his head, the light spewing forth from the portable headlamp that was strapped to his forehead. It penetrated through the darkness and up towards what looked like a light stand. Yet it appeared not to be wired with electricity or a bulb for that matter. Another thing on Corstine's "to do" list. He swatted repeatedly as several bugs tried to dive bomb towards him. He watched as the small winged rainforest inhabitants fluttered in his headlamp light for a moment, before flying off into the darkness.

"The only thing missing is marshmallows," Josiah said playfully, trying his best to remain positive and upbeat.

Nat smiled and then turned and looked towards Downs. "We'll stay here for the night and then head out tomorrow on the rest of our trip."

Despite her calm and pleasant demeanor, there was a nervous tension that filled the air. It was still extremely humid, and Downs would have paid an ungodly sum of money for a cool San Francisco breeze to come rolling in, but such was not the case. Beads of sweat continued to meticulously make their way down his forehead.

Downs had already communicated to Nat that he would have first watch, and she seconded the idea that the group couldn't just lay down in lieu of the day's events without someone keeping a watchful eye out. Max and Josiah had bedded down in their tight and cramped mosquito-netted sleeping bags.

Downs stood to his feet and left the group, making his way towards the railing. As he approached the canopy, the thick and sticky air was abuzz with various insect chatter that only seemed to be getting louder with its symphonic pitch. As he neared the growth, his mind went back to the discussion earlier in the day about picking up various insects from rainforest ecosystems in order to discover brand new scientific species.

His headlamp illuminated the vegetation as he stared out. Several bugs annoyingly fluttered in and around his line of sight, undoubtedly drawn to the bright, beaming light, something they most likely were not accustomed to. He wondered and assumed that everything here had probably never seen anything but the shining of the moon high above, and that thought fascinated him for a few random seconds. However, if Corstine's boardwalk officially came true, he wondered how that would affect them?

More and more insects were coming out of the woodwork, flying in and out of the light like a type of dance. Downs was just about to flick off his headlamp when he thought he heard something.

Faint and distant at first, it sounded like a crunching sound. Downs focused his attention, but as he swiveled his headlamp in the direction of the noise, it suddenly died down, and the usual sounds of the jungle instantly overtook it. A hand from behind him touched down upon his back.

"Sorry about that," Nat said. "Figured you could use some company and a nice relaxing cup of tea. Well, at least I can offer you the company part."

"I'm good," he replied. "Something out there in those trees caught my attention. Sounded like a crunching sound, but it died down the minute I shone some light on it though."

Max and Josiah were now awake and beside the two, their short-lived sleep nothing more than a rhythmic dance of tossing and turning upon a hard and uncomfortable surface.

"Well, maybe we need to shine some more light on the situation," Josiah said. His tone of voice, whether it was meant as a joke or not, was unknown. No one replied though.

Downs flicked off his headlamp, instructing everyone else to do the same as well. At first the act of killing the lights seemed to do nothing, but about twenty five seconds or so after removing light from the equation, the unmistakable crunching sound that Downs had heard earlier returned.

Downs looked over at Nat, the only light between the two being offered by the full moon. Without warning she suddenly flicked her headlamp back on, and once again, as expected, the crunching came to a stop just like that. Downs flicked his light back on as well, with Max and Josiah following suit also.

"Strange," Nat said, her finger about ready to push the lights out once again.

Downs tapped Nat on the shoulder and mouthed the word "go" to her. Simultaneously all four of them flicked off their lights.

Immediately the crunching was followed by the breaking and snapping of branches as it sounded like something lurched forward, and then stopped. For a moment there was silence, the entire jungle itself had fallen quiet as well, before the all too familiar crunching sound returned again.

Downs could feel his heart rate accelerate as he suddenly switched on his headlamp. He moved his head ever so gently to the right, passing the outstretched limbs of vegetation with the light. It was thick in this part and seemed to be a tangled impenetrable wall, but as Downs moved his head back several feet to the left, he saw something staring at them. He had almost missed it, almost passed right on by it the first time. Staring at them was a giant eyeball.

"Um, please," Max said, his voice wavering in fear. "Please turn off your headlamp."

CHAPTER TWENTY-TWO

"What better way then to see this place than at night through the eyes of an investor, boys. Screw through the eyes of a guest. Through the eyes of an investor," William Jamison announced, holding his hands up in the air, seemingly soaking in the very essence of the night air itself.

All three of them were equipped with headlamps as well. Ridley Bells nodded his head and began to take in the night. Ringing the amphitheater were several dozen torches. The torches flickered back and forth to life, apparently running off of solar energy. Since they were at the top of the canopy, direct sunlight was practically available all day, whereas light availability at the bottom of the forest floor was limited, causing vines and other plant life to bend and to twist their way towards what sun filtered in through the dense canopy high above.

Frederick looked up towards the stands. He could see that solar bamboo torches also ringed the circular amphitheater at the top as well, giving the whole area a sort of medieval vibe.

"Any plans," Frederick said, standing next to Jamison who was busy gazing up at the full moon.

"Well," Jamison replied. "I say we experience the entire night here, see what this place is like when the lights go out, and ultimately see why a tourist would want to pay top dollar to come to Corstine's little invention here."

"I second that," Ridley said. "Before I throw my hard earned dollars into something, I want to see it from the angle of the consumer, the potential customer, the family that has saved up the entire year for a trip like this. I want to look at things from the end-users perspective."

A vibration, although not massive, but big enough to register beneath their feet, suddenly caught them off guard, causing an uncomfortable ripple through the human body. No one budged. Ten seconds passed before another vibration could be felt beneath their feet, this time more intense, and it seemed to be getting closer.

Suddenly, like a tidal wave of repressed and potential energy, something began moving straight for them beneath the boardwalk.

"Quick to the stands," Jamison shouted, but it was too late.

Huge lumbering breaths of air heaved in and out. There was a wheezing whir of a sound at the end of each breath. The scent of rotting and decaying meat wafted its way up through the cracks and openings in the boards of the boardwalk. Something large was hanging directly beneath them.

CHAPTER TWENTY-THREE

N at pulled Downs back just as something lashed out at them with startling speed. Downs stumbled backwards, instantly losing visual sight of Nat and the others.

As Downs rose to his feet, he noticed a smattering of a foamy substance across the front of his shirt. Nat was behind him as she stumbled to get up as well.

"What the hell was that?" her voice quivered, grabbing his shoulders from behind and peering out towards the green.

Downs' shirt was wet with a spittle type of substance, as if he had been licked. A whirring and clacking sound rang out from inside the trees as the vegetation shook and rumbled with life. Josiah and Max's headlamps were both on full bore, as the light shone brightly on the shaking patch of vegetation. The whirring and clacking sound appeared to be retreating as the light continued to shine brightly on the scene.

Nat's eyes were still wide with terror, wide like some type of nocturnal creature out and about in the heart of the night.

They continued to stare and listen, until the whirring and clacking was all but a faint whisper in the jungle air. Suddenly, the faint whisper eventually turned to nothingness as the accompanying sounds of the jungle came back to their usual audible level as if someone had slowly turned the volume back up.

Max turned and looked at Downs' shirt and was just about to reach for his Swiss Army knife when he scratched that thought entirely. Instead he reached out with his hand towards the foamy spittle. It was warm to the touch.

"Warm blooded," Max mumbled to himself.

"Perhaps you should have taken that knife out. Something's out there," Josiah muttered in fear. "Something's been out there, and it's not going away."

"A tongue," Downs said. "Something licked me. A big slobbering tongue burst out from the trees and knocked me to the ground."

Max's face crumpled up into one of complete concentration, though it hinged more on the fear side of things. "Just going through a mental catalogue of species in my head would lead me to believe we're dealing with something new to science here. Most likely some sort of undocumented species, and if that tooth is indeed linked to it, we're dealing with something big, a predator, a carnivore, an apex predator at the top of the food chain, at the very top of the canopy here."

A branch suddenly snapped from somewhere out in the canopy. The conversation died down as the group listened. At first there was nothing, but the whirring and clacking sound soon returned.

"Is something being dragged?" Josiah whispered.

Max took the question. "Sure as hell sounds like it. Like something is being dragged by another something through the trees."

The words out of Max's mouth needed no deciphering, no processing. The audible sounds before them supported Max's observation. Something of substantial size was being forced and ripped against its will through the vegetation and branches by an equally bigger "something."

Max held up his finger. "It's getting further away from us."

The sound of breaking branches kept moving further and further away but was still distinguishable nonetheless. This was followed by a short-lived violent struggle, and directly after that a high pitched shriek of a scream cut through the air.

The treetops fell silent.

CHAPTER TWENTY-FOUR

The attackers came at William Jamison and the others with both speed and aggression, traveling low to the ground, propelling themselves forward with their long front limbs and powerful hind limbs. Though they were juveniles and small, they were still deadly, nonetheless. That coupled with their ferocious appetite and need to constantly keep honing their skills as a top apex predator, made for an explosive combination. One day they would grow to massive size, but for now they were dog-sized and moved extremely fast as they raced forward, their three-toed-padded feet making them not the most graceful of runners, but they were still adept at moving quickly, nonetheless.

Jamison saw everything playing out, courtesy of his headlamp, as if he were back on the hardwood floors of the NBA. Frederick and Ridley were spaced out to essentially where the three point line would be, and there were four aggressive pursuers coming straight for him, as if his body itself represented the basket. Jamison reached for something that neither of his two colleagues had known he had been carrying all along. Out of the side of one of his deep cargo shorts pockets, he extracted a 9 inch extreme tactical kukri knife. One of the youngsters was headed his way, and fast at that.

It exploded from the ground, catapulting itself up and into the air, seeming to be on a crash collision with Jamison's jugular. Jamison performed a series of intricate maneuvers with the knife before he thrust the blade into the soft under-region of the little creature. The kukri knife sunk deep into the neck, the creature howling in intense pain as Jamison surgically retracted the weapon.

The creature hit the boardwalk and was sent skidding, its legs now rendered useless as it slid towards the edge. Jamison quickly saw his opportunity and seized it. With several large and commanding steps, he bounded forward towards the skidding youngster and booted it as if it were a soccer ball.

The power with which his right foot struck the creature undoubtedly crippled it, sending the screaming little thing over the edge of the boardwalk as it plummeted and fell away into darkness.

Quickly Jamison spun around to assess the situation. There should have only been three left, but his eyes suddenly registered five. Two others must have come out of the vegetation from somewhere.

With the bloody kukri knife still in his hand, he began sprinting towards Ridley who was in over his head with three of the small creatures now pursuing him. However, as he made his way, the corner of his right eye caught the tail end of Frederick making a bee line as fast as his slightly out-of-shape body could muster.

Jamison's eyes darted back to Ridley, and that was all it took. He sprinted all out in that direction, the knife ready to attack at a moment's notice. One of the creatures propelled itself up off the boardwalk and towards the stomach region of Ridley Bells. It's talons were outstretched and Jamison could see it was trying to rip the television mogul wide open.

Jamison slashed at the right hind limb of the little creature, drawing blood and delivering a deep gash, but not severing it as the creature continued to sail through the air. Ridley performed an athletic move that seemed more complicated than he was capable of, hitting the ground and rolling as if it were a routine fire drill.

As if on some predestined course of action, the creature could not stop its intended route, and it went flying over Ridley as he was still performing his drop-and-roll tactic. The creature hit the board-walk and immediately was sent skidding, but this time it was able to stop itself just short of the edge. It regained its momentum and was heading towards Ridley again, but the man was already up and to his feet. Jamison was on it quickly though, wielding the kukri knife like the thing never left his side, but now there were three of the creatures in hot pursuit of him.

Frederick's urgent voice rang out from somewhere. "Over here."

Jamison, only seconds earlier, had spotted Frederick doing some-thing that he couldn't have imagined and which seemed highly improbable, but he wasn't about to question it at this point. Only moments prior, Frederick hurried over to an area in the amphi-theater cordoned off by rope with a sign that read: AUTHORIZED PERSONNEL ONLY BEYOND THIS POINT.

Frederick found what seemed to be a trap door that led down to an area beneath the boardwalk, possibly a storage unit. Ridley saw it as well and headed in that direction. Jamison followed closely, yet the three creatures were upon him.

Jamison had no time to raise the kukri knife, as a mouthful of hungry teeth went hurtling through the air towards him. Doing the only thing he could muster, he lifted up his massive right forearm and closed his hand tightly into a fist, delivering a swift punch to the side of the animal, yet it still raked his exposed skin on his forearm with its teeth and talons on its back limbs.

The creature was batted down from the air, like a football in the NFL being swatted down by an aggressive defender. Jamison watched momentarily as the creature hit the deck, but instead of resurrecting to its feet, something happened, something Jamison himself didn't see coming. The other two of its kind turned on it in an act of true cannibalism, taking full advantage of the situation of their unfortunate fallen comrade.

Jamison hung around just long enough to witness the two as they ripped into the other, using their impressive arsenal of teeth and already sharp talons for nothing more than pure killing. The dog-sized creature that had initially launched an aerial attack against Jamison was being eaten alive as it thrashed about wildly on its back. Jamison watched with horror as one of the creatures gouged its comrade's eyes out while the other pulled the forked lizard-like tongue straight from the screaming youngster's mouth.

Jamison's mind snapped him back into action, and with that he headed for the trap door.

CHAPTER TWENTY-FIVE

"Mr. Corstine, are you here?" Collin Fairbanks called out, still seated in front of the computer monitor as he toggled back and forth between one security camera after another. The whole scene was nothing more than a blatant attempt to make it look like he was diligently working. "Sir, are you here?"

Collin stood to his feet as his back cracked, his eyes sick of looking at the same stupid monitor screen for hours on end. Just to be certain he was indeed alone he called out once more. "Sir?"

The silence confirmed what he already knew. John Corstine had left the building once again. He wasn't quite certain when, but by now he predicted that Corstine was drinking his favorite adult libation, red sangria from the comfort of his bungalow patio.

"Ladies and gentlemen, Elvis has left the building," Collin joked with a sarcastic smile.

Corstine's assistant left behind the computer monitors with their varying views of different security cameras as he made his way, but before he officially exited the room he took one last look towards the monitor.

"If he needs security, why the hell doesn't he hire the staff necessary to pull off such a feat," he muttered to himself in disgust. "Cheap bastard. Should have purchased the domain name www.Cheapest. com way back in the day and built an online memorial to himself. Flipping unbelievable."

Collin shook his head once more in disgust and exited the room. He hated picking up the slack for what he commonly referred to as Corstine's shrewdness. Although Collin himself had never actively built and put together a company, he was acutely aware of how one would have to be shrewd in terms of spending capital judiciously if one were to succeed in the business landscape at large. Despite this though, he believed Corstine was being too cheap, cutting far too many corners, that in the end would essentially come back to burn them as well as ultimately spell doom for the boardwalk. There had to be a limit, and he believed Corstine had already treaded close to the edge, crossing that limit, and was now in freefall.

Collin smiled and chuckled quietly to himself while at the same time patting himself on the back for exploiting some of Corstine's cheapness. Corstine had failed to set up a better system of checks and balances, and with Collin essentially needing no signature other than his own to sign checks, he had free reign over the readily available capital which had been set aside to fund the early stages of the boardwalk.

What Corstine didn't know, whether out of sheer neglect or stupidity, or the possibility of simply being too busy, was that the pullout by several of his investors was not the only hit to his direct capital pipeline. Collin Fairbanks had been stealing from him for going on two years now, not stealing in a major sense, but still stealing nonetheless. Collin started out small, seeing whether

Corstine would notice the modest amounts of cash being siphoned out each month. When nearly seven thousand dollars was stolen over the course of two months, Collin decided it was time to up the ante a bit.

Collin had heard of the rush that thieves often spoke of when they robbed a bank or even a convenience store, and he was starting to feel the intoxicating effects of that very rush. It was like nothing he had ever experienced before, the pure rush of stealing but more importantly stealing and getting away with it.

Just thinking about the fact that he had gotten away with stealing from Corstine's vast fortune for the better part of two years, gave him goose bumps and a rush the likes of which he knew he may never experience again in his lifetime. He took several deep breaths, wanting to remain cool, calm, and collected for his next set of intricate maneuvers. He would need to keep his wits about him in order to pull it all off.

The thought of $1.1 million in one shot was enough to send his pulse skyrocketing through the roof. Quickly his mind harkened back to his days of working in the sales world, making $22,000 per year plus commission.

Plus commission, he thought to himself. *What a flippin' joke.*

Collin had been an Account Executive for a computer start-up company called Creative Computing Solutions, Inc. Over the course of nine months he had worked his way up to Senior Account Executive, a title as well as an achievement that heralded great praise from those around him. Yet he wasn't happy; the long hours and the low pay led to a demoralizing outlook on life. Coupled with the fact that the company refused to offer him stock options angered him to the core.

The jump from Account Executive to Senior Account Executive meant he saw his pay increase from $22,000 to $30,000 per year, a far cry from the high six figure salaries that he saw many of his close friends making. He needed an out so he quit and moved back to Nebraska with his parents.

It was there in Omaha, Nebraska, that he happened upon a chance encounter with John Corstine. He didn't actually meet Corstine first but he had met one of Corstine's business partners who took quite a fancy to the young Nebraskan's command of the English language as well as the way he carried himself. To put it in the words of the business partner, "I like the way you carry yourself, young man. Keep that up and you just may be the boss of many one day."

Collin had never been one to want to grow in a company to a position of power. Yet upon meeting Corstine he happily lied, citing that he was hungry to start at the bottom and work his way to the top. That was precisely the response that Corstine must have been looking for, because after a quick period that literally consisted of a couple of phone calls, Corstine asked him to be his personal assistant.

With the hiring, Collin once again worked his magic, convincing Corstine that he was up to the task of managing several new and emerging revenue streams that Corstine's company currently had in the works. It was planned for Collin to play an instrumental role in the launch and early stages of Ecological Television, but for now Corstine had tasked Collin with helping him to get the boardwalk fully funded and up and running. He had even gone to meetings in Denver, New York, and Chicago. Each time he with a different group of investors, and he tried to persuade them that plopping down large sums of money into the boardwalk was indeed a sound business move.

Collin had failed each and every time he went out and pitched the boardwalk to investors, but Corstine liked his can-do attitude and kept him on the task of raising private money. Corstine viewed himself, ultimately, as the best scavenger for the job, taking money from any source he could and not overlooking anyone as a potential investor.

Collin remembered the time when Corstine had traveled to the Tenderloin district of San Francisco, a dangerous part of the city known for its seedy characters and drug dealers. Corstine had happily made his way to the fifth floor of an old and extremely dilapidated apartment building, opting to take the stairs for fear of encountering problems in the run down and neglected elevator shaft.

Collin could still vividly recall Corstine recanting the idea that one never knew the financial standing of someone, despite the outward or physical appearance that he or she may have portrayed to the world. The fifth floor of that old and dilapidated apartment building was occupied by a man with a net worth just shy of $50 million, and on that grim San Francisco day, he cut Corstine a check for $5 million dollars for one of his business endeavors.

Never underestimate anyone, Collin would always think to himself. *You never know what type of cards that special someone has up his or her sleeves.*

Corstine had taught Collin a very important lesson, but the teacher failed to pay close attention to the pupil. Now the pupil was about to make the teacher pay in a very big way.

CHAPTER TWENTY-SIX

The silence lasted for all but thirty seconds as the familiar sounds of the jungle crept back in. Without warning, that was shattered by something hurled in the dark at Downs and the group. Immediately Downs knew there were watchful eyes fixed upon them and flicked his headlamp on once again, the others following his lead.

Rising up like an angry swarm of bees, the overwhelming smell of something dead stung deeply in their nostrils. As Downs moved his head, his light penetrating through the darkness, he could see something, something huge and elongated. Spanning roughly eighteen feet and laid out before them was a reticulated python, or at least what was left of it. Downs knew it right away to be just that, as no other snake in Indonesia could match a retic pound for pound in terms of length. Downs bent down, although part of him wanted to pull back, never having been the biggest fan of snakes to begin with, but what lay before him was a true gargantuan in every sense of the word.

Max was already on it though, coming immediately to the conclusion that the thing was dead. As the zoologist approached closer, he could see deep gouge marks that had been inflicted upon the python's massive siding, deep penetrating wounds as if something had raked the living hell out of the huge snake, scraping and shredding it on both sides. The snake was as wide as a small tree trunk. Max lifted the heavy tail up and let it flop back to the ground, the heavy thunk on the boardwalk reinforcing just how truly massive the snake was.

"What the hell's going on here?" Josiah muttered, his eyes matching the equally wide eyes of the others. "Dead animals and pieces of the human body being flung from every corner of this jungle. Either there's one really angry and large monkey playing games with us, or I don't know what to think. It's just all too much."

They were barely even able to digest Josiah's words when the sounds of breaking and snapping branches came rushing towards them again. The forest was being bent, twisted, battered, broken, and beaten into submission.

<hr />

William Jamison lowered his huge body and ducked into the small shelter that Frederick and Ridley had escaped into only moments prior.

"Damn good thing I'm still in tip top shape," Jamison said as he hurried inside. Frederick let the door down on top of them, sealing them inside from below with the latch. Had it not been for their headlamps still going full bore, they would have been immersed in total darkness.

The pitter patter of movement could be heard directly above them, but for the moment they were safe. The suffocating crowded conditions inside were all engulfing. Jamison put his hand above his head, realizing that the ceiling above his head was only three inches at best, meaning their tight and confined compartment was only seven feet tall.

The dangling and blackened light bulb that hung down over them reminded Jamison of his grandmother's basement. There was a similar light bulb that hung down over one of the cars. He had never liked that setting for that particular reason, and he didn't like what he was currently seeing.

Like the kind of place where your life would end, Jamison thought grimly to himself.

There were very few things in this world that scared William Jamison, but one of them was the idea of being in a tight and confined space, especially one that was accompanied by black, dingy, piece of crap light bulbs. He would manage and conquer it though, he always did. Just for shits and giggles, Jamison pulled the chain attached to the light bulb. He rolled his eyes, seeing the act immediately to be a stupid one. Obviously, it didn't work. Why would anything work down below when basically nothing was working up above.

"Not much workin' here on Corstine's boardwalk," Jamison said with an air of disgust, as if he were a man who had already made up his mind.

The light exuding forth from Jamison's headlamp managed to capture the terrified expression of Ridley Bells. The television entrepreneur seemed as if he had encountered the devil himself. Suddenly Ridley's eyes shot up towards the boardwalk. "What's at work up there?"

Jamison pulled out a half-smoked, unlit Cuban cigar from his back pocket and stuffed it firmly between his teeth, a habit that he had been known to do from time to time. He didn't necessarily enjoy smoking them, but he certainly enjoyed chewing them. "Not our problem."

Ridley seemed enraged as he stepped forward towards the big man. "Not our problem. Not our freaking problem. Are you completely insane? Of course, it's our problem. It's very much our problem. We're trapped inside a shithole of a storage compartment, and you have the nerve to tell me it's not our problem. I surely as hell don't see who else's problem it would be."

Jamison pulled the unlit cigar from his mouth and grinned down at the man who stood before him. He then shone the light back on Frederick who was crowded almost cowardly in a corner behind him. "Not exactly the two I'd like to be holed away with in a bunker, smack dab in the middle of a war, but we'll have to make do. We always do."

Frederick turned away from the others, hardly even understanding the comment as he stared at the wall, stared at all four corners for that matter. "Um, this appears to be some type of ammunition and weaponry storage bin."

Clearly, Jamison thought to himself, trying to focus on something other than the claustrophobic conditions.

Basic rudimentary shelving held dozens and dozens of weapons and high-powered assault rifles as they lined all four of the walls surrounding the men. Everywhere they looked they were surrounded by instruments of death.

Jamison considered himself to be a hunter in life, and for some odd reason he believed in the notion that he had been a hunter in a previous life as well. He held to the belief that hunting was a spiritual endeavor which should only be done using the skill and expertise of the hunter, preferentially with bow and arrow. This was the way it all started, the way that it should be.

Ridley reached up and grabbed one of the high-powered assault rifles and took it down from its perch. He ran his hand along it and examined the thing as if he were a kid who had just discovered his father's gun.

"Quit playin' around," Jamison said, grabbing the barrel of the rifle and ripping it out of Ridley's hand as if it were a toothpick.

"At least the safety's on," Jamison remarked as he carefully placed the rifle back in its position on the shelf.

"Apparently, Corstine's got a few secrets regarding this place," Frederick said. "And by the looks of it, this place might have some type of infestation problem with whatever it was that attacked us from above."

Jamison strained his ears for a second. Nothing. Whatever these creatures were had apparently left the area, at least for the time being.

Or they're waitin' to pounce the minute we open up and come back out, Jamison thought.

"Well, fellas," Jamison said. "Seems pretty clear why construction on this little side project of Corstine's came to a halt. There's something runnin' around up there. Something that shouldn't exist."

"That coupled with the death of the Indonesian," Ridley added.

"Death?" Jamison asked, slightly confused.

Ridley returned a befuddled look to him. "You didn't know. A man died here a few weeks ago. A worker, to be exact. Reports said he was hunted down by some type of creature or beast. Something that defies all logic."

Frederick gave a half ass smile, though it reflected someone scared shitless rather than smiling. "We're in trouble here. What's the plan?"

"The plan," Jamison said with a wide grin, his attention focusing towards five huge bows housed in the far corner. "The plan is we're gonna hunt down whatever it is that produced those little shits up there. Whatever it is that severed that Komodo dragon in two like it was nothing. That's what we're going after. And those five bows will help us do just that. That's the plan, fellas."

CHAPTER TWENTY-SEVEN

Downs had always been a man who believed in the unbelievable, believed in the everyday miracle, believed in things that defied explanation, but what he saw before him defied every logic thought pattern that the human brain possessed. He turned to witness an explosion of branches, leaves, and vegetation as an enormous being let itself down from the canopy and crashed down hard onto the boardwalk. The explosion mixed with the potential energy sent a coursing vibration that rippled through the structure.

As they ran, Downs was taking in the entire scene for the first time, clear and unobstructed. The whole creature looked like a horrific science experiment gone wrong. Its forest green reptilian skin provided a base, and it had several large red and brown swirls of coloring on its back and sides. It sported a thin yet spiky row of hair that ran atop its back, up and onto the neck and head, giving it a Mohawk appearance. Its skin was beady and reptilian, it had talons that hinted towards a lineage from the raptor family, and it possessed a plush prehensile tale that screamed primate in nature. It must have stood close to nine feet tall when resting on its four manhole-sized feet, each foot equipped with three basket-ball-sized suction cups. The creature possessed a head that any ancient prehistoric animal would have run from. The head was a solid three feet in length and was lined with row upon row of sharp and serrated shark-like teeth, teeth designed to deliver a devastating bite.

The foul smelling breath of the creature instantly rose up as saliva dripped from its serrated teeth. In a moment in which time itself appeared to stand still, the creature seemed to be taking in the entire scene, observing the humans as they fled. Downs paused as well, before several voices cut in, causing him to snap back to reality.

"Come on," Nat shouted, from a bend up ahead. "Come on."

With that Downs took off running as Nat disappeared out of sight around a corner.

⸻

Collin Fairbanks entered the numbers 7, 13, 27, and 31 into the safe. He had done this before, although it had been some time. On his second try, he managed to nail it.

He was in.

The safe housed what John Corstine commonly referred to as the petty cash fund. The funny thing was there was $100,000 dollars in there, $100,000 that was supposed to be used for small knick-knack purchases. This served as a convenience because the Indonesians commonly did not accept credit cards and happily accepted American currency.

Collin held a stack of $5,000 up closely to his nose and breathed it in as if it were the very pages of a book. He loved the smell of money, and that was why he was going about on a personal quest to acquire more of it. By his own admission, he wanted to go about acquiring as much of it as was humanly possible.

The money that he intended to steal from Corstine was going to change his life. It wouldn't make him set and free for life. He would still have to work, but it was going to give him one hell of a head start on his quest to working solely for himself. Collin had already sketched out the details pretty meticulously what he planned to do with the money. Ever since his early teens, he had wanted to get into real estate investing, and Corstine's money was going to help him do just that.

Collin was going to start anew in Brazil, Sao Paulo to be exact. In a country and city so big, he would blend right in. He hoped the masses would swallow him up and he'd never be heard from again, at least not by the authorities and all involved in Corstine's endeavors.

His proposed realty empire would be set up as such, courtesy of a business model from a guy who his sister had once dated. He would start modestly and purchase a small apartment building, three to five units to be exact. However, he Collin Fairbanks, would not be purchasing the building himself. His company that he would start would officially be purchasing the building and the apartment would be held in the company name. Furthering that model would be the small property management company that he planned to set up. This company would be responsible for managing the day-to-day aspects of the building itself as well as handling the monthly cash flow statements. When he needed to visit the building or future buildings he planned to purchase, he would simply introduce himself as the property manager instead of the building owner.

It all made sense to him, perfect sense indeed, and he wondered why more weren't following these proposed strategies.

Their problem, not mine.

His hand reached further into the safe and grabbed another stack of $5,000, bringing him firmly back to the present and out of la la land. He smelled the stack of crisp bills once more.

That smell never gets old.

In his right hand he now held $10,000 dollars in cash. He knew that Corstine's safe housed $100,000 dollars. At least that's the amount that should have been in there, give or take a few thousand. He wanted to have cold hard cash on him for his journey out of Indonesia and to Sao Paolo.

Collin grabbed six more stacks of bills, bringing the total in his hand to a cool $40,000 dollars. This left $60,000 in the safe. Odd as it sounded, he reached into his pocket and pulled out a few pens and put them beneath the other stacks of bills in the safe. He propped up the bills on top of the pens, angling the money in such a way that it seemed as if the existing bills were still there. Not that it really mattered anyway, but he wondered hard for a moment why he wasn't stealing all of it, concluding that $40,000 in cash was more than enough. He had never even seen Corstine go into the safe, and even on day one of the job when Corstine alerted him to the existence of the safe, the real estate tycoon had to search through countless sets of papers just to find the combination.

Collin paused for a moment as the overwhelming urge to steal all the money from the safe radiated powerfully through his body. He stood there for another few seconds poised deeply in thought. Corstine would never know the money was gone, would never know and would never miss it. There was simply too much on his plate, and Collin knew it.

Despite this he shook his head. No. Forty grand was more than enough. Besides he had bigger fish to fry, more importantly $1.1 million. With that Collin Fairbanks closed the safe and was off to the next leg of his journey.

CHAPTER TWENTY-EIGHT

Jai Constantine had been driving for nearly two hours in the dark of the night. The rain soaked jungle road was still a sloshy mess at best as a result of an earlier heavy rainstorm. The darkness was all encompassing around him, except for the two front headlights of the beat up old Land Cruiser that illuminated the jungle road ahead. Things had gone from bad to worse, and what had once been a trail of sorts was now resembling a waterlogged mess, with the soil fully saturated and not able to hold any more water. The conditions were almost non-navigable, but still the vehicle trudged on.

The beat up black Land Cruiser had no stereo. It had been stolen years ago. Jai figured that the poor kids who most likely stole and hawked it had in some small way improved their meager existence. He was perfectly fine with that. As a result Jai had been forced to listen to the rhythmic sound of the vehicle vibrating and making its way along the makeshift dirt road.

"Dear Christos," Jai muttered to himself, barely managing a sharper than expected turn and nearly averting crashing into a large branch that extended out and over the road. The Land Cruiser spit mud out everywhere as the tires scrambled to gain traction. They finally regained their hold of the road and allowed Jai to continue on his way. He had driven these jungle roads before, but the monsoon rain that had swept through the area a few days prior had left everything almost impassable.

Jai was 75% Indonesian mixed with 25% Dutch, although he wanted to acknowledge himself more with the Dutch than the Indonesians. He was sick of being a so-called jungle boy, sick of the brutal heat and humidity mixed with deplorable living conditions. He wanted out desperately, and believed he had figured out a plan, or at least sketched a rough outline of one.

His plan was to take the money that Collin Fairbanks was offering him, $9,000 in cold hard cash, for a ride to the coastal airport. From there he would personally hightail his way to Madrid where he had a good friend. There he would live rent free for awhile as he pursued a new career and life. He could put some money into savings while treating himself to a nice little holiday with the rest of the leftover money.

He thought long and hard about that plan, about the proposed $9,000. He already had $4,500 in the glove compartment to his right, with the other $4,500 to come once the journey with Collin was complete. Slowly, he took his foot off the gas and carefully reached over to the passenger side glove compartment. He opened it, letting it crash down, before finally returning both hands to the steering wheel.

He glanced over and saw the stack of American currency, smiling pleasantly to himself. $9,000 was more than he could save in quite a few years of work. In fact he was so tired at the moment that he couldn't even do the necessary calculations to determine how many years that in fact was. Yet he knew that it added up to many, many years of work.

His eyes made their way from the glove compartment back to the muddy jungle road, and he drove for about five minutes or so before his eyes made their way back to the glove compartment. Several inches to the right of the stack of $4,500 was a sleek 9mm handgun.

Plan "dos" as he had been playfully referring to it. Plan "dos." The thought swirled back and forth in his head.

Jai knew that Collin had money, although he obviously had not pinpointed it down to an actual direct number. He knew the assistant had money, nonetheless. How much remained to be seen, but his mind had been toying with it for several days now. The notion of doing away with Collin Fairbanks entirely, wiping him from existence on this earth, in the damn middle of this nowhere jungle, appealed greatly to him.

He knew that Collin would have money on hand for his journey to the coast, and the two of them would essentially be on roads traveled by very few people, if any at all. It would be easy to murder someone and dispose of the body and let the jungle quickly discard of the evidence. The insects, maggots, worms, and countless other rainforest creatures had a way of rendering a full grown man to nothing but bones in a short amount of time. The jungle never wasted anything. Everything was always being used and reused in one continuous never ending recycling process, and Jai loved that fact about the rainforest.

Jai let the thought hang in his mind before his back finally screamed loud and clear. It had had enough of the forced sitting along with the fact that he had to pee. He brought the Land Cruiser to a halt and quickly parked it. He then proceeded to step outside, down and onto an area of the jungle road that was surprisingly firm despite the squishy conditions he encountered earlier on his trip.

Instantly, his ears were greeted with the low but constant rhythmic groans of several tree frogs. Now with the vehicle off and no headlights, he was totally immersed in the full darkness of the jungle night. He found it both exhilarating and terrifying at the same time, and he decided it best not to move more than a step or two from the Land Cruiser.

Jai had always found the jungle to be a peaceful place as he unzipped his pants and began to relieve himself. It felt good. He had been needing to go for quite some time. His head tilted upwards, towards where he thought the groan of a few tree frogs were happily calling out.

He jumped, peeing on himself in the process. Something had startled him high up in the canopy, startled him to the very core. When he looked back up, whatever it was, had disappeared.

He wiped his eyes, and for the first time he realized just how tired he, in fact, was. He could have sworn that he saw a pair of huge black beady eyes staring down at him. It had been a brief encounter, the exchange lasting not more than a half a second at best, but it seemed so very real.

Jai shook his head, dismissing it all as nothing more than sleep deprivation. When it was all over, he planned on having some serious rest and relaxation. With thoughts of sleep and a better life in mind, he climbed back into the old Land Cruiser and continued on his way.

CHAPTER TWENTY-NINE

The sickening sound of the creature's taloned feet touching down on the boardwalk behind Downs sent him moving at quite possibly the fastest pace of his life. He flew around the turn where he had seen Nat and the others disappear.

He kept moving though as he had no choice. Something behind him, an aberration that defied all logic, was chasing him. Finally up ahead on the far left, Downs saw part of an arm frantically waving him over. It looked like Nat's arm. She had surprisingly disappeared beneath the boardwalk, and now she was somehow waving him on from beneath.

"Come on," she yelled. "Come on. It's on your heels. We can smell it. Hurry. Hurry."

Downs slowed as he approached the partial arm still waving him in and crouched down, grabbing hold of her arm.

Downs ducked low to the ground and with the help of her guiding arm maneuvered his way beneath the railing.

For a moment, his eyes locked with the sheer heights at which they were, and he thought he was going to plummet to his death. He soon felt strong hands grasping his legs as Josiah pulled him through the side opening and down to the platform they were on. "Boy, am I glad to see you guys," Downs said, finally standing to his feet, but barely at that, his head only able to clear by half a foot or so. Immediately Downs motioned for them to flip the headlamps off. They killed the lights.

An overwhelming stench began to float and seep down towards them in the darkness as the boards above vibrated with life, heralding the arrival of the creature in all its glory. Methodically all of them looked up, the darkness of the jungle was slowly materializing into bits and pieces of light.

The intense vibrations from up above finally began to settle down. Time itself seemed to stand still. The creature was just above them now, breathing slow yet powerful lumbering breaths. There was also that distinct odor again. Not being able to fully place it, it smelled like the rotting remains of road kill mixed with raw feces.

Definitely a carnivore, Downs thought. *And most likely what big predators like t-rex would have smelled like. A big hot stinking mess.*

Deep breaths wheezed in and out of its lungs. Then something glimmered in the early morning light. Slowly it was coming into focus that the creature appeared to have a reptilian gleam about its skin.

Downs saw Max adjust himself ever so slightly, and then the reasoning for him even moving in the first place came sliding down between the gaps in the boards above. With minimal visibility, they could, however, make out saliva as it dripped down from one of the openings. Downs watched as it made its way in one continuous stream down towards the floor.

Downs moved himself, making sure he stayed away from the clear gooey substance still coming down in copious amounts. He could now make out the head of the creature above. It was easily three feet in length and almost equally as long in width. The head was massive, to say the least, and the breath spewing from its mouth smelled downright putrid.

It took all of their will power not to wretch, and it was becoming abundantly clear that they were in the presence of something ancient and primordial. It was a relic that had somehow managed to survive in this isolated part of the world, something that might have harkened back to the age of the dinosaurs. It had most likely been stalking, hunting, and eating whatever it wanted for eons now.

The creature turned its head, its attention and gaze focused on something that caught its eyes back in the foliage. As it did so, a new trail of saliva dripped down from the cracks and to the very boards beneath them. Two drippy gooey saliva trails were now running in continuous downward motion, just as one might expect to see from a Komodo dragon.

With that the creature bounded off, propelling itself up and into the air, before disappearing into the green vegetation. The only reminder of it being there in the first place was the swaying back and forth of several branches that had absorbed the impact as it sent itself plunging full force into the rainforest.

"How could something that big just up and disappear?" Josiah asked, making sure to still be using his best library voice.

"Who's to say it's gone," Max chimed back. "Could simply be toying with us, concealing itself just out yonder."

The wretched smell had dissipated somewhat, and for that each and every one of them was thankful. The group now took in what seemed to be a catwalk, quite possibly used by the staff to perform routine maintenance on the boardwalk. At least that seemed to be the most logical thought.

Josiah spoke. "What are we dealing with here?"

All of them looked at Max who smiled. "Guys, this is something brand new to science. Beats me what the hell it is. One thing seems very clear though. It is toying with us. If it had wanted to kill us, it would have already done so."

CHAPTER THIRTY

"Then you're going to have to kill it," Ridley Bells fired back at William Jamison.

Jamison's eyes widened somewhat, confused a little by the rude and arrogant tone of the television mogul, but he appeared more intrigued by the way in which the statement had been delivered. Jamison liked and respected forthright people. You could say that he had a special affinity and place in his heart for them.

Jamison smiled before he was about to speak, but Ridley cut him off.

Ridley spoke. "With all this high powered weaponry available at our fingertips, we'd be foolish not to take advantage of it and knock off whatever those damn things are up there."

Jamison smiled. "But what fun would that be?"

Ridley looked over at Frederick, as if waiting for some type of visual signal that the man sided with his reasoning. Frederick remained stone cold and showed no emotions.

Ridley threw his hands up in the air. "Don't tell me you're siding with him on this?"

Frederick responded in his usual monotone voice. "I am not siding with anyone, Mr. Bells. I am a business man, nothing more, nothing less. I prefer to weigh all angles, taking everything into account, therefore leaving no stone unturned."

"Great, just great," Ridley let out. "I can't believe you would even take this lunacy into consideration. The simple fact of you considering the bow and arrow scenario versus the option of blasting these creatures into oblivion is in itself an exercise in insanity."

Jamison puffed his chest out, making himself seem as big as humanly possible. Whether to visually intimidate the others, or merely to remind himself that he was fully capable of taking the creature or creatures out with nothing more than his God given talents and a bow, he continued to puff his chest out.

Ridley shook his head and turned away. "I just don't get it. This is lunacy, sheer and absolute lunacy. I simply just don't get it."

Jamison paid no attention to the television mogul, turning away and focusing all of his attention on the abundant assortment of bows that were perched before him. He felt like a kid in a candy store with so many to choose from. There were long bows, short bows, and cross bows. Each was no doubt strung to a different draw weight. Jamison picked up one of the bows and started to pull the string back ever so slightly. He knew that the draw weight had to be strung at around thirty five pounds or so, knowing full well that for truly big game such as an elk or moose, fifty pounds was the suggested draw weight. He needed something with that capability, if not more, to take down what he was attempting to take down.

Jamison put it back in place and took a step back, folding his arms and scrunching up his face in the process. Could he kill the creature and its young with such weaponry? And the fact that there was young more than likely indicated there would be an adult male and female creature, unless of course it reproduced asexually.

Primitive, he thought. *The ultimate test of man versus beast.*

Jamison liked the idea of taking these creatures out with such primitive weaponry so much so that the vision of him standing triumphantly with one foot smashed down over one of the adults was already reigning supreme in his head. He had already painted that picture as if it were something straight out of the pages of the magazine Solider of Fortune itself.

"This is insane," Ridley whispered in Jamison's ears. "Absolutely insane. We have all this at our disposal and your eyes only look to that crap."

"Made up my mind long time ago, brother," Jamison replied, almost as if he were in a trancelike state.

Ridley pulled away from him, shaking his head, and looked over at Frederick who moved towards them with his eyes on the bows as well.

Great, Ridley thought to himself. *Just splendid. Now we have two loonies.*

"How would we do it?" Frederick asked, grabbing hold of one of the crossbows.

Jamison chuckled a bit. "Very tactically and precisely. Must be no mistakes. Can't afford to make a mistake when you only have a bow and a few arrows."

Frederick looked back at Ridley, who still had the look of frustration plastered squarely across his face. Frederick then glanced back at Jamison, the big man intently focused on killing with his own skill instead of relying on a high-powered rifle with a scope.

Frederick took one more look at the bows and then back towards Jamison. Quietly and nonchalantly he stepped back towards Ridley and nodded to the television mogul.

Jamison noticed this out of the corner of his eyes and turned to glare at the two men who now seemed to be on opposite ends of the spectrum regarding how they should be protecting themselves.

Frederick now stood confidently next to Ridley, signaling his wish to use high powered weaponry versus raw skill.

"Fine fellas," Jamison said. "Nobody's stopping you from using what you want, and the same goes for me. Nobody's gonna stop me from takin' down the ultimate predator using nothing but my own skills. Nobody."

CHAPTER THIRTY-ONE

Collin Fairbanks had settled on $40,000 in cash as the number that he would steal from John Corstine's petty cash fund. For as long as he had known Corstine, he had found it an oddity that someone could refer to $100,000 as merely petty cash. One hundred thousand to Collin could quite possibly have been someone's life savings. Both of his parents had passed away, but when they were alive they were rural farmers in Nebraska. The idea of $100,000 to them would have been representative of potentially an entire lifetime's worth of money, a number that took years and years of grinding away to achieve.

So as Collin felt around in his right pocket and touched the $40,000, he knew that he had almost half of someone's life savings, and, most importantly, he had acquired it in one tax free shot. The fact that it was cash was the best part of all. He patted it once again as he loved that feeling of cold hard cash. There was no feeling like it. No drug available on the market that could produce such a high for him. There simply was no substitute for the wonderfully warm spreading feeling he got when he touched money. He removed his hand from his pocket and patted at his pocket from the outside. He couldn't get enough of it.

Collin looked down at his watch and began to work out his plan for high tailing off to Brazil and what he would consider to be the good life. At least he began to plant the necessary seeds in order to get him to the good life. Never one to get ahead of himself though, he was only focusing on the next step in that evolution, and that next step involved Jai Constantine.

The plan was simple enough, yet Collin did not want to take any chances with Corstine catching him. That fact alone added detail to the getaway. Collin had originally told Jai to meet him at the grand staircase entrance to the boardwalk, where Corstine housed two gas powered Jeeps below on the ground level of the jungle. Occasionally, in the early days during the construction phase of the boardwalk, he and Corstine would hop into one of those gas powered Jeeps and drive the road beneath the boardwalk that stretched the length of it to survey and make routine checks.

Collin thought about if he should have scheduled his pickup at the staircase to the boardwalk. He shook his head in disapproval. That would have been the easy way out, the sloppy solution, and, most importantly, it might have been the solution that allowed John Corstine to catch him red-handed in the act of stealing from him. He did not want that, did not want that in the least bit.

Collin had arranged for Jai Constantine to pick him up at approximately what was deemed the middle or dead center of the boardwalk. By his calculations Nat and the group should have already passed that midway point by now. By the time he got there, they would be long gone, but he hadn't really been paying close attention to the cameras. He was simply making an educated guess at this point.

Once picked up and successfully down from the boardwalk, he and Jai would make their way to the airport through a rough yet drivable road that had been hacked and cut out of the jungle. He laughed quietly to himself at the fact that Corstine still had the issue of making that jungle road navigable for buses and other commercial vehicles. Corstine still had that hurdle to jump and overcome, and Collin knew it would indeed be a difficult one.

It had crossed Collin's mind once or twice that he could simply commandeer one of Corstine's gas powered Jeeps and drive himself out of the area, but once again it sounded too simple. Therefore, he dismissed it as nothing more than a badly devised plan.

Collin grabbed his Jansport backpack, stuffing a few random energy bars in it. Lastly, he grabbed several bottled waters and stuffed them inside as well.

He paused for a moment, pondering the idea of bottled water. It had always fascinated him how someone came up with the concept of people paying outrageous amounts of money for water. He shook his head. He'd have plenty of time to think up the next multi-million dollar idea once he settled in Brazil and had things up and running for which he had already worked and planned.

Collin took one last look at his surroundings, and with that he opened the sliding glass door and made his way out onto the boardwalk.

⊷⊶

Jai Constantine had driven for a solid hour in one long passage, the silence of the jungle road itself had been getting to him somewhat and the urge to pee had once again been tugging at his last nerve. His legs, back, and hamstrings ached beyond belief, and he would also use that time to do some much needed stretching. Jai figured with the money Collin Fairbanks was paying him, he would visit a nice chiropractor when it was all over, preferably one who worked on a white, pristine sandy beach.

For now he had drunk way too much water before departing on his journey, and he knew better than to do that, but his system had felt dehydrated and he was merely trying to quench his thirst.

His bladder throbbed with pain, and now he was paying the consequences for his water drinking binge earlier. Jai slowly brought the Land Cruiser to a halt in an area that was overgrown with vegetation in an almost seamless mat of growth. As he put the car in park, his eyes gravitated towards the thick mass of vines and branches above him. In fact, to say that things were overgrown was an understatement. It seemed as though the very canopy itself had been lowered all the way down to some fifteen feet above the forest floor. That was the height he estimated the thick matting of growth to be above him. Though he was tired of it, the rainforest never ceased to amaze him in the way it produced vegetation, the likes of which appeared to be on steroids.

A sliver of movement flashed in and out of view in a quick dash above him. Instantly Jai's senses went on heightened alert as he continued to peer upwards at the thick matting of vegetation from the driver's seat.

There was something up there, but whatever it was, was gone or had suddenly disappeared. The burning sensation in his bladder once again returned to the forefront of his mind. Jai reached for the handle to the door to let himself out, but just as he was about to do so an explosion of glass came bursting through the windshield, sending shards of glass as they came raining down onto the dashboard.

There was no time for Jai to scream, panic, or make sense of it all, as an enormous limb came through the open windshield, ripping him from his seat and pulling him violently up and out of the vehicle and into the dense foliage above.

CHAPTER THIRTY-TWO

The maintenance level to the boardwalk that Downs and the others were on, extended for what looked like another hundred yards or so. Downs' ability to estimate yardages was perfected from many years of playing the municipal golf courses in his home city of San Francisco. Here yardages were tracked by the golfers' own calculations instead of being labeled properly by the golf courses themselves, and it was here that Downs learned to judge distances so well.

"We have to get back up to the surface," Nat said.

"And face whatever's up there," Josiah replied, although the paleontologist's rebuttal seemed more like someone cowering in fear rather than a call to arms.

Downs looked over at Max, who had somehow crawled his way into a tight corner and looked like a little kid huddling with his knees pulled tightly towards his chest.

"Not going anywhere," Max muttered to himself. "Not going anywhere. Going to stay here where it's nice and safe. Nice and safe here. Nice and safe. So very safe."

Downs made his way to where the zoologist was curled up. Just to be careful, in case there were any low hanging objects, Downs hunched over as he crept forward towards Max.

"Not going anywhere," Max continued to mutter to himself. "So very warm and nice here. Not moving."

Downs looked back at Nat who returned a confused look as well. Slowly, Downs bent down towards him.

"Hey Max, you okay man?"

Max continued to clutch tightly at his knees while muttering the same garbled and repeated phrase. "Not going anywhere. Not going anywhere. Nice and safe here. Nice and safe. Oh, so very safe."

Downs could see that the zoologist's body was trembling as he grabbed his right hand and gently placed his own hand on top of Max's. Still that had no effect as Max continued to mutter in a trance-like state while his body shook.

Downs thought to himself for a moment this was not getting anywhere. Then he noticed that Max was clutching at something, clutching something tightly in his left hand for all it was worth.

Slowly and rather deliberately Downs touched Max's left hand, and he began to pull the fingers away, one by one until Downs had in his own hand what Max had been clutching so tightly.

"Not going anywhere," Max mumbled once again. "It's going to rip us all to shreds. Rip us all to shreds. Rip. Rip. Rip."

"Rip or RIP," Nat jokingly said to no one in particular.

Downs looked to his hand and saw a massive tooth. It was serrated and about three inches in length. It was a massive piece of weaponry. He looked at the tooth once more and then up towards Max. "Hang right here, pal. It's going to be okay. We're going to get out of this together. Okay. The key word is together."

Downs stood to his feet and quickly made his way over towards the others. Nat immediately took possession and grabbed hold of the tooth. She looked up through the openings in the boards to the top of the boardwalk, where the creature had been standing, and where the overwhelming smell that seemed to follow it everywhere still lingered ever so faintly.

Josiah crowded in around the tooth as well. "A killing instrument that only the most apex of predators would evolve to both need and have, the very top of the food chain. Imagining this tooth digging into you would be like trying to picture being stabbed at once by dozens of knives. Not a pretty picture at all."

Downs looked over towards Max who was still clutching his knees tightly to his chest. "He's in no condition to provide us with any real help at all."

"No," Nat said, shaking her head, "but whatever it is, seems pretty clear we're dealing with something that lives and hunts in the forest canopy. And it will use that to its fullest advantage. Up here in the treetops we are very much out of our element."

Josiah nodded. "Like a shark hunting a weak swimmer in open water. We're completely out of our element up high in this canopy. Doesn't seem plausible though, makes not one bit of scientific sense whatsoever, but I honestly have no argument with which to counter back. It appears we're dealing with something that is not only massive, but which moves with ease in the trees by means of some type of miraculous adaptation."

Downs' eyes turned towards the foliage. The usual constant buzz and drone of the rainforest had returned, offering them some sort of semblance and normalcy to the situation.

Nat looked back towards Max. "What'll we do with him?"

"Give me a second," Downs replied.

Downs made his way back towards the zoologist. Max seemed to have calmed down a bit, as he was no longer muttering to himself, but he was still clutching his legs tightly to his chest. Bending down next to him, Downs gave it a moment before he spoke.

"Max," he whispered. "Hey, buddy, we need to get outta here ASAP. You don't even need to respond. We just need to get out of here quickly, buddy."

A few seconds passed before it seemed as though he was finally coming around. Still pale as a ghost, Max turned, faced Downs, and spoke.

"We're all going to die."

CHAPTER THIRTY-THREE

William Jamison had chosen his bow. He had come to the conclusion and made up his mind that whatever the creatures were, he was going to take them down using nothing more than his sheer raw athletic ability. That's the way he wanted it, and that's the way the final kill scene had already played out in his head. He could still see himself posing for the media with his foot on top of one of the fallen beasts and the other planted on terra firma, his bow slung over his wide chest and a grin plastered across his face from ear to ear.

Ridley Bells had chose an AK-47 rifle, and Frederick, who had never even handled a gun let alone fired one, found himself garnering a sleek 9mm handgun.

Jamison looked at the rag tag group as he pulled the string tightly back on his bow, testing the strength of it. He knew that the bow could easily kill something formidable like a boar, but could it take down what it was that appeared to be stalking them.

Jamison made eye contact with Frederick. "Just do me a favor, partner, don't shoot me in the face. The legs or the arms I can handle, just not this pretty mug. Got it?"

Jamison flexed his arms and patted his powerful legs. "These babies can deal with a gunshot, just not this pretty face. You dig?"

Frederick nodded. "Which side is the killing end again?" He smiled.

Jamison rolled his eyes and focused his attention on the trap door above them. "You fellas ready? I've got my choice for a weapon, and you both have chosen yours. Can't be no mistakes up on the surface."

Ridley tightened his grip on the AK-47. The feeling of having something so powerful in his hands was an intoxicating one. He liked it, despite the fact that he had only fired a weapon a handful of times at the local gun range across from the golf course that he frequented regularly.

Jamison positioned himself directly under the door and held onto the latch that would lead them back up to the surface. He looked back once again at the two men, one a television mogul, and the other an online magazine entrepreneur. Though highly successful in their chosen endeavors, they were quirky, nonetheless.

Not exactly the type of warriors you want with you in the heat of a battle, Jamison thought to himself.

However, that didn't matter now. Jamison fully intended on killing the creature or creatures and its young entirely on his own. That was the final thought in his head as he pushed up on the trap door with his left forearm.

CHAPTER THIRTY-FOUR

Collin Fairbanks stood with his two feet firmly planted on the boardwalk, quadrant one, and not more than ten feet or so from the glass door through which he had let himself out. He wiped at his scalp, sweat already building up atop his forehead and trickling down into his eyes. To make matters worse, it was still early morning and would only get hotter as the day progressed.

Although he would have to learn to deal with it, he didn't like the oppressive heat. That was primarily one of the reasons why he left his parents farm in rural Nebraska and made the move to San Francisco. There always seemed to be a cool breeze coming one's way and the summers weren't so downright intense. The humid conditions of the Indonesian jungle seemed to be having their effect upon him, and as his feet kept him still as a statue, he knew that he had a good 17.5 miles to walk by foot until he would meet up with Jai at the intended pickup locale. By his own calculations, he placed it at somewhere between quadrants three and four, although quadrant four was a better guess than three, but he would know the area when he arrived.

He swatted at a bug that was flying close to his left eye. Collin missed, providing a narrow window of opportunity for the small insect to flutter and make its getaway, up and into the warm jungle air it flew as it made its way out of sight.

Collin hated the outdoors. His setting was the downtown type with fancy bars lined with high scale shopping centers and upscale restaurants that lit up his eyes. This damn humid weather mixed with every bug imaginable was driving him crazy. It was that reason why Collin had pretty much stayed indoors, minding his business, and helping Corstine build a small empire in the middle of the sweltering God awful nowhere.

Just think of Brazil and the seven to one girl to guy ratio. At least there he could lounge by the beach or pool if he so choose to. The conditions there would be quite hot as well, but they would seem oh so much better as he began to grow his small property empire.

The thought itself got his legs in gear, and with that he headed out.

⋯

Jai Constantine was not dead, although he wished that he was. Most of his ribs felt broken. His jaw hung motionless so that speaking or even screaming was extremely painful. His mind was operating slowly, very slowly, yet still able to process the excruciating pain he was in. He was being carried, but to where and by what, it was all so confusing. Focusing all the attention he could muster, and nearly passing out in the process, he could see that he was wedged in a tight embrace in the arm, up near the shoulder of something horrific. They were oddly enough moving from tree to tree through the jungle, often scraping and dragging their way through vegetation that seemed to not want to be penetrated. He watched as the creature suction cupped its left limb to the base of a tree and then pulled itself to the nearby tree with its right limb.

Although he had a jumbled mess of thoughts and senses at best, he could see that they were moving quite easily high atop the jungle. The creature continued to reach out and pull itself from tree to tree. Jai felt as if he were dreaming of gliding through the rainforest. It was like he was flying.

His mind was now focusing on his present danger, and all of a sudden he went into full panic mode. The creature had gripped him tightly along the waistline, and as he kicked with his legs, a strange thing occurred. The creature jerked him even tighter, perhaps reminding him of the effortless power that it possessed, or simply to remind Jai that he was his property now. Whatever the reason was, the power being exerted on Jai now was almost unbearable, as if he were in the terrifying clutches of a vice.

Jai's brain was sending the signal to move his legs, but nothing was happening. He managed to swing his left arm at the scaly massive limb of the creature, the act itself resembling a child trying to punch a full grown adult. It was comical and pointless but he managed to punch the creature again, each time it felt like punching into a concrete wall as he wrapped his knuckles against solid muscle.

The green world around him was now spinning, and Jai did the only thing he could think of at that moment in time. He let out the most blood curdling of cries. He screamed again and again, then came to the stunning realization that he had not been screaming at all. His tongue was gone. It had been ripped out.

And then he saw it, the bulbous little eyes of the youngster that the immense creature was also carrying atop its back. The small creature tilted its head back and swallowed something down. Jai couldn't take it anymore, couldn't take what he was seeing. He let his head flop downward and fixed his gaze on the forest floor below. Jai Constantine wished for death as the huge creature reached out with its right limb and continued pulling all of them deeper and deeper into the entangled jungle.

CHAPTER THIRTY-FIVE

Downs turned back to Nat who was looking at him and shaking her head slowly back and forth. Downs looked over at the zoologist, still clutching at his knees as if they were his safeguard in an unsafe world.

"He's done for, man," Josiah whispered into Downs' ear while grabbing at his shoulder. "I mean damn, man, I feel overwhelmed by the situation at hand, but he's completely gone head over heels back to the googo gaga thumb-sucking stage on us."

Downs lowered his head and made his way over towards Max. He knelt down. "Max, we really need to get going man. Can you walk? We need you. All of us need you. I need you."

To everyone's surprise, Max turned, faced Downs, and spoke, although his face was still pale and sickly white.

Max nodded. "I can do it."

"Let me give you a hand," Downs said, gently grabbing at his shoulder and pulling the zoologist up.

Max dusted himself off as if nothing had happened, as if nothing in the entire world had happened and he had merely fallen to his feet. All eyes were on him as he made his way towards the foliage that appeared to be creeping in by the second. Here the jungle was thick, and the boardwalk's maintenance level, if that was in fact what they were on, would be completely overtaken with vegetation and growth in a short amount of time.

Max hung his body out and stared at the foliage. Then spinning back around like someone possessed, he spoke. His speech was surprisingly calm and composed for someone who had only moments prior looked as though he were part of some distant world.

"It will return," Max said. "My intuition tells me it's still in the general vicinity. Could be watching us right now, much like a great white shark will leave the area but still be watching from afar. Watching, always watching."

There was that pang of uneasiness again, as the tension of the situation seemed to rise up from the very boards beneath Downs' feet. It made its way to his beating heart and spread out over the rest of his body, finally by ascending all the way to his wild thoughts housed deep within the brain. Despite this, Downs breathed a subtle sigh of relief and was visibly glad to see that Max had snapped out of whatever dark hole into which he seemed to have crawled.

"Well we can't stay down here," Nat said. "Besides, this only goes on for a little while longer. So it looks like the underground party is over down here."

Max smiled at Nat's comment, perhaps letting them know he was okay, at least for the immediate moment.

"What in the hell is the purpose of this lower platform?" Josiah asked.

"Maintenance, most likely," Downs replied. "Haven't you ever been to Disneyland?"

Josiah returned an inquisitive look. "I have. What's that gotta do with anything?"

Downs began to pace back and forth. "Well, just like any other major park or theme park, routine maintenance must be performed.

And at Disneyland there is an entire underground city beneath the actual park itself. Maintenance can work at any time and fix problems as they occur while the park stays open. I'm assuming Corstine was trying to mimic the same conditions here, on a much more minor level of course."

"And a much more incomplete level," Josiah cracked, realizing that this surely was no underground city.

Max was suddenly gone from beside the three of them. Downs spun around and his eyes located the zoologist some fifty yards from where they stood. He was fidgeting with a door of sorts that led back and up to the surface.

By the time everyone quickly scurried over, Max already had a staircase that folded out from what was the boardwalk above. It resembled what one would expect to find coming out of a ceiling leading up and into an upstair's attic.

"Our doorway back up to the surface," Max proudly announced, almost not believing it himself.

Josiah stood behind him slightly. "Our doorway back up to get eaten. Shit man, we're screwed. At least down here it gives off the air of safety."

Downs grabbed hold of Josiah's shoulders. "Stay with us, okay man. We're going to get through this ordeal together. There will be no lurking down here in the shadows."

Nat's face once again scrunched up into a look of seriousness and concern. "I'm sorry for leading you guys into this ordeal, whatever it may be that we're indeed dealing with up there. Corstine never made mention of any concerns or worries, other than acquiring new investors."

"Let me see it again" Max said, as he grabbed and regained possession of the tooth from Nat.

All eyes were once again on the tooth and Max's outstretched hands. It was big, far larger than seemed possible for a creature living this high up in the canopy. It would have stacked up formidably in terms of size against any of the giant carnivores throughout history.

Downs looked back towards where he had seen the saliva dripping, only minutes prior. This seemed like an eternity ago. The humid jungle seemed to have that effect on all of them, that time was indeed moving at a snail's pace, and every hour seemed as long as an entire day. He could hardly believe they had survived the night.

"Well, we can't stay here," Nat once again stressed.

Downs positioned himself at the bottom of the opening to the stairway and stared straight up for a moment. The blue sky above, mixed with overhanging tree limbs, greeted his view. His eyes quickly made their way back down towards the others. In a short but brief exchange, the four of them nodded to one another, not a word was said, nothing needed to be said. The seriousness of the situation spoke louder than words ever could.

And just like that Max was first, but not before stuffing the tooth into his back pocket. He began to climb the stairs back up to the surface of the boardwalk.

CHAPTER THIRTY-SIX

John Corstine quietly opened the door to his small and modest, yet entirely comfortable, two-story residence three quarters of a mile from his offices at the boardwalk. He had taken one of the gas powered Jeeps and traversed a small maintenance road that had been plowed solely for the purpose of allowing him to drive to and from while he was in this part of the world overseeing the project.

It had been a bone of contention among several of the early investors in the boardwalk who had found out that such a road had been constructed. With the construction came the demise of the hundreds of trees and vegetation that populated the area. The investors questioned how someone who was supposedly trying to save patches of rainforest in this part of the world, and who was trying with every last ditch effort to bring Ecological Television to fruition, would destroy a small yet still considerable size area all in the name of convenience to get to and from his residence. But it all simply added to the mystique and mystery that was John Corstine.

Corstine let himself in through the elegantly designed bamboo door. Bypassing the living room, he made his way to the kitchen. He was in desperate need of a drink. A nice cold glass of sangria, his personal favorite would do the trick just nicely. He knew his limits, never drank himself to oblivion, but enjoyed his late afternoon drink with regularity.

He poured himself the drink, sat in the kitchen for a moment, before making his way further through the house until he reached a glass door. He unlatched it and let himself out to what was his back veranda, a small brick patio, some twenty by twenty feet, with a nice view of the dense and entangled jungle.

Corstine sat down on one of the outside patio chairs and took a sip of his cold and refreshing sangria. He just wanted to unwind a bit and let his thoughts roam.

Running things from a remote control standpoint had been something that many investors had disliked of John Corstine, and the way in which he had gone about doing things in the past as well as the present didn't help either. He had once purchased a strip mall development on the outskirts of Dallas, Texas, with the help of a consortium of ten or so investors, and was accused of never once visiting the site, not one single time. Corstine admittedly denied it though, citing he was on site twice and had hired a fulltime property manager to conduct business and oversee the redevelopment phase.

Corstine took another sip of his sangria. Despite the lavish and jet-setting lifestyle that he portrayed to his investors and those closest to him, he was in debt, in trouble, and he knew it. He took another sip of his drink and gently rattled the two remaining ice cubes at the bottom of the glass.

Corstine was in trouble with many of his projects and investments, and had already foreclosed on three large apartment buildings in the Northern California area. Several others in the Phoenix and Dallas areas were in danger of going under as well. He simply could not let that happen. He had to win, whatever the cost would be.

He reclined in his seat and stared out at the thick, solid wall of vegetation consisting of vines, branches, and leaves as the jungle melded into a wall of green. A tree frog could be heard croaking somewhere, and that triggered a few more to chime in from the surrounding limbs and branches.

Corstine needed the boardwalk to be a success, both for his personal as well as his financial growth. He had been hoping to use the profits to pay off the debts that his other properties had taken on over the years. He was also banking on the fact that people from all over the globe would take to the idea of being able to hike and experience the rainforest from what was essentially a road high in the sky.

Corstine reached over and pulled out a pair of beat up old binoculars lined with a leather casing. He placed his glass down on the small table to the side of him. Something had caught his attention out yonder. Slowly he did his best to steady his focus.

There was something up in the trees, and whatever it was there were sounds buzzing in and around it. At first Corstine almost missed it, but as he once again steadied the binoculars and backtracked about ten feet or so down and to the left, it vaguely looked like the ragged remains of a human body.

Corstine stood to his feet so quickly that he nearly made himself lightheaded. Out about a hundred yards or so and seventy five feet up, entwined and dangling amongst the dense vine growth was a human body.

Corstine's blood went icy cold.

CHAPTER THIRTY-SEVEN

William Jamison had chosen the aggressive and commanding route as he pushed and climbed back up to the surface. As he pulled himself up and out of the dark shadowy storage compartment of a hole and stood to his feet, his senses were back on heightened alert. Blessed with superior vision and hand eye coordination, along with blistering speed and power, he was launched into professional sports, more specifically the National Basketball Association.

He knew though that he would have to use every bit of those talents and then some to take down what he knew was out there waiting for them, not to mention the pack of ravenous youngsters. Jamison quickly went on the offensive with the bow ready to fire at a moment's notice as he did a quick 360 degree sweep of the area.

His eyes scanned the boardwalk, looking for any possible hiding areas in which the small youngsters could be lurking. Noise from behind rustled in the foliage and he spun around just as Frederick and Ridley had come to the top of the boardwalk, their weapons also raised, resembling a makeshift special forces unit at best.

Noise and chaos came bursting forth from the green foliage as several birds appeared to have been flushed from their perches. Jamison ducked as the three tropical birds made a beeline for it and flew over his head, flying tightly and lowly for a few brief seconds before finally rising up and out of view.

Jamison spun back around again, having let down his attention momentarily, and by his standards that was too long. The branches that hung over the railing once again fluttered to life and out stepped a lime green bird. It hopped down off the railing and bounced along on two weak yet still functioning legs.

Jamison immediately saw that the bird's right wing was broken, as it dangled limply at its side. Noise once again rustled from the foliage and the bird promptly stopped and turned around to have a look. More rustling of the leaves followed, and the bird quickly turned around and began hopping away.

Both Ridley and Frederick smiled to one another playfully as they let their weapons drop to their sides. Jamison, however, did not, his attention still intently focused on the patch of vegetation from which the bird had come. It was at that point that the attack came, but from the completely opposite direction.

Frederick spotted the intruders out of the corner of his eye, but they were moving quickly in his direction, giving him little time to react let alone process fully what was happening. As he attempted to raise the 9mm into an offensive position, the first of the small creatures leaped towards him, mouth wide open, talons outstretched.

Frederick almost had the weapon leveled when the creature came sailing through the air and slashed at him with its talons, gouging deeply into his neck before finally gravity took hold, sending the animal back down to the ground. Frederick howled in pain and was now bleeding profusely as the handgun clunked down hard on the boardwalk.

The creature was coming back for more, and it was not alone. An intense shooting pain registered at Frederick's left calf as one of the speedy predators slashed a deep gouge and then retreated. One by one, little by little, they were trying to pick the stumbling human apart, and bring him crashing to his knees. Frederick screamed again. The creature had torn his calf muscle wide open and along with it shredded part of his pant leg.

With the weapon now on the ground, bleeding considerably, and in a world of immense pain, Frederick made a last fleeting attempt to retrieve the weapon. Once again the youngsters were bearing down hard on him, attempting to launch a high speed aerial assault. Seeing this he did the only thing that seemed logical. He began to run as fast as he could as the three speedy young predators pursued him.

Both Jamison and Ridley were under attack themselves, and they could do nothing for their injured comrade as he raced off into the distance.

All Ridley saw were rows upon rows of small yet sharply pronounced teeth and equally razor sharp talons as they were being propelled towards him like falling meteorites. He unloaded several rounds into the air, spraying bullets everywhere, yet surprisingly hitting one youngster in the process. It let out a sharp piercing wail as its body flopped down on the boardwalk.

William Jamison, meanwhile, had gotten down on one knee, steadied himself, and released an arrow that pierced through the neck of one of the oncoming attackers. It was killed on the spot mid-flight as the dead weight of the thing immediately hit the deck skidding. Quickly Jamison acted and in one swift move that would have done any competitive soccer player justice, he kicked the dead youngster over the side of the boardwalk with his size sixteen's.

The little creature could be heard falling hard through several branches as it plummeted downward towards the jungle floor. The sound of the commotion finally faded off into the distance.

⟞⟝

Frederick Douglass took a brief glance over his shoulders. He had miraculously managed to put some distance between himself and the young creatures. His peripheral vision on both sides told him that the vegetation had become extremely heavy. The growth hung over the railings, crowding everything in and giving it a tightly confined feeling as that of being in a maze. He managed to look down at his torn calf and saw a big open gash, but he kept running, kept moving as best he could.

From his right ear he heard breaking limbs and branches. This all caught his attention. The foliage was coming alive as something massive seemed to be moving about. His pace and pulse quickened considerably, his feet continuing to move him forward at a frantic pace.

Then from behind him, he heard the blood-curdling cries of the youngsters. They caught up to him and were now moving relatively quickly, galloping like a pack of reptilian carnivorous dogs.

Frederick pushed himself beyond what he believed he was capable of. He had placed the unbearable pain to the back of his brain, as he was now in full on survival mode. One of the youngsters sped up on his left side and nosed out just ahead of the pace he was setting. It took a swipe at him, but he narrowly avoided the small yet razor sharp talons as he darted quickly to the right. The little creature swiped several more times, missing each time, but with each swipe Frederick was being pushed further and further towards the right side of the boardwalk, closer to the railing.

This cat and mouse chase continued for another hundred yards or so, before Frederick finally realized that the youngster was not purposely trying to harm him. Rather it was pushing him as far as it could to the right, herding and corralling him in the same way a sheepdog might herd cattle into a desired location.

Frederick had just about been pushed to the edge of the right side of the boardwalk, any closer and he'd be riding the railing itself as he continued to run. Thunderous snapping and cracking sounds followed as a giant predator suddenly emerged from the foliage and bore down upon the scrambling dot com entrepreneur.

CHAPTER THIRTY-EIGHT

The constant drone of insects, combined with the sounds of the jungle was driving Collin Fairbanks to the edge of insanity. To relieve this feeling, he delved his hand into his pocket to feel the cold hard cash he had stolen from Corstine's safe. Almost immediately he felt the soothing effects course through his body.

Collin's mind kept focusing on flashes of images here and there: past, present, and the future. He was doing his best to ensure that he stayed on track mentally. Collin kept reminding himself of a tropical beach setting with throngs of good looking women as he began to build a small property empire in Brazil away from the constraints of the United States government. He didn't care about the prospect of being a slum lord; that title would suit him just fine as long as it was his own empire he was building and not someone else's.

Collin had already walked several miles, although it felt like about twenty as the oppressive and sweltering humidity rose with each passing hour. He dropped his backpack to the ground and wiped at a solid stream of sweat that had been continually running down the side of his face for quite some time. It was hot, damn hot. He pulled a blue bandana out of his back pocket and ran it quickly through his hair that had once been neatly gelled. Although he considered it to be an exercise in futility as the sweat would start accumulating and running almost as soon as he stuffed the bandana away in his back pocket.

Collin sipped at his water bottle, deciding to chase it with some Gatorade, a combination he had been doing since his graduate school days. Slowly the future visions that were flooding his memories gave way to his present situation as he took in the endless sea of green splaying out in all directions. Collin didn't like nature, never had, and most likely never would, but the idea of capitalizing and making money off of nature suited him just fine. He was after capital, lots of it to be exact. After all he was going to need it to initially fund and get his small empire off the ground without the help or backing of outside investors.

Collin gulped down another swig of water and took in his last panoramic view of the place, fully absorbing Corstine's damned ridiculous vision. Stuffing the bottle back into his backpack, he decided it was high time he continued on his way. His rendezvous with Jai Constantine awaited him.

CHAPTER THIRTY-NINE

Downs watched as Max's rear end made its way up the hanging staircase and out of view, trying his best to keep a sense of humor in such dire situations. He found it encouraging that the zoologist had agreed to go first, coming to the full realization as a whole that the group was far better off with an intelligent and sane Max Caldwell, than they were with a bumbling, thumb-sucking child.

Max pulled himself through the opening, stood to his feet atop the boardwalk, brushed himself off, and peered back down towards the others below. He then crouched low to the boardwalk, out of view as much as he could muster. Listening for a moment, he motioned that the coast was clear with a wave of his right hand.

Responding to the call of duty, Nat grabbed the ladder and began the short climb.

Josiah turned to Downs and rolled his eyes. "Old Maxy's trying to beat us both to the punch."

Downs chuckled lightly, although now wasn't the time for such joking. "We got bigger issues."

"That we do," Josiah said, craning his head up towards the opening as Nat continued to ascend.

He waited until Nat had finally climbed her way to the surface before beginning on his own short journey. Just as Josiah was about to push off with his right foot, Downs felt a small tingling vibration beneath his feet.

Josiah immediately turned towards Downs, neither of them speaking a word. Downs wondered if something large had been flung atop the boardwalk, or if they were indeed in the presence of the real deal.

"You guys good up there?" Josiah asked in a low but certainly not a whisper of a tone.

Nat peered down through the hole towards them, but before she could even utter a response, the boardwalk was hit with a second tingling vibration. This time the shockwave resounded and had some staying power, as things shook with a slight vibration for a few long and unnerving seconds.

All at once, four eyes peered down at Josiah and Downs. Not giving it a second thought, Downs nudged Josiah and began to push him up towards the surface. Josiah didn't say a word, quickly hurrying himself up the ladder towards the others. Whatever it was, they would face it together, as a team, and wouldn't fancy the crowded and tight confining spaces of the maintenance level anymore.

Downs took one last look around at the surroundings, and with that grabbed hold of the ladder and began climbing. As he pulled himself through the opening, his eyes quickly took in the entire scene. The group was scattered on either side of the boardwalk, peering out as best they could into the jungle that surrounded them from every angle.

Nat stood for the first time with the pistol raised in front of Max who was pointing with his hand to some random point out in the vegetation. She looked ready to fire at a whim's notice, with the possibility of shooting first and asking questions second.

Downs glanced over at Josiah who had removed his own six inch retractable knife from his backpack. Together the team was no match for whatever was waiting for them in the deep vegetation, and they truly embodied the term ragtag in every aspect.

Without warning the vegetation at Downs' back rumbled to life with the sound of branches and limbs being obliterated. As quickly as the rumbling began, it ended. This time, however, the rumbling now came from beneath the boardwalk, and before any of them even had time to react, the vegetation in front of Max and Nat was alive with life.

All fell silent as Downs' eyes naturally gravitated towards Nat's, but they were intercepted by the glare of Max. He looked surprisingly calm and in control of his emotions, a far cry from the whimpering school kid from earlier.

Another terrifyingly long thirty seconds of silence ensued before the team could hear movement once again from below the board-walk. It was making its way back towards where Josiah and Downs were standing.

Downs' eyes met with Max's for one last fleeting moment, before the zoologist belted at the top of his lungs for all it was worth.

"RUN."

CHAPTER FORTY

"Now what?" Ridley Bells asked, looking Jamison square in the eyes. "Gotta go after him. Can't just leave him."

"No," Jamison replied. "No, we can't, but we certainly can't go runnin' into no bloody massacre either. You dig, brotha?" Jamison knew and had physically seen Frederick run further along this part of the boardwalk that they were on, but where Frederick had gone was truly the unknown.

Ridley rolled his eyes. "Yeah, I dig real clear. I dig that you don't give a shit about Frederick over there, and you're happy to see him get munched on by God knows whatever it is that's living in this rainforest."

Jamison smiled, looked down at the ground, and wiped at some sweat that had accumulated nicely under his chin. "Look, all I'm sayin' is I don't want to go get either of us killed. What's done is done, and let's face it, by now he may be done. Nothing more than some limp skin and bones."

Ridley was not certain where he stood with Jamison's comment, but he did see that the big man had a point. They now sat here conversing, wasting precious seconds, knowing full well that Frederick may have already been long gone.

They were in the presence of a power unlike anything that any of them had ever seen before. Despite that, Ridley had to go after him, had to know. He did see Jamison's point, but he couldn't just leave Frederick to fend for himself.

He simply had to go in pursuit of his fellow colleague.

CHAPTER FORTY-ONE

Frederick came to a panting stop, breathing hard as he reached down for his knees. Most of his mind was still in complete shock at what he had just seen only moments prior, a massive head that would have given any dinosaur or prehistoric creature from the past a run for its money. Despite the innate fear that gripped him the moment the huge creature had emerged from the growth, he forced himself onward.

Surprisingly the thing had not given up chase. Frederick felt as though he had outrun the land version of a great white shark, and that thought alone made him feel on top of the world as he stood upright and put his hands over his head, still trying desperately to catch his breath.

He knew he was out of shape. It had been quite some time since he had last exercised. Starting a giant online company usually had that type of 24/7 grip on people. The fact that he was still alive though, still breathing the warm jungle air, was about as intoxicating a feeling as he had ever experienced or even hoped for back in his trial and error drug days of his youth.

Nope, he thought to himself, once again keeling over and feeling as if he was going to vomit. *Not feeling good.*

He coughed several times, but it appeared to be nothing more than the dry heaves, the worst by his own accord. At least vomiting would provide immediate relief. He continued to dry heave for a while before he was able to fully stand to his feet, and with saliva plastered across his face he looked back down the boardwalk, expecting to see the creatures still giving chase, but all was silent, eerily silent.

Resting his arm on the railing of the boardwalk, he realized for the first time just how dense the growth was in this section. It hung and formed a canopy high above the boardwalk, intertwining itself, making things quite a bit darker than they should have been.

Instinctively, he backed away, somewhat intimidated by the lack of visibility that lay before and above him in the dense, dark growth. The lack of light made it difficult to see, but his eyes caught a break in the vines and branches. With his pulse quickening, he blinked several times, uncertain at what he was observing.

Within another second all was revealed. About ten feet or so away, almost completely invisible in the vegetation, laid two large baseball-sized bulbous eyes. Frederick almost missed them, and even as he was staring wide eyed as a child, he was still unsure if what he was looking at was indeed real or not. Suddenly one of the eyes swiveled and turned directly towards him.

His brain screamed loudly for him to run, screamed for him to turn and sprint, but his heart began pounding. Whether it was the tension or the sheer terror of it all, a jumbled message was sent to his brain. His feet got tripped up, sending him tumbling backwards as he fell with an awkward thump on his backside.

Before his brain could even make sense of any of it, the vegetation came alive as the creature burst forward in a blur. Frederick quickly tried to force himself up but was pinned down by an enormous three-toed manhole-sized foot. Instantly he could feel that several of his ribs were broken as the predator continued to crush him with relative ease, not killing him, but still crushing him, nonetheless, as if it had both a plan and use for him.

The pressure atop his chest felt as if he were being wedged beneath a small car. It became absolutely unbearable, and he struggled with each breath, each one now coming in short and labored intervals. The creature pushed down with a little more pressure, and there snapped another one of his ribs. He felt no pain, as pure wild terror coursed through his veins.

Frederick began to flail wildly with his hands, striking the massive foot that held him pinned down, but he was no match for the creature. It merely upped the exertion power that it had on him. He managed to lift his head just enough to see the jaw of the predator. He knew that once the animal bit down, the only way to escape the bite would be to travel down the throat. Back would not be an option, meaning the creature's throat and belly would be the only alternative.

The creature seemed to be a nightmarish mix of different prehistoric life forms that had come to fruition in Earth's history, but it was very much alive as it continued to crush him.

Frederick's vision suddenly became spotted and blurry. Fear and terror soon gave way to a wish, one last final wish that it would all end and he would pass from this world to the next. Frederick closed his eyes shut and gritted his teeth together, wishing and praying for death, his breathing now next to nothing.

Spots and colors filled his vision as the world slowly began to fade away into nothingness. Frederick Douglass managed to open his eyes one last time to see the jaws of the huge creature open wide and close down over his head.

CHAPTER FORTY-TWO

Collin Fairbanks stopped dead in his tracks and stared at the structure that lay before his eyes. He knew it would be there, as he had had many a discussion about it with Corstine early on in the architectural blueprints days of the boardwalk. He hadn't actually seen it in the light of day yet, but he was greatly anticipating it.

There it is.

He took a few more steps forward and then stumbled a few feet beyond that before finally coming to a stop. Before him was the restaurant that he had both heard about and discussed on numerous occasions, a restaurant high atop the forest canopy offering guests and patrons broad sweeping views of the endless sea of vegetation in a dining experience. However, it was currently on a part of the boardwalk deemed the maintenance section, but it was clear as day that patrons were supposed to be funneled towards it just as soon as it was completed and open to the public.

"Odd to see the thing just sitting here," he muttered to himself.

As he stood there he tried hard to think how long it had been since he had actually been out and about on the boardwalk, he realized it had been quite some time. There had been those days when he was busy supervising and overseeing construction in and around both his and Corstine's offices. Yet now that he really thought about it, his memory did not recall ever being this far out on the boardwalk.

Yep. That was correct. By his account he had never ventured out to this part of the boardwalk. Momentarily, he was distracted by a large branch that had grown over the boardwalk. Collin grabbed hold of it and attempted to push it back, trying to jam and wedge the thing behind the railing, before letting go of it and realizing it was far too large to manipulate in such a manner.

Collin laughed to himself. That was Corstine's problem now along with the rest of the mess that he wouldn't be there to clean up and oversee. The boardwalk was a mess, an incomplete and utter mess as he continued to look at the makeshift building.

Suddenly though and without warning, Collin thought it odd that he felt some remorse for what he was doing and had done. Maybe it was the fact that Corstine had taken a chance on him and showed him some loyalty. Or maybe it was just plain remorse for a criminal act. After all, he had never even received so much as a parking ticket in his life, let alone commit a full fledged criminal act such as the one he was currently undertaking.

His eyes darted back towards the restaurant, and for a moment, a strange moment, he felt as though there were eyes on him. He didn't care much for nature, but he had forced himself to grin and bare it with the creation of the boardwalk. Now as his pulse quickened somewhat, he felt damn positive that something was watching him from afar.

The idea of remorse for his act of wrongdoing at this point in time quickly turned to fear as the vegetation moved with life. The wind blew though, and Collin shook his head.

He was doing his best to stay in and focused on the moment, but his brain was still screaming that he was being watched. His gut instinct had been something he had learned to trust over the years.

The width of the boardwalk around the actual restaurant widened to about eighty-five feet, an astonishing width given the heights at which they were currently situated.

That feeling of uneasiness had finally reached a tipping point inside Collin's head, and with that in mind he quickly hurried towards the entrance to the small building.

⚔ ⚔

Downs' mind was spinning, wild with fear, a fear that wanted to cripple and paralyze him. He wouldn't allow that though, and fought with every shred of mental energy he had to rid the fear while pushing it away.

The boardwalk strained under the immense weight of the creature, and in its fierce arrival out of the vegetation, it had become turned around, Downs was greeted by both its backside and its long prehensile tail that swished vigorously back and forth in the air.

Quickly though and with surprising speed, the creature righted itself and spun around, offering Downs a clear and unobstructed view of its ugly mug. Hanging downward like a drooping flower from its massive jaws was the limp and lifeless body of Frederick Douglass, the poor dot com entrepreneur pinned in place by the massive teeth.

Downs felt a cold shudder run through his body; the sight of the online magazine entrepreneur's morbid body dangling there like a rag doll caught him completely off guard. The creature's bulbous eyes looked more menacing and crazed than ever, as it jerked its head back and forth from side to side, as if announcing that this was its kill. Frederick's head and legs bobbed back and forth as the creature continued to shake.

And then just like that, Downs decided to high tail it out of there.

Whether the creature was caught off guard by his surprising speed, or it simply felt weighed down a bit by the dead weight of

153

Frederick's body, it did not react and took a few moments before finally deciding to give up chase.

There was no roar though, no menacing cry that followed. With Frederick's body still firmly clenched in its jaws, it bounded after Downs, but, thankfully, the thirty-year old had already been able to put about fifty yards or so between him and it.

The creature was fast, but not insanely fast. Its three-toed manhole-sized feet coupled with its huge size made it incapable of reaching great speeds plus it had the added burden of a full grown man still dangling from its jaws. But regardless of all that it was still moving at a good speed. Once again and not to his surprise, Downs saw the hand of Nat up ahead waving him on.

They must have gone under the boardwalk again.

Behind him the creature was now letting out a low resonating growl, like a person trying to speak with a mouth full of food. In one sweeping movement, Downs lowered himself and prepared to hang his body over the edge of the boardwalk, but several hands grabbed out to pull him from below. He was not ready for that.

Suddenly, he felt his body falling.

CHAPTER FORTY-THREE

William Jamison and Ridley Bells had been moving at a brisk pace for quite some time. They had little to no sign that their colleague and fellow investor Frederick Douglass had ever even made his way across this part of the boardwalk.

Finally, they were starting to see the first visible signs of blood, gradually changing from drops here and there to large puddles with, large smear stains. Both of them slowly came to a stop and bent down around a shallow pool of blood approximately four inches in diameter.

Ridley shook his head, his eyes sinking as he squatted down. "Oh, man."

"Doesn't look good, brotha, doesn't look good at all," Jamison said as he stood to his feet, his attitude steely and cold as ever, not showing the least bit of human emotion.

Ridley remained in a squat position, his eyes taking in the small pool of blood, his heart not wanting to give in, but his mind knowing full well what the blood more than likely meant and signified. His eyes spotted sizeable portions of blood that made their way out and away from where he was squatting.

Ridley stood to his feet and followed the blood trail as Jamison came round. Instantly, Jamison could see that the blood was making its way towards the creeping vegetation, and he didn't like the sight of that.

Jamison pulled the bow from his side and set the arrow firmly in place. He wasn't taking any chances, and the blood, combined with the fact that his eyes could see several of the leaves drenched with blood, made him feel on edge. Slowly, he crept forward with the bow raised and ready to fire.

CHAPTER FORTY-FOUR

Collin Fairbanks made his way forward towards the makeshift restaurant, pausing at the entrance where two life-size wooden Indian elephants greeted would-be guests, the scene and imagery itself seeming to be heavily inspired by the concepts of the Rainforest Café. Strangely he wondered to himself for a moment if his traveling via several of the maintenances passages below from time to time had been necessary? There were times when he decided that he would use them, opting for secrecy and stealth, before he finally popped back up to the boardwalk just a short distance from where he knew the restaurant would be. Collin knew that the investor tour was on the main guided part of the boardwalk, and what he was on would be closed to the public for still sometime. But he had chosen his route for maximum privacy in order to pull off his plan.

His eyes focused back on the restaurant, wondering when Corstine would officially open up this section of the boardwalk. Collin was not the biggest nature buff in the world, but he knew the two wooden elephants were Indian elephants because of the small ears they had, another random tidbit of information that he would be happy to forget in the future. He stood there for a moment, dwarfed by the huge elephants, and paused to reflect on John Corstine's boardwalk concept once again.

It took a few seconds to fully kick in, but he felt it. Collin could feel the overwhelming power that Corstine had spoken of time and time again. The power that would take an ordinary human being from a thriving metropolis or suburb of the world and make him or her feel the power and importance of conserving the rainforests of the world. Collin could definitely feel it, and as he turned around to look at the immense sea of green, he saw what Corstine had seen all along.

There was that guilt again as it rose up in his stomach, guilt for not only stealing directly from Corstine, but for betraying his trust. The guilt caused him to stop dead in his tracks, and he once again focused on the two Indian elephants. He stepped closer towards the elephant on his right and smiled. They weren't actually made of wood at all, as they first appeared to be.

They were made of something entirely different, although he didn't know what. All he knew was that they weren't wooden. Corstine claimed to be too much of a tree hugger to blatantly chop down trees in the name of creating something, although that was entirely debatable as far as Collin was concerned. In fact, one of Corstine's main pitches to the public was that everything on the boardwalk was constructed using no wood whatsoever. Essentially, Corstine had resurrected an Ikea in the sky, Ikea being the grand master of making things look, like wood which were in fact not. Collin's thoughts quickly rotated to that of the road that had been plowed on the rainforest floor below, allowing Corstine direct access to his bungalow dwelling. He shook his head once more, knowing full well the amount of trees that had been cut down in order to make that road a possibility. The old fool Corstine at times made absolutely no sense whatsoever.

The thought of an Ikea in the sky caused Collin to chuckle quietly to himself. He let out a deep breath, trying to push away the feelings of guilt that he now had. He began to focus once again on launching his small property empire in Brazil.

Determining he had enough guilt as well as elephant statue time, he proceeded to make his way through the double doors. He pushed them open and immediately was bathed in dim lighting, the kind of dim fading light that one would expect to see as the shadows crept in on the end of a day in the rainforest.

Collin was not overtly impressed with what he saw. The place looked capable of holding around a hundred guests or so, and it offered comfortable booth dining. He thought the place resembled Outback Steakhouse both in the layout and in the way it felt. To his right he saw a rectangular sports bar area, minus the flat screen televisions broadcasting every sport imaginable.

He made his way towards the bar area, realizing that Corstine himself must have been copying a strategy straight from Yosemite National Park itself. His idea was to take the concept of nature, mix it with alcohol, and then selling it to the public for an insane profit. Collin knew that a trip to Yosemite ensured guests would get to connect with nature and get away from things such as the internet and television. Yet the ever important revenue stream known as alcohol would always be a flowing part of the equation. Corstine's boardwalk appeared to be enlisting that very same strategy. Collin shrugged his shoulders as he didn't blame Corstine one bit for the revenue stream and continued to move forward.

His eyes continued to scan. There was a women's and men's bathroom to the right, and then his eyes locked onto the kitchen to the slight left. Without even thinking, he began moving towards it. As he was just about ready to push his way through the traditional double doors with two glass circular windows on each one, the overwhelming smell of decaying meat met and greeted both his nostrils and stomach. Wanting to recoil back and vomit, it was too late; his hands were already in motion as he pushed through into the kitchen.

Immediately near one of the stoves, as clear as could be, was a badly decaying severed arm.

CHAPTER FORTY-FIVE

A powerful hand reached out and grabbed Downs, cradling him around the waist, and reeling him in. The reunion between Josiah and Downs was short-lived though, as their eyes met for a quick fleeting moment. Then the high pitched screams of Nat and Max broke in. Quickly, Downs looked behind them and could see a thick black swarming and seemingly endless mass that was moving and twitching about everywhere and anywhere there was space.

"Go," Max shouted. "Go. Just freaking go."

The zoologist's hands pushed Downs and Josiah out from the maintenance platform. Downs had failed to notice that several enormous tree limbs and branches were gathered in a tight configuration, supported from below by a myriad of other trees, producing a giant makeshift platform of sorts that lay horizontally with a slight decline. A handful of other limbs pinched and leaned in from close by. Quickly the four of them made their way off the maintenance level and onto the primary fallen limb. The group continued to move out, moving with hesitant yet cautious steps. They used the three limbs to the side which acted as a rail all the while continuing to place careful steps on the enormous tree limb beneath them.

"Just go," Max continued. "Don't look back."

But Downs managed to look back, just enough to have a peek, and he could see a black swarming mass that had completely invaded the maintenance perch.

Ants, his brain registered. *A swarming, hungry, uncontrollable mass of ants, ready to engulf everything and anything in their path.*

They looked furious, absolutely in some type of whipped up frenzy. The ants were substantially larger than modern day bullet ants, and probably no less aggressive. Downs turned back around as they continued down the decline, the limb wide enough to walk on, yet still requiring extreme concentration.

Max continued periodically to look behind, making damn sure the swarming mass was not in pursuit. To his relief it was not. Up ahead, he could see green vegetation and growth that had already begun to invade and grow around the broken off limbs. And beyond that Max knew it fell away to the forest floor below.

"That was close," Josiah said, breathing a slight sigh of relief as they slowed and came to a stop, still on edge given that they were easily a good eighty feet up in the air.

Downs looked around though, knowing full well whatever it was that was hunting them moved with ease through the forest. That coupled with the heights they were at made his pulse continue to skip beats. "We can't stay here unfortunately. There can be no such thing."

Downs moved closer and felt with his hand along the other limbs that were butted up against the end of the enormous tree limb they were on, the bark of those trees providing somewhat of a stable base to ease his mind. He was still somewhat uneasy about the idea of being so high up, and on a gathering of disconnected treelimbs to make matters worse. Since arriving on the boardwalk he had felt uneasy about everything, and now that they were being hunted seemed to be the culmination of all those bad vibes he had experienced earlier.

"Bick's right," Max chimed back. "We're not safe here either. We're not safe anywhere, to put it bluntly, with something like that moving where it wants, when it wants."

"Yeah, but at least we're safe from those ants." Nat winced in pain just thinking about how bad that would be. "Those things make bullet ants look cute and cuddly."

Downs was quite confused as well. Nothing seemingly was making sense atop Corstine's boardwalk. "What the hell happened back there? I've never seen a swarming mass of ants move like that before?"

"Well," Max replied, his eyes already trying to take in as much as they could. " Um, this is a whole new ecosystem up here with discoveries most likely abounding with every new insect that is uncovered. It's also possible that the flies and ants that we've experienced so far might be acting in some type of symbiotic relationship to this creature, much like pilot fish do to a shark."

"How something that large moves like that, and at these heights, is beyond me," Nat said, folding her arms and giving off the impression of extreme worry.

The silence of the rainforest was downright unnerving, as the thick and humid air was devoid of sound, the kind of silence that meant the creatures and insects knew that a predator was close by. All of their eyes shot ninety degrees to the right as several birds came to a noisy squawk of a landing on a nearby branch. They watched with baited breath as the three birds screamed loudly as if almost in protest to one another. One of them took a peck at the other with its beak, and then with several more loud squawks, they lifted up into the air and out of view.

"How far to the chopper rendezvous point?" Josiah asked, his eyes deadlocked on Nat.

Nat pulled out an old-fashioned map from her backpack. She did her best to estimate where they were in relation to where Corstine had originally planned for them to meet his private helicopter at what he informally called "the rendezvous point," or that was at least what his assistant Collin Fairbanks had told them.

Fairbanks, Downs thought to himself momentarily, reciting Collin's name in his head. He didn't like the name one bit. Sounded like the name of a scam artist, but he had no facts or figures to back that up. It was just the way it sounded and felt when he shook the personal assistant's hand.

"We have approximately 3.7 miles," Nat announced, "according to my calculations, give or take a half-mile here or there. Once we get back up to the boardwalk of course."

Downs let out a deep sigh, now fully back in the moment. "Not a crazy distance, but with something hunting us at our backs, and from all around, may as well be a thousand miles."

"Let's just cut right to the chase," Josiah remarked, folding his arms across his wide chest. "No b.s., just straightforward talk. What are we dealing with here? You dig, brothas?"

The group chuckled at his last line as it offered a moment of reprieve.

"Sorry," Josiah said, "just had to get in a quick William Jamison jab. But seriously, do we know what the hell we're dealing with here?"

With the question posed, Downs had his own personal opinions, but naturally his eyes gravitated towards Max, giving the zoologist the stage alone.

"Geez, you guys," Max said, showing both signs of nervousness and tension. "You guys really know how to put the pressure on a fella."

Max looked at Downs, Downs giving him a quick nod of approval, hopefully egging him on in the process, and giving him the confidence to deliver his best scientific opinion.

Max took a deep breath. "Okay, you guys, here it is. Mind you, I'm a zoologist, and to truly find out what that thing is, we'd have to get a blood sample, take it back to the lab, and perform a series of tests on it."

Nat smiled a tired smile. "I think all of us would settle for just getting the hell out of here."

"I second that," Josiah replied. "Come on Max, just tell us what ya think we're dealin' with and, more importantly, how we can defeat it. You know, possible weaknesses and things like that."

Max's face scrunched up into a ball of concentration, undoubtedly the face that his colleagues back at his day job in the lab saw on a daily basis. "What we're dealing with here appears to be some type of monstrous hybrid of a mixture of different animals, both from the past and the present."

Max was heading in the direction that Downs had thought as well, but he still wasn't quite certain where the young zoologist was going to take it. It was obvious that Max wanted to pace back and forth, undoubtedly, his forte for long-winded explanations, but he remained firmly rooted at where he stood for obvious reasons.

"Where do I begin with this creature?" Max continued with. "The jaw or the skull itself, in my opinion resembles the extinct predator Koolasuchus, a gigantic amphibian that lived some 137 to 112 million years ago."

"Possessed a flat and spade-shaped head," Downs added.

Max turned and looked at him. "You know your prehistory. I'm impressed."

Downs nodded and smiled. "Spent many a night as a kid watching Discovery Channel. But what do you make of the teeth of this thing?"

Max shook his head, most likely somewhat confused himself. "That's where the hybrid, almost insane, part of this creature begins. The shape of the head seems straight out of the pages of Koolasuchus, while the teeth themselves point towards a resemblance to the Great White Shark lineage. And if the tooth in my back pocket is any indication as to the size of a shark under the water, it'd be a giant shark by any estimation. Twenty feet plus."

No one said a thing as Max continued on. "The body of this creature is extremely muscular and heavily built, and the way that it maneuvers hints at a possible big cat relationship, like the giant cats that stalk the African plains, and possibly affirming some type of Smilodon relationship, once again though just speculation on my part. Yet the way it moves and the fact that it can propel its massive body from tree to tree via a prehensile tail affirms some type of primate relationship."

Max snapped his fingers and smiled. "Bingo. And it has feet that resemble a tree frog, allowing it to suction cup to a firm base and climb."

"Yet with the talons and weaponry of a full-on killing machine, Nat added.

"Treetop canopies," Downs said with a smile as he looked in Josiah's direction.

"Yeah I know," Nat said. "An undiscovered ecosystem, but something this size. Don't you think it would have been discovered by now?"

Downs shook his head and looked at his feet, deciding to step into the conversation. "In this part of the world, a lot goes unnoticed and unreported in third world countries, and given just how off the beaten path we are, I'm surprised anything makes it out and into the news. Take shark attacks for instance. It's tough to get an accurate worldwide number of how many people are bitten and attacked by sharks each year because so many people live in third world countries where the attacks are never reported and tabulated."

"You got that straight from "Shark Week" on Discovery Channel, didn't you?" Josiah commented with a wry smile on his face.

Downs raised his head up. "Damn straight."

In as blunt a tone as Downs had ever used in his entire lifetime, he spoke directly to no one in particular. "Now to the important issue. How do we kill this thing?"

CHAPTER FORTY-SIX

C ollin Fairbanks wasn't certain how he had done it, but he had somehow managed to suppress the revolting urge to vomit. His eyes saw a badly decaying and severed human arm, and before he knew it, his eyes found what looked like the mangled and partially devoured chunk of an adult human thigh close by. Now his mind was reeling uncontrollably fast, and in a strange out-of-body experience he staggered forward with his hands covering his nose, offering partial relief to replace the putrid smell.

Collin hunched over, hands still covering his nose, and stumbled clumsily into the gas-powered stove with a loud thump. Now his body was leaning over the stove, and that's when he saw what an absolute disaster the kitchen was. Blood was splattered in thick splotches on both the walls and floor, indicating that a struggle had taken place.

He recoiled at the sight of what was more than likely a pile of ragged, shredded flesh, and it had the unmistakable look of being human. Collin's mind continued to race with frantic, wild scenarios of what had gone down in the kitchen.

Now that he was close to the pile of flesh, flies buzzed in and out and in close proximity to him. He saw a black mound beyond the pile of flesh, and then upon closer examination, the black mound was molting, moving, turning over as if it were a living, breathing entity.

And then that's when Collin saw it, an eyeball that stared lifelessly back at him as the severed head of a man jarred to one side, offering him a partial view of the forehead region as well as the eyeball. The black mass once again turned over, and just like that the eyeball and the head disappeared.

Collin felt as though he was on the verge of unconsciousness.

Breathe, he told himself. *Just breathe. You must breathe.*

⟫⟨ ⟩⟪

William Jamison and Ridley Bells had come upon the only small building that the boardwalk currently had. Despite this most interesting and unexpected of discoveries, it had all become somewhat of a blur for Ridley, whose attention and mind was surprisingly still firmly wrapped around the idea of Ecological Television. Ridley was positive, just downright positive that the concept would be enough to sustain a twenty-four hour television network. He, unfortunately, was downright positive as well that they would never see fellow investor Frederick Douglass again. The thought was and had been weighing on him as they moved further and further across the boardwalk and started to see more evidence that hinted towards the idea of Frederick's demise.

Ridley had already made ungodly sums of money in his entrepreneurial career, and if he played his cards right, there would be more ungodly sums filtering and flowing his way soon again. He and Corstine had been working on the idea for a little over a year when he read the headlines that Al Gore had sold their television network called Current T.V. to the Aljazeera Television Network for a reported

$500 million dollar payday, with Gore's personal cut of the endeavor valued at $200 million dollars.

Reading that only wet Ridley's own personal quest to launch another large television network. The first television network had found him to be a scrappy entrepreneur just eager and grateful enough to have a group of investors who were willing to invest in his idea. When the idea was officially up and running, it was voted on by the small board of directors that they would sell early, not wanting to officially see the idea through to years down the road, and rather wanting to cash in on a guaranteed and quick profit.

Ridley's personal cut was just shy of $250,000, not exactly chump change, but certainly not enough with which to think about retiring on. With the sale of his second television network, his cut was bumped up to an impressive twenty million. Now for the first time in his life, a life that had seen several business ideas come and go before finally hitting on a winner, he was ready to launch his third television network and, hopefully, if all went well, receive an even bigger percentage of the company than before.

Ridley had been so preoccupied with his thoughts that he had failed to see that both he and Jamison were now crouched some fifty feet behind what appeared to be the back entrance to some type of building. Jamison slung the bow over his shoulder as his strong and powerful legs remained in a crouch position low to the ground. He looked at the structure before them and then up towards the roof, instantly seeing two vents. Jamison studied the metallic-colored vents for a moment and then looked back towards the small and ordinary looking back door.

"What the hell is this place?" Jamison said scratching his chin, deep in thought.

"Huh," Ridley said, as if he had been awakened from a dream.

Jamison turned to Ridley in frustration, knowing immediately that his partner was not fully entrenched in the moment.

"Wakeup, brotha," Jamison said abruptly. "We're about to enter through that backdoor. There may be some supplies in there that we can use."

Ridley nodded at Jamison's statement. "Right."

Jamison turned to him with as intense a glare as he'd ever seen before. "Are you with me? No mistakes."

Ridley nodded as his grip tightened on the Ak-47.

"Okay then," Jamison said. "Let's move in."

CHAPTER FORTY-SEVEN

Jepson Ray realized what must have happened just as the first shrill scream rang out through the old dilapidated Brazilian school bus. He turned and was overwhelmed with the sight as a middle-aged Brazilian woman was hastily making her way towards him down the crowded and narrow aisle of the bus. Her outstretched arms begged and pleaded for him to help her, as if by some weird quirk of fate she knew he was responsible for her predicament.

Her upper arms and neck were engulfed in a traveling mass of black as she continued to panic and scream, making her way closer to him. Then out of nowhere, an elderly bald gentlemen stood to his feet, as if answering the call to duty. The two collided violently in the aisle; the momentum that the woman had was almost enough to knock the old man to the ground as he stumbled back a few steps. He managed to cling on to one of the seats, keeping himself upright, yet barely at that.

The old man pushed off the seat and edged himself forward towards the woman once again. Yet strangely it was as if she did not want the man's help, and she tried to push her way through him towards Jepson. The man was now up against her, close to her crawling skin.

Jepson could see it all from where he stood. He saw that the oversized Indonesian ants, easily thirty percent larger than that of a normal bullet ant, were repeatedly stinging the woman and violently shaking themselves at the same time, thereby releasing miniature versions of their adult selves onto her panic stricken skin. The miniatures were now hastily making their way from the woman's skin onto the man's skin, as if rushing to claim a new territory.

The man's ungodly screams signaled that an attack had indeed been launched by the hungry and voracious miniatures. The bus erupted into complete and utter chaos, as not a single soul remained calm. Husbands shouted tirelessly, mothers tried relentlessly to protect their babies and young children, and Jepson Ray, the only white Caucasian male on the bus to Sao Paulo, continued to stand where his carry on bag was stowed.

One man stood and pointed at Jepson while shouting out phrases in Portuguesse, signaling towards the lone Caucasian. Jepson knew that the man was insinuating that this was all because of him, that he was responsible for the madness, but the commotion and stir that the man was causing was soon drowned out by the overall madness taking place inside the bus. Jepson had, after all, agreed to take the voracious new species of Indonesian ants that Collin Fairbanks had sent him out onto the black market to see what the huge ferocious ants would fetch in terms of a pure dollar amount.

As all out chaos ensued, Jepson turned in horror to see the bus driver slumped over the wheel of the bus as the vehicle hit a large bump, sending many of the still screaming passengers up and into the air momentarily. Jepson raced over towards the driver. Whether the large man suffered a heart attack, passed out from shock, or had been bitten and inflicted with bites, Jepson did not know. All he knew was the man was slumped over the wheel and there was no one driving the out-of-control bus. Jepson was just about to put his two fingers up to the man's neck to check his pulse, when the bus hit another violent bump. It was now evident that they were heading off the side of the road and were going to plummet down the steep hillside.

For a split second Jepson thought he would take the wheel of the bus, attempting to save the forty foot out-of-control moving mass, but it was too late. The slumped over bus driver was far too heavy to try and move at this point.

Just as the bus went careening over the edge of the road and down the steep embankment, Jepson managed to look back towards the main part of the bus to see the man and woman's body piled on top of each other in the middle aisle of the bus, more than likely both dead. Jepson knew what was happening next as even more shrill, panicked screams filled the bus. The predatory ants were leaving the dead bodies and going after the terrified bus patrons.

Screams of terror and pain filled the air as the bus crashed through a healthy sized branch and continued its reckless descent down the Brazilian hillside.

CHAPTER FORTY-EIGHT

John Corstine knew he was under attack as a piece of unknown flying substance went sailing through the bottom lower window of his quaint little bungalow with a loud shattering sound. Corstine hastily gathered the papers he had been reviewing and stuffed them back into the manila colored folder. Quickly, he made his way to the door, pausing for a moment to have a look back. Just as he did so, the wall to his left was once again splattered with a substance.

"What the hell?"

Bending down quickly, despite his aging knees, the substance had the unmistakable and disgusting odor of raw feces.

Could it actually be? Corstine thought to himself. The ground to the left of him was littered with what seemed like dried animal feces.

Corstine quickly slammed the door and spun around in the little house. He wasn't quite certain what to do next, but as another small window in his living room was shattered, he knew he needed to leave. He looked down to the rug to see several large balls of what he now knew were more than likely animal feces.

"Jeez," he muttered to himself, his eyes looking up the stairways to the two bedrooms that were on the second floor.

Quickly, he made his way up the stairs with the manila envelope still tucked firmly at his side. Once up on the second level, Corstine scurried past his small bedroom and towards the room that served as his office. Another shattered window from an unknown location somewhere in the house caused Corstine to move with more urgency.

Quickly he threw open the desk drawers and began shuffling through papers. Not finding what he was looking for in the first drawer, he slammed it shut and opened the second drawer. Once again his hands were working at a feverish pace, fumbling through all sorts of papers and documents.

Corstine's heart was pounding inside his already nervous chest. He needed to find those papers as his hands continued to make quick work of all the other excess paperwork that had built up from years and years of not cleaning out the desk drawers.

His eyes spotted something though, the key words he was looking for. Still moving at a frantic pace and forcing himself to take deep, fulfilling breaths for fear of passing out, he saw the word CRYPTOZOOLOGY written in big bold letters atop the official document. He quickly shuffled through the rest of the seven pages that were paper clipped to the title page and closed the drawer. Corstine had the documents for which he had been searching.

The sound of feet shuffling and scurrying about from the bottom floor of the living room quickly caught his attention as his body went as stiff as a board. He peered out of the second story window to the ground below. He thought about it for a moment, but the fact that there was no lower level to which he could jump meant he would have to jump two stories down to the dirt of the jungle below. It wasn't worth breaking an ankle or far worse. Then he would truly be done for.

The noise and scurrying from below in the living room was becoming louder and more pronounced as Corstine heard one of his vases atop his mantle fall and shatter to the ground. Quickly, he needed a plan of action. Going out the office window would not suffice. His eyes scanned the room for anything, anything at all that could serve him well. Nothing seemed of any use to him except for a lone pitching wedge, a friendly reminder to his favorite past time of golf. It greeted his eager eyes, and it would have to do as he hastily grabbed the golf club, making his way out of the office and in the direction from which the noise was coming.

CHAPTER FORTY-NINE

"It's a must that we start a feeding frenzy," Downs announced, the words stumbling quickly out of his mouth.

The others looked at him. Downs' eyes locked with those of Max's, who had a wide grin on his face.

"To bide much-needed time for ourselves," Downs added.

Nat looked back down at the map once again. "Only about 3.7 miles to the rendezvous point, but what are you getting at, Bick?"

"Everybody likes a free meal, right," Downs said, his eyes making contact with each and every one of them. "I'm proposing that we take something down and start the ultimate feeding frenzy to give us some much needed time to make our getaway to this so called "rendezvous point." Even just a little snippet of time could make the difference between life and death."

Max scratched his chin. It was obvious that the gears were churning inside the zoologist's head. "Not a bad plan, not a bad plan at all, but what would we take down at these staggering heights?"

Downs looked around, the nearby branches, vines, and leaves greeted his vision. Beyond that endless mile after mile of green tree-top canopies continued on and on.

Downs let out a long and drawn out sigh. "What about capturing and taking down another reticulated python?"

"A retic," Max said, his eyes almost popping out of his head in disbelief. "Would be an extremely difficult task this high up. The one that we encountered was most likely taken from somewhere lower in the canopy if not from the forest floor itself or a nearby stream or water source."

Downs sighed once more.

"Well," Josiah joked. "We could always hope that another fully grown Komodo dragon gets tossed our way."

"Um, fat chance," Max said. "The fact that it already happened seems like a one in a million chance. If we are even to hypothesize that we can fully execute Bick's plan, we need something fresh. Nothing rings the dinner bell harder than fresh meat."

"Well, it happened before," Nat said, trying her best to be as positive about the situation as she could.

"Yeah, and that's why I want to get the hell outta here," Josiah insisted. "That thing out there's just playing games with us."

"It is." Max said, "Make no doubt we all could have already been dead, but we're not. It's kept us around, for whatever reason."

Max's words hung in the air.

"Well, first thing's first," Downs said. "We need to get back on terra firma."

"Terra firma, the ground, or terra firma, the boardwalk?" Josiah asked as he smiled.

Downs smiled. "Terra firma, the ground, would be great, but for right now the boardwalk sounds better than being stuck out here."

Max turned himself in the direction from where they had come. "Not if that swarm is still going strong."

"Yeah man, what's up with that?" Josiah asked. "What kind of ants are they, if you can even call them that?"

Max shook his head. "They're definitely something that hasn't been documented, or at least I certainly have never gotten wind of them. My gut instinct tells me that the tribal and local people of this region have been dealing with these ants for millennia. It's possible they could be directly linked to the creature by some type of symbiotic relationship, yet at this moment I don't see how the creature would benefit. Just like pilot fish swim close to sharks and feed off the entrails from dead kills, these ants might be doing the same thing to this here creature of ours. Merely speculation on my part though."

Downs nodded as he fully absorbed everything that Max had said, knowing full well that there was nothing to prove that what he was saying was correct, but it certainly seemed plausible. Downs knew that the third world, in general, was a great hoarder of secrets from the rest of the civilized world, hoarding such secrets as official shark attack numbers and statistics, people being bitten by poisonous insects and reptiles, and medicinal plants which possibly held the cures to diseases deep within the rainforests of the world. By and large, it seemed as though the third world never wanted to relinquish its secrets.

Such was the case with whatever it was that was hunting them. It was no doubt a secret, something that had hunted and survived high in the relatively unexplored Indonesian rainforest canopy. Downs knew they were not dealing with a myth or some monster created from men gathering round a fire and speaking of tales from the primeval past. They were dealing with a living, breathing creature, one that seemed to have only assets and no liabilities. They were dealing with a living relic, something from a time gone by, something that appeared as though it would have blended in perfectly with the world that the dinosaurs once called home.

Then suddenly, and without warning, something reached out and grabbed Nat.

CHAPTER FIFTY

William Jamison and Ridley Bells entered the back side of the building about as secretly and as unassumingly as they had stumbled upon it. Jamison was first to enter through the back door. Crouched low to the ground and with his senses on heightened alert, he took several large but quiet steps into what looked like a kitchen, coming to a stop just behind a large stainless steel refrigerator. There he crouched for a full thirty seconds, mired in silence and waiting to see what clues his environment would give him. When all seemed clear, he motioned with his hand for Ridley to begin coming forward.

Ridley did so, but with quite a bit of trepidation. With his hands still firmly wrapped around the AK-47, he began to edge forward towards where Jamison was waiting for him. He was moving slowly, as if each uncertain step were being taken on an ice sheet above a frozen lake.

Jamison motioned with his arms for the television entrepreneur to quicken his pace, but he let out a quiet sigh when he saw that Ridley was locked firmly at one speed and one speed only. Jamison quietly turned around and stood softly to his feet, the bow still locked in a firing position.

Jamison began inching his way forward towards yet another stainless steel refrigerator that stood some ten feet away, but his eyes were focused on making his way further to the gas stoves that lay just beyond. He could hear Ridley behind him and didn't know if the man was crawling on all fours, crouching, or walking slowly upright, and, quite frankly, he didn't care. Jamison could hear the man behind him, and for him that was good enough.

Meanwhile, Ridley's eyes were beginning to take in the entire scene. He saw dark and forbidding red patches on the far wall, his eyes straining to make sense of it all. It sure as hell looked like blood. He saw more dark red patches on the wall as if some great struggle had taken place.

Ridley let out a deep breath and focused all of his attention on the broad and powerful shoulders of William Jamison up ahead. But just before he did that, something caught his attention on the front side of the second stainless steel refrigerator as he passed it on his left. He came to a complete stop and watched as several enormous ants were traveling in both directions across the surface of the refrigerator. Some were moving up while others were moving down in pure working fashion, similar to the way leaf cutter ants behave. Like faithful workers, they traversed the industrial-sized refrigerator.

He was just about to wave in an attempt to get Jamison's attention when out of the corner of his eye he saw the big man come to a halt, his hand looking as though it was about ready to release an arrow.

Ridley's breathing became slow and deliberate, his ears straining to hear what his eyes could not see. To his mind, the silence was deafening. He had always hated silence, had always tried to fill the void by talking, but now was not the case as the silence persisted. Ridley held on for about another twenty-five seconds or so when he saw exactly what Jamison had probably seen a split second earlier.

Jamison had just released the first arrow and was busy quickly reloading the second as the black apparition rose up from the ground and came at him with surprising speed. Ridley sprinted to get a better view, stopping some ten feet behind where Jamison stood as the black mass raced forward with Jamison's first brightly colored arrow protruding out of it.

"What the hell?" the words just fell out of Ridley's mouth at the shock of what he was seeing.

Cool, calm, collected, and with the steady and ice cold nerves that only a former professional athlete could possess, Jamison moved to the side and steadied himself as he fired the second arrow and placed it several inches to the right of where the first arrow jutted out from.

Ridley felt his knees, along with the rest of his insides, reduce to jello as a limb outstretched towards the top and brushed away vigorously, exposing the unmistakable eyes, nose, and face of Collin Fairbanks. Amidst the black and crawling mass, Collin pushed to keep his face free of the vicious oversized attacking ants. John Corstine's personal assistant was totally engulfed and under attack as he held out his arms, completely covered by a moving mass of black as he managed to mouth the words "help me."

It was then that both Jamison and Ridley realized why no words had escaped the assistant's mouth. Overflowing like a small cascading waterfall out of Collin's mouth were more of the ants, which quickly covered up his exposed face and replaced it with black once again. It was hard to consider that under that swarming mass there still was a living breathing human.

In one final act of desperation, the black mass managed to propel and rush itself forward with outstretched arms, but it was too late as Jamison had already put a third and final arrow into the personal assistant's chest, the black mass stumbling and twisting sideways before keeling over and hitting the kitchen floor. The minute the body hit the ground, it was as if a beehive had been dropped out of a tree from up high above, as ants poured out and scattered in all directions.

"Let's go," Jamison shouted. "He's done. It's over. Move out."

And with that Jamison leaped and bounded over the mess, hitting the ground on the other side with ease as he made his way towards the doors that led back into the restaurant. Jamison pushed through the double doors and was gone.

Ridley stood stunned, half of his brain in complete shock while the other half was running wild with fear.

Go, Ridley, get outta here, his subconscious shouted to him. *Ridley, get the hell outta here now*."

When the rational part of his brain had finally won, he ran and leaped over the remains that were once Collin Fairbanks and headed for the double doors through which Jamison had exited.

CHAPTER FIFTY-ONE

John Corstine was slightly winded and breathing heavily as he approached the stairs and slowed himself somewhat, having sprinted the entire length of the hallway just to get there. He held the golf club like a baseball bat as he slowly began to make his way down the stairs, taking it one step at a time. He felt as though he had been awakened suddenly in the night by a burglar, and was now the stereotypical husband clutching the Lousville Slugger baseball bat, waiting to confront the intruder.

For a split second, Corstine's mind gravitated back towards his own son, his only child. Had it really been a year since they had last seen one another? His son made residence in Maui and was responsible for acting as the official property manager to the investment properties that Corstine had on the islands. Corstine shook his head, trying to clear those thoughts and firmly establishing himself back in the present moment as he was now almost halfway down the stairs.

Corstine had his first glimpse of the living room, and it was a befuddling one. He saw that two of the three couch cushions had been uprooted and the stuffing had been ripped out of them, looking as though a dog had a field day with them. He gripped the golf club even tighter as he continued down the stairs, one painfully slow step at a time, his pulse now beating out of his ears.

As he finally got down to the last few stairs, he heard a sharp and crisp tearing sound, the sound of another one of his cushions being ripped apart. Then he saw the culprit as he stepped down and onto the living room floor.

It was a small creature, and if it weren't for the forest green coloration adorning its body, Corstine might have thought as though he had stumbled upon some type of wild dog. Then his eyes saw the small, three-toed taloned feet, the well-defined prehensile tail swishing back and forth, and the beady, scaly skin of a reptile.

The little creature continued to tear viciously at the cushion. Corstine had only taken one step forward on the floor when all of a sudden one of the boards that he stepped on let out a loud creak and groan. He froze. Surely the little creature had heard him, but to his surprise it continued to pull the stuffing from the cushion as if it were a chew toy.

As Corstine took a few steps towards it, he was granted a more defined view of its distinguishable features: razor sharp talons adorning its feet, prehensile tail, thin layer of blackish hair rising up several inches or so like a Mohawk atop its head and continuing on through the tail, and the gleam and shine of beady, reptilian skin.

It was then Corstine remembered the documents that he had been holding. They weren't under his arm anymore as he was still clutching the pitching wedge. A moment of confusion followed, and then he remembered he had stuffed them into his back pocket just before he acquired the golf club. He touched the papers with his right hand, realizing that it didn't matter what they said or from what official organization they were. Here was the living proof right before him, ripping his couch cushions to shreds.

The creature stopped tearing and lifted its head out of the fabric of the cushion, its body going rigid as it straightened itself upright. It was then that Corstine could see the extensive damage that had been done to his window. The whole thing looked like it had been blown out. Surely the little thing before him could not have been solely responsible for that.

Something came through the window, something that downright chilled Corstine to the core. It appeared wet and lathery and was a spectacular light blue in coloration, like that of a tropical fish. Corstine moved himself a few inches to the right to gain a better vantage point.

CHAPTER FIFTY-TWO

Time seemed to be moving in an absolute blur, nothing making sense, only sounds, shapes, and color reigning supreme. Something dripped on top of Downs, and instinctively his head shot upwards. He had been hit in the face, and as he reached his hand to his face...

It was blood, human blood that had dripped down on him from above.

Josiah's voice rang out high above all the chaos though.

"Run," Josiah shouted. "Back to the boardwalk."

Downs turned to follow, but just as he did so he cocked his head back up to the branches and witnessed Nat's body as it flopped backwards, her legs appearing to be wedged in between a jumbled mess of tightly configured vines and branches. Something had shoved and stashed her there momentarily. Her outstretched arms and hands dangled down towards him as blood dripped from the ends of her fingers.

A powerful hand collided with Downs' shoulder, and he turned, eyes wide with terror.

"Come on, she's a goner."

It was Josiah, and he wasn't waiting for a reply. As they started to scamper their way back to the boardwalk, Downs managed to sneak one more peek up towards where Nat was. He witnessed in disturbing fashion Nat's limp and lifeless arms be pulled and disappear further into the vegetation and out of view.

He shook his head, still in shock of it all, but following Josiah as he moved quickly. Max was up ahead.

None of them stopped. They just kept plowing through, past the point from which they might have thought the menacing swarm of ants would have begun invading the tree limbs. Quickly Downs watched as Josiah made his way past Max, showing them the escape route, climbing powerfully up the siding to the boardwalk, making his way up and past the maintenance level, and finally reaching the top of it.

Max was next, although he looked back at Downs with a bit of apprehension.

"Take it one foot at a time," Downs said, trying his best to calm the zoologist, although his own head was spinning. "Now go."

Max turned and diligently began to climb his way up, just as Josiah had done. He moved at a surprising speed that he maintained continuously until he finally climbed up and over the railing and the bottoms of his feet disappeared. Quickly Downs took one rushed look behind him. All was clear, and as he turned and began to focus his attention on climbing quickly, he had the overwhelming feeling that something would rip him from his perch.

With that thought in mind, he ascended until he finally made his way up and over the railing. Like a newborn lamb, he flopped helplessly onto the deck for a brief second.

Downs, who lost all ability to walk, pulled himself forward several feet towards Max and Josiah, who were both hunched over like two fellas that had just witnessed a gruesome crime scene and needed to yack their guts out. It seemed like a mini lifetime in its own right before Downs was finally able to pull himself up and stagger to his feet.

"I can't believe that just happened!" Max gasped, and after that it was too late, as fluid spewed forth from his mouth. He had vomited, and Downs could only hope that it provided him some immediate relief from the awful feeling that his stomach must have been experiencing. As he continued to speak, it became evident that he was suffering from far more than just an upset stomach.

"She's gone," Max cried. "She's gone. Gone. Gone. Gone." And with that the zoologist dropped to his knees and began to sob uncontrollably, tears streaming forward.

Downs too felt the sting of the pain and a tear welled up in the corner of his eye. Despite this, he picked Max up, and spoke directly into the zoologist's eyes. "We have no time. You've got to get it together. We need you."

The boardwalk rumbled under the immense weight as the creature slammed down onto the boards, having propelled itself from the surrounding vegetation. Six human eyeballs turned to see the grizzly thing just standing there, looking down from about a height of nine feet, its dirty mouth a mixture of blood and raw meat.

"Oh God," Max whimpered.

The creature lunged towards them, mouth open and screaming mad.

CHAPTER FIFTY-THREE

The sound of something being pierced and crashing to the floor caught Ridley Bells' attention as he pushed through the double doors that led out of the kitchen and into the restaurant. Jamison had shot one of the juvenile creatures, and the animal now wiggled violently on the floor as it bled out just in front of the rectangular bar setting.

Jamison rushed forward and instead of wasting another one of his precious arrows, he took his size sixteen's and sent his huge foot crashing down through the creature's skull, caving the head in and putting the thing out of its misery. The sound of shot glasses falling and shattering to the floor could be heard as another one of the juveniles had jumped up onto the bar counter, mouth wide open, flaring its small sharp teeth. With a loud piercing cry, it lunged off the bar and towards Jamison.

Jamison got down on one knee and steadied himself as the creature came at him. He exhaled and released the arrow. It grazed the top of the creature's bristled Mohawk-style hair atop its back, but the juvenile continued to bound hungrily towards him.

191

Not being one to panic and always fully believing in both himself as well as his God-given talents, Jamison calmly reached behind him and pulled another arrow. Quickly setting it into place, he once again exhaled a breath and let go of the arrow. The arrow glanced off the right front limb of the youngster as the hearty little thing charged on, its eyes fierce and red with menace.

Jamison, still on one knee, reached into the quill of arrows on his back, and in a split-second decision decided to switch it up. He lay the bow down on the ground, resurrecting to his feet like an NFL running back who had just recovered the football and headed full sprint towards the creature.

Meanwhile, Ridley continued to watch, half stunned at what he was seeing.

The little creature propelled up and into the air, and to Ridley's surprised eyes, Jamison did the same. Ridley watched as the 6'9" 265 pound Jamison leaped up and into the air, easily capable of still dunking a basketball, and in a moment of blur and sheer speed, managed to pull the kukri knife from his side while changing his course of attack in the air.

As the creature was now full stride in the air, Jamison came at it from the side and plunged the kukri knife deep into its back, tearing through sinew and muscle before he finally retracted the weapon and landed firmly back down on the ground.

With the bloody knife still in his hand, Jamison pivoted, his full attention focusing solely on the creature that he had just stabbed, but he had delivered the death blow. The young creature staggered a few steps and collapsed under its own weight.

Jamison reached for a towel that had fallen to the ground in the skirmish, choosing to remove as much of the blood as he could, figuring he didn't want to be walking around with the equivalent of a bag of chum in a hungry ocean full of sharks. He didn't even know that Ridley was in the room until the man let out a loud shriek.

Instinctively, Jamison's gaze fired back to the door that led to the kitchen, but that did not produce Ridley Bells. Several more seconds followed before he finally spotted the television entrepreneur. Ridley was being pursued by two of the creatures, but these creatures were bigger, about as large as a one hundred pound dog, but amped up several more times on the vicious scale.

Jamison reached back to pull an arrow, but suddenly he realized that the bow was still on the ground some fifteen feet from where he stood, past the two dead young creatures. His eyes darted back towards Ridley. The television entrepreneur was in serious trouble.

Jamison remained stymied about what to do, but when noise came dashing out of the kitchen and bounding his way, he knew he had his own pressing issues. He was under attack as well as two small creatures came scurrying out from the kitchen double doors. He also acknowledged that he would let the television mogul fend for himself, and whatever horrible fate awaited him, he most certainly deserved what was coming to him. Jamison had been fully aware of Ridley's past shady business practices.

Jamison gripped the knife tightly in his right hand as he braced for the attack. Choosing to stay grounded this time instead of going air-born, he slashed violently as the first creature came bounding for his calves, most likely wanting to strip muscle from bone in an attempt to take down the much larger prey.

Jamison inflicted a serious gouge in the first of the attackers as it scampered on by him, wounded, but not down and out for the count. The second one leaped up and into the air, as Jamison wasted no time slashing at the thing, trying literally to decapitate the youngster with one powerful blow. Suddenly, as Jamison flung himself and the knife at the thing, it found another level and ascended higher and up and over his head, kicking and scratching at his forehead with the talons attached to its back foot.

Simultaneously, as the creature landed on the ground, Jamison realized he had been torn open a bit by the creature's back talons, as a steady stream of blood trickled down from his forehead and over his face. He wiped at the wound with his forearm, smearing both his face and the side of his arm in blood as liquid continued to pulse from the gash. There was no time for bandaging though.

The second creature collided with the first and the two viciously snapped at one another, seemingly trying to end the other's life. Ridley's cries for help then rang out loud and clear, as if the proverbial dinner bell had been rung. The two creatures took one last look at Jamison, still in the crouched and ready position to take them on, and that was all it took as they bounded off after the television entrepreneur.

CHAPTER FIFTY-FOUR

John Corstine stood both awed and dumbstruck at what was standing just outside his living room window. A creature more massive and awe inspiring than he could have ever imagined stood absolutely still and motionless as it quickly retracted its long and lathery forked tongue back into its mouth and away from the youngster. Corstine stood frozen, absolutely frozen in time, his muscles incapable of moving while his brain was working at lightning-fast speed trying to figure out what in the hell it was at which he was looking.

His mind quickly raced back to the death of one of his workers, the Indonesian man. Surely the death and disappearance of the man had come at the hands of the beast that now stood before him.

He had never seen a head like it, and the way it stared at him reminded him of the emotionless stare of a snake or a crocodile. Its forked tongue rested just inside its mouth while its huge bulbous eyes stared at him. Corstine noticed that the juvenile, a miniature version of the giant just outside the window, was now staring directly at him as well. The real estate tycoon now had both creatures' full attention.

The huge creature once again let a little portion of its forked tongue come out of its mouth, wiggling it back and forth like a snake would, possibly smelling at the air. Perhaps it was smelling Corstine? Perhaps it could smell the sixty year old man's fear. Perhaps that fear itself was exuding from the very pores of his skin.

Whatever the case, while Corstine continued to hold the golf club as if it were a baseball bat, he slowly started taking baby steps backward. His head was tilted ever so slightly downward so he could see the Turkish rug beneath him while still maintaining a view of the two creatures.

Corstine continued to move backwards, ever so gently, following the design patterns in the rug to know his location in relation to the couch, the coffee table, and the end tables that furnished his living room. When his shoes finally hit the laminate floor, he knew he was no more than fifteen feet from his front door.

If he exited quickly, would the creatures give up chase through the house or would they possibly run around it? Would they make their way over the roof, or would they just continue to stand there like great prehistoric statues, relics of an ancient time in a modern world? These questions swirled and churned in Corstine's head as he was now five feet from the door knob, still staring down at the ground in as non-threatening a manner as he could muster while maintaining a slight visual of both of them.

Corstine knew that he was aligned properly with the door as his eyes made out a small dent in his floor, the result of one of his dinner guests a year ago dropping a drink glass on the floor, and delivering a knick in his practically spotless floor.

Idiot drunk, Corstine thought to himself.

The party and get together had been an event that he hosted at the small yet surprisingly well-decorated home for the early investors in the boardwalk, the people who were the ones to hear the business pitch by Corstine himself. It felt like a lifetime ago, as Corstine was now staring directly at what had possibly scared off those early investors. Wild, irrational, almost delusional claims that there were predators that called the forest canopy home, and now Corstine was in the presence of two of them. Two things that defied all that comprised and defined logic.

How many could there be? Corstine wondered, his hand making contact with the front door, missing the doorknob probably by a foot or so.

There Corstine stood, poised and still, with his palm now firmly on the door itself, but still not yet at the doorknob. He watched as the adult retracted its tongue, and it was then that Corstine noticed the array of teeth that gave the inside of its mouth a shark-like appearance. Yet the rest of the face along with the tongue seemed to resemble a reptilian lineage, like the thing had crawled straight out of the primordial swamps of eons ago.

Corstine saw the warning sign, the telltale sign that a creature was going to strike, as a snake would behave just moments before the attack. The adult tensed up a bit and lurched ever so slightly backwards, seemingly setting itself up like a driver might set himself up for a tight turn. And then it struck.

CHAPTER FIFTY-FIVE

Downs saw a mouth open impossibly wide, exposing teeth the likes of which he had only seen before in documentaries on television. The creature possessed a nightmarish mouth full of serrated weaponry.

Downs stumbled backwards at the sight of the charging open mouth that was pounding towards him. Out of the corner of his eye, he saw two blurry human shapes moving out and away from him followed by indecipherable shouting, the likes of which could not audibly be made out. What Downs saw next he almost didn't quite believe. It was too late though, his body half expecting to bounce off of the railing, the railing that was supposed to be there. As Downs had gotten jammed near where the railing should have been, it was too late, his intended course of direction had already been locked and set into place. Part of the railing somehow had broken off.

Downs knew he was going over the edge backwards, yet it all seemed so distant and otherworldly in his final attempt to right himself. However, he continued on, falling backwards and away from the boardwalk as a huge limb with outstretched talons took a fleeting swipe at him from above, followed by a terrifying roar that rang through the jungle.

The boardwalk and the terra firma that he knew began to fade away like a distant drifting memory, and then, everything went black.

CHAPTER FIFTY-SIX

Ridley Bells collapsed on all fours now that he was outside on the boardwalk and began crawling, trying helplessly to keep himself moving forward. The television mogul was injured badly and bleeding profusely from multiple places. He had lacerations along his neck, forearms, and face, and each wound seemed to be serious enough to end his life.

However, the most serious problem was his stomach. He had been ripped wide open several excruciating inches along the lower abdomen. He looked down in horror and could partially see into his stomach, a sight that he had never thought in a million years he would be looking at. It had all happened so quickly and at a blurryingly fast speed as one of the youngsters had gotten hold of him, ripping his stomach wide open, razor sharp talons doing exactly what nature and evolution had evolved them to do, to dismember prey and kill.

As Ridley continued to crawl on all fours along the boardwalk, his life began flashing before him in disjointed bits and pieces. He saw his college years mixed with the struggles, trials, and tribulations that he had endured before getting his first television network up and running. Most of these were business related with a few social interactions mixed in here and there. It wasn't necessarily with the first television network that he began openly exploiting people. It was with the creation of the second network that he began doing so, and with routine regularity.

The second television network, for all intents and purposes, had been much easier to get up and running. It was during the development of the second network that the majority of the budget and capital had been allocated towards creating content for the channel. The funneling of a significant percentage of the capital towards content meant that the marketing and advertising budget went down the tube. Hiring the correct number of personnel was also abandoned. The lack of an advertising campaign meant that Ridley had to be creative once again and think like a scrappy startup entrepreneur instead of an established one who had already successfully launched an earlier channel.

Ridley felt the squeeze early on from the investors he had taken on, the pressure mounting on him to get word out about the channel like a pounding migraine headache building and building with intensity as each day passed. For a period of several weeks he was like a walking zombie, working twenty, sometimes twenty-two hours a day, and sleeping two to three hours a day, only to rise daily like a well-oiled machine and do it all over again.

Ridley knew damn well that they were taking good care of the content part of the channel, but it was the marketing side that he felt was lacking. That was what preoccupied his thoughts almost to an obsession. He became obsessed with the channel's official launch day, and began establishing relationships with bloggers, owners of websites, and people who had established a proven track record of high traffic to their YouTube pages in an effort to get the word out.

Ridley began reaching out to these people, making wild promises to them, promising to help them with their own business endeavors if they did all they could to help promote the launch of the channel as well as the television channel's official website. Ridley even went as far as to reach out to one individual who was posting the link to the television channel's website in thousands and thousands of strategically located blogs, chatrooms, and websites across the internet. He promised to help this individual with the idea that he had come up with for his own television network. This young entrepreneur was counting on Ridley to help him with his network idea, and Ridley had willingly promised to introduce him to other investors and television personnel, promising to bend over backwards for the kid in order to help him. Ridley did all this knowing that he had no intention of ever helping the young kid, or the others for that matter, and the minute his channel was fully up and running and well-established, he would discard the kid and the fleet of others like an obsolete computer.

Ridley shuddered in pain once more as he looked down at his exposed stomach, forcing himself to continue on. He didn't even have to look back. He heard noise on the boardwalk and knew he had company. Not being able to inch himself forward anymore, he collapsed onto his stomach with his full body weight. Ridley wiggled to get his arms out, but he couldn't manage the task, as they remained bent and contorted beneath his body.

Something that possessed an enormous bite force clamped down on both sides of his body, puncturing through his skin and lifting him up and off the ground like a forklift. He felt hot panting breath on his neck and the overwhelming smell of raw dead and decaying meat. The massive adult creature shook its head back and forth vigorously, like a crocodile might do to its prey. It continued to shake Ridley's body back and forth as if he were a ragdoll, before finally dropping the television entrepreneur from its mouth, his body plunking down hard on the boardwalk.

The huge beast retreated some twenty feet away from its kill and began to pace back and forth, much like a lion might do. Ridley somehow managed to right himself onto his back, looking up and over at the menacing creature, knowing full well the horror that most surely awaited him. He saw the creature's mouth full of sharklike teeth, and he wondered what in the hell it was. He wondered if the thing had persisted since the time of the dinosaurs? Had it roamed, stalked, and hunted in the primordial jungles millions and millions of years ago? But more importantly, how in the age of media and the internet had such a creature gone undetected and undocumented?

Ridley watched as the creature suddenly shook itself like a wet dog, and from atop its back jumped down two hungry mouths, mouths that he hadn't even known were there. The youngsters hopped around on the boardwalk and let out small yet piercing cries, heralding their own arrivals.

And as any good mother would do, the huge creature pushed forward its young towards the fallen television entrepreneur.

CHAPTER FIFTY-SEVEN

John Corstine's hand fumbled for the front doorknob as if he were a nervous teenager on a first date. As the massive creature and its young came charging straight for him, they upended and destroyed everything in his living room in the process. Eventually Corstine's hands did the trick, and the front door to his two-story bungalow served as the real-estate entrepreneur's escape route. Now outside, he slammed the door hard and pumped his legs for all they were worth, sprinting as fast as he could muster towards the gas-powered Jeep that still sat in the dirt driveway.

Slightly winded and definitely out-of-shape, he pushed himself, doing his best to hop up and over the side of the Jeep and into the driver's seat just as the sound of a massive mound of muscle rocked his small house to the core. Thankfully, the Jeep fired right up.

The wall to his bungalow had held up, and inside the adult creature and its young still could be heard, scraping and clawing, trying to get out, but Corstine knew it wouldn't hold forever. With that thought in mind, he backed up hastily, put the Jeep in drive, and floored the pedal to the metal, peeling out of his driveway and leaving a plume of rising dust behind him as he sped off.

Quickly, Corstine got the vehicle up to speed, reaching thirty-five miles per hour as the jungle habitat passed by on both sides. It was at this time that he had serious regrets about installing a governor in the vehicle in the first place. Forty-miles per hour was the top speed, and he was flooring it as far as the accelerator would allow for. He wasn't certain how far away he was from his residence when he heard several explosions of windows shattering.

"Damn," he cursed, knowing full well that the creatures were most likely now out and about.

Corstine looked over to his driver's side mirror and adjusted it ever so slightly to have a better view of the road behind him. Nothing yet as he kept his foot firmly on the pedal, but he was expecting that to change at any given moment.

Corstine swerved suddenly, nearly toppling the gas-powered Jeep over, as a large branch lay in all its glory partially covering the road.

That's odd, Corstine thought. *Where in the hell did that come from?*

The branch hadn't been there on the way over, less than an hour before. As Corstine looked back in the rear view mirror, he could see it just lying there. It was huge, possibly twenty-five feet in length. As soon as the answer came to him, a massive mound of reptilian skin, talons, and ferocity swung down and out of the foliage via a prehensile tail at the car with its jaws wide open. The creature went flying over the top of the Jeep, but not before taking a swipe at both Corstine and his windshield, the prehensile tail whipping by and striking Corstine's back.

Corstine howled in pain but managed to stay the course, continuing to fly down the dirt road. Meanwhile, the adult male creature with all its forward momentum was not able to stop, hitting the ground and tumbling further into the jungle, rolling end over end before finally coming to rest at the base of a giant tree. It quickly righted itself, letting out a huge roar as it got back up and onto the road. It immediately took up chase once again, making its way through the clouds of dust that the Jeep had left behind.

Corstine could now see the creature bounding after him, and then, in horror, he could also see that out of the passenger side mirror several other smaller versions of the creature were giving up chase as well. The creatures were closing the gap on him. Corstine knew there was no way they could get their bodies up to the speed at which he was traveling. Or could they?

Corstine could see through the rear view mirror that now it wasn't just the huge adult. It was an all out attack on him and his gas-powered Jeep. The three youngsters ran speedily at the feet of the huge monster, moving like a pack of tyrannosaurs chasing down triceratops on the plains of North America some sixty-five million years ago, with the young tyrannosaurs doing the high speed chasing.

Suddenly, with both speed and blinding acceleration, the youngsters took off like miniature-sized, high-powered performance vehicles from beneath the huge lumbering adult. They immediately put a considerable amount of distance between themselves and the adult. Corstine could now see the youngsters, some the size of small dogs, while one of them appeared larger, roughly the size of a leopard or a cheetah. They were fast, possibly reaching big cat speed out in the open.

The speedy youngsters reached the Jeep and were quickly hovering around the tires of the vehicle like flies on dung. Corstine even saw one of the small ones slip under the vehicle, only to emerge out seconds later on the opposite side. Another of the small creatures slashed repeatedly at the back tire with its talons, but the tires were too thick and the Jeep was moving too quickly.

Corstine continued on, his mind hell bent on escaping the pack of creatures that the wise subconscious part of his mind knew had existed all along. How could he have been so stupid to have waved off the red flag warning signs? They were there all along, from the talks with local elders about strange beast-like creatures known to inhabit the jungles for years, right up until the mysterious death of the Indonesian worker.

An unexplained death with only a pair of teeth to account for, the thought nearly leaping out of Corstine's brain and into the humid jungle air.

The Jeep hit a slight depression, and Corstine struggled to regain control, almost veering completely off the road and into the forbidding jungle. At the last second he "righted the ship." *Smash.* The Jeep hit what appeared to be another pothole.

Suddenly Corstine saw it, rather he saw all of them, like parade lights under the banner of a dark night sky. What he had originally thought to be a jungle road filled with potholes and depressions, seemed to be a game trail full of mud footprints of the creatures. Clearly some of them were huge, manhole size to be exact, while a host of them were modest size, no bigger than the common household dog.

A gametrail, Corstine thought.

A distinct growl suddenly rang out from the backseat. Corstine turned to see one of the juvenile creatures perched there staring at him, eyes flaring with intensity and talons poised to strike.

CHAPTER FIFTY-EIGHT

Over the span of about seven minutes, the young creatures had been feeding on Ridley Bells. Almost toying with the entrepreneur, they would approach, sometimes with caution, other times brazenly, bite and lock down on some part of his body, and tear away a piece of him. Each terrifying time the television entrepreneur would beg for mercy, but the creatures, knowing nothing more than gut instinct, continued to feed on him, little by little reducing him to nothing more than bits and ragged pieces.

Ridley lay in several pools of blood on the boardwalk, patches of his skin along with a good percentage of the muscle and tissue in his legs and biceps had been taken. What was left of him lay completely wide open and exposed, but, unfortunately, for him he was still alive, still barely clinging to life, breathing slowly while being conscious just enough to realize he was indeed being eaten alive. For a flash of a moment, he pictured downed WWII pilots floating and bobbing in the cold waters of the Pacific as sharks swam in and around them, biting and taking pieces of them before eventually returning to finish the grizzly task. He had never envisioned the ending to his life, thinking like many successful entrepreneurs that he would find a way to live forever, like the way that he time and time again would save his companies. But this time it was different. This time he was not in control and was at the mercy of things that had no plausible explanation.

One of the creatures came up unexpectedly, and without giving it any thought sunk its teeth deep into Ridley's thigh and began to pull as if it were a tug-a-war contest between it and the fallen man. Several others joined in, plunging their teeth deep into Ridley's leg as well.

Ridley screamed with every last shred of energy he could muster as his leg eventually gave way and tore off. The adult suddenly swiped at the original attacking juvenile with its prehensile tail, sending the juvenile skidding back across the boardwalk.

As Ridley barely raised his head, he could see the entire scene. The hulking adult creature bounded toward the frightened and whimpering youngster, and let out a low resonating growl. That was all it took as the pack of the rest of the youngsters turned on the creature in an act of pure cannibalism.

In no time it was an all out feeding frenzy as the helpless little creature was ripped limb from limb. Nothing went to waste in the frenzy.

Meanwhile Ridley had been observing the entire scene, his whole body and mind literally numb with pain and shock at what had happened to him. He gasped when his eyes finally took in the damage that had been inflicted upon him. Bits, chunks, and now limbs had been removed. He wished for death, wished for it all to be over; and somewhere in the far corners of his brain, he couldn't help but think he was getting what he so rightfully deserved. He had treated people like crap for quite some time, making wild claims and false promises to help those that had helped him, often using the phrase "help me and I'll bend over backwards to help you." He repeated this time and time again, until he had a small army of workers around the globe helping him promote his companies and television networks, resulting in success after success.

He coughed and spat blood on the boardwalk. He was beginning to choke on his own blood, and that's when it hit him: if he just lay back he could probably choke to death, ending his suffering and putting him out of his misery. There was no coming back from the damage that had been done to him, and it had all happened so dizzyingly fast.

The adult creature once again took a renewed interest in the downed entrepreneur and was on him quickly. Ridley had no time to further contemplate his own demise. In one swift move, the jaws of the huge beast opened wide and collapsed over the weeping and blood-strewn head, plunging the man into darkness and officially putting Ridley Bells on the extinct list.

CHAPTER FIFTY-NINE

John Corstine momentarily took his eyes off the road as the Jeep went down on its left side and into another depression. The youngster launched itself from the back seat, screaming as it flew through the air with its talons outstretched and ready to strike. It slashed powerfully and with precision at Corstine's neck, leaving bleeding gouges and then pushing off of the man's neck, landing on the passenger side seat with the nimbleness and balance of a house cat.

Corstine howled in pain, his hand immediately going to his neck, and coming away colored with blood, as the creature hissed at him from the passenger seat. Corstine managed to right the vehicle, bringing it back up and onto the dirt road just as another one of the youngsters made its way up and into the cabin of the Jeep.

This time Corstine was on it and delivered a swift blow to its stomach region with his elbow, sending the youngster tumbling down from its perch and back onto the jungle road. The creature immediately rose to its feet, shook itself, and once again gave chase.

Corstine had managed to reach down into the paneling of the driver side door and retrieved his pistol, but it was too late. The creature to the right of him once again jumped on top of his shoulders while tearing off part of his shirt.

He fired the pistol, grazing the creature's tale as it jumped off the speeding vehicle and landed down and onto the road. Its small prehensile tail had been hit and was bleeding. To Corstine's surprise, out of his driver-side rear view mirror, he saw more of the young creatures pouring out from the dense vegetation. They descended on the wounded youngster into a feeding frenzy, a rolling ball of carnage as the Jeep continued to speed on.

Corstine gripped the wheel with two hands tightly, his eyes wide with fear at what he had just seen. These weren't just a few random undocumented creatures. This was a small colony of them, and he wondered how many adults there could possibly be to produce such a litter.

"The adults," he muttered to himself.

Where the hell had they gone? He quickly adjusted the rearview mirror to get a better view of the road behind him. He saw one of them still bounding forward, about twenty feet or so behind a small pack of the young who were closing the gap on the vehicle by the second.

"Like raptors," Corstine breathed.

The scene was playing out like any dinosaur enthusiast would have imagined, the young creatures chasing down the gas powered Jeep like velociraptors speeding through their Gobi Desert habitat trying to tackle and take down much larger prey. Corstine was now seeing shapes of all sizes, realizing that creatures of varying growth stages surrounded him.

Corstine set the Jeep up for the turn, swinging the vehicle wide a bit and then pulling it tight, accelerating through the turn. As he did so a few youngsters who were clinging to the back exhaust pipe were thrown off. Corstine saw what appeared to be a teenage version of one of the creatures through the rear view mirror. He watched as the teenager stepped on one of the youngsters that had been thrown from the exhaust, more than likely snapping its neck in the process. As the teenager continued on after the Jeep, everything behind it converged on the crippled creature in another feeding frenzy ball.

"Jeez," Corstine said with a shake of the head, setting his eyes back on the road ahead once again.

Corstine felf a bit dizzy and knew that he needed to get back to safety, and quickly at that. The two feeding frenzies had slowed and distracted most of the predators, and it seemed at least for the moment that the huge adult was nowhere to be seen. But where was the original adult that had invaded his home? Corstine again shook his head. He could clearly see the teenager that had crippled the other youngster, was quickly closing the gap and almost upon the Jeep.

With powerful long strides it moved as if it were a modern day Cheetah. It must have been a solid two hundred pounds in weight, and would probably grow another eight hundred pounds or so before fully grown, growing in length and height as well.

Corstine glanced down at the pistol resting in between his left hand and the steering wheel, vibrating and chattering as the Jeep continued to bump its way down the dirt path back towards the entrance to the boardwalk. He hadn't even had a chance to think about how he would extricate himself from the situation, or exit from the Jeep that had so far delivered him to safety. He had every intention of getting out alive. He had all the world to live for, all the investments, business pursuits, not to the mention the boardwalk itself, but it was the fact that he hadn't seen his son in a little over a year that kept him going strong.

Corstine had to find a safe way out, he simply had to, but, more importantly, he needed to see his son again.

CHAPTER SIXTY

A sharp stabbing pain brought Downs back, and as if being awakened violently from a nightmare, he shot straight up, as if in bed, and sucked in a huge but necessary breath.

"Holy shit," the words spilled out of his mouth while breathing like there was no tomorrow.

In an instant it all came flashing back to him. He saw himself falling helplessly back and away from the boardwalk as something monstrous swiped at him from above, and then after that, the memory went black on him, like it had been wiped or erased from its very existence.

Downs let out a quiet gasp of agony, and he remembered the sharp intense pain from behind. It was hard to imagine he had forgotten it had been there in the first place. He reached into his back pocket and extracted a claw, a killing claw to be exact. It was from the late Cretaceous predator, Velociraptor. Downs had always carried this dinosaur's killing claw in his back pocket, figuring if he ever got confronted in a dark alley back in the real world, it would be his last line of defense. He had always loved dinosaurs, and he had been carrying it in his back pocket since his early teen days. Downs' mind rotated suddenly to his quaint little action sports store back home. He had to get back there. He had big plans for the store, plans for how to get it to turn a profit and plans for how to incorporate his physical brick and mortar action sports store into a more hip and sleek place that would be able to survive in the age of e-commerce and corporate titans like Amazon. However, for now he continued to fumble the killing claw nervously in his right hand.

Slowly, with eyes beginning to come into clearer focus, he began to take in his surroundings. Downs could see the tall tualang trees that extended and grew all around him, and as he took in more he could see that the massive trees surrounded him on all sides in a tight circle. Rather gingerly he stood to his feet, tucking the claw into his back pocket once again. Nothing seemed broken, albeit a few incredibly sore spots primarily around the rear end region, but all appeared to be in good working order. The ground beneath him was stable yet gave off the air of being soft, fluffy, and cushiony all at the same time.

Downs took a few cautious steps forward, realizing in a moment of stunned confusion that he was walking on bedded down leaves, fronds, vines, branches, twigs, and just about everything else that the rainforest could offer up. As wild and crazy as it sounded, it looked like he was in a nest, and as he marveled at the sheer size of the very thing upon which he was standing, a quick mental calculation tabbed it at some ninety five feet in width and equally as long. The nest was weaved in and out of about a dozen or so of the massive tualang trees. It was enormous and almost too much to comprehend, although everything that had happened to Downs and the others high atop Corstine's boardwalk could be construed as not believable.

Instinctively, Downs began to scan the nest for eggs, eggs that would ensure the very survival of the species itself. He had no way of knowing whether the creatures gave birth to live young or did so via the laying of eggs. It was that first thought that made his senses once again go on heightened alert, the idea of live and deadly young, ready to stalk and take down prey even in their sheer infancy.

His eyes suddenly shot upward, in the direction from which he had fallen. He could see the boardwalk and the opening through which he had slipped as he must have fallen some forty feet. The soft, cushiony bed of leaves and materials in the nest broke his harrowing fall. The nest had saved his life. He also knew that the nest had the ability to ultimately end his life as well.

Downs looked up once again and resisted the urge to call out, realizing that if someone were still up there, they probably would have been doing the exact same thing to him. It was then that he began to realize the long shadows that the jungle was beginning to cast, signaling late afternoon. Downs knew that he had been knocked unconsciousness. Had he been out several hours or several minutes? He scratched his head and let out a deep breath. He had no clue. The days, hours, and minutes were all melding into one long and confusing life age.

And where were the others? What the hell had happened to them? He feared the worst for his friends and colleagues.

The hairs on the back of his neck began to tingle, possibly in an effort to prepare him for something. Downs had learned over the years to trust his gut instinct, trust what his body was telling him, trust what his nerves were telling him, but, most importantly, to trust himself. And right now his entire body was screaming that he was not alone in the nest.

Quickly, his eyes did their best to scan the area, turning up nothing. His body was screaming for him to listen. The hairs on the back of his neck continued to stand straight up, and he knew, just knew, that something was with him.

Downs had just begun to reach into his back pocket to remove the velociraptor claw, when, without warning; something rose up from behind him.

CHAPTER SIXTY-ONE

Beyond his hands still intently gripping the steering wheel, Corstine could see the grand staircase entrance to the boardwalk. He was no more than one hundred yards from it, the mere size of a football field, yet the objective may as well have been a million miles away. As Corstine swerved the Jeep, he tried to avoid the slashing attack by the teenager behind him, but it was too late. The creature's already enormous and elongated talons had managed to puncture his back right tire.

Corstine tried continuing to maintain control, but with what appeared to be effortless strength as well as the ability to change course of direction on a dime, the teenager spun itself and clawed down on the back left tire. It clamped down with vice-like power and punctured its thick rubbery core. Yet it didn't stop there. With both of its three-toed paws, it dug deeply into the tire, while planting its back legs into the dirt road. It attempted to bring the still moving vehicle to a halt.

Corstine's gas-powered Jeep now had two flat tires. Still the vehicle continued on though. Corstine was shocked at the raw power of the creature as it felt as though he were having a tug of war with the teenage predator still clamping down on the back left tire.

The teenager continued to pull with unbelievable power, like that of a world strong man in competition pulling a small plane or large bus. At one point Corstine felt as though the vehicle was actually in reverse, being pulled towards the teenager that possessed awe-inspiring power.

Finally Corstine and the Jeep gave up the struggle and came to a complete stop, only some fifty yards or so from the staircase that led up to the boardwalk. Corstine's hands remained firmly gripped on the steering wheel, as did the pistol, wedged between his left hand and the wheel. He stared straight ahead for a moment, as if he had just been pulled over by the highway patrol and was trying to play it cool.

Corstine knew better than to make any sudden movements, and he certainly knew better than attempt to make a run for it. He would be tracked down before he even began. Ever so gingerly he switched the gun from his left to his right hand, and he adjusted the driver side mirror with his now free left hand.

He breathed softly as he could see the creature, still crouched down by the back left flattened tire, as if guarding its kill. Corstine watched out of the driver side mirror as the creature began licking its paws with its forked tongue. Was it wounded? Perhaps it had suffered some cuts and scrapes during the all out battle to bring the heavy Jeep to a stunning halt.

Whatever the case was, the teenager was not acting swiftly. Rather it took its time, still licking its wounds and behaving more like an animal than some type of blood thirsty monster. It was not acting malicious or giving off warning signs of an attack whatsoever.

Meanwhile, Corstine continued to sit frozen. He wasn't quite certain how he felt about the situation, having observed similar scenarios on safari in Africa, with lions feeding and hunting on the plains of the Serengeti. It felt all too familiar. There was a large predator just outside his vehicle. Yet despite that, it was not showing malice or ill will towards him. Rather it just seemed to be going about its life as nature had always intended it to do.

Corstine continued to watch from the mirror as the creature picked itself up off the ground and stood on all fours. He felt his senses on overload, eyeing the creature the entire time from the mirror. John Corstine's heart skipped a beat as the creature suddenly locked its gaze onto his, staring the real-estate tycoon straight in the eyes via the driver-side mirror.

CHAPTER SIXTY-TWO

"Keep quiet, brotha," the voice whispered into Downs' right ear, while an enormous and equally powerful hand covered his mouth, and seemingly most of his face for that matter. "Keep quiet or we'll both be toast."

It had been a whisper, merely just a whisper, but the voice was none other than William Jamison's, his unmistakable tone and command of the English language on full display.

Jamison released Downs slowly from his paralyzing grip and watched as the man stumbled forward, immediately turning round to see him. It was odd seeing him there, and as Downs looked up at the man, he realized just how large and imposing Jamison's 6'9" presence was.

Jamison had both a confident and cocky glow about his face, but also one which hinted at the seriousness of the situation. Before Downs could even speak a word, Jamison cut him off.

"No time for small talk, brotha. They're all gone. I'm assuming the same for you on your end?" Jamison said.

Josiah and Max suddenly popped into Downs' head. He had been trying with every last shred of mental energy to put the image of Nat and what had happened to her out of sight.

"I don't know," Downs replied. "It all happened so quickly when I fell."

Downs didn't wait for Jamison to reply and spoke just as the big man was about to open his mouth. "We need to create a feeding frenzy. Something that will draw everything in, divert the attention to this place, and allow us to get up and out once and for all."

Jamison smiled and replied. "I thought you'd never ask. That dawned on me earlier today as well."

Downs remained emotionless. He wasn't certain if Jamison had come up with the concept as he was insinuating, if he was simply lying through his teeth, or if he simply could not stand the idea of Downs coming up with a plan with which he was not intellectually capable of devising. Either way, as Downs continued to stand there still as a statue, none of that mattered. All that mattered now was that the plan was executed to the T.

"Okay," Downs said, bending down as if he were a coach sketching out the next team play. "Here's what we're going to do."

Jamison rolled his eyes to himself but bent down as well to have a look.

CHAPTER SIXTY-THREE

The sound of something piercing and cutting through the air caught the attention of Corstine's left ear, as if an object itself had just sailed by it, and quickly at that. Suddenly, Corstine heard howling, the howling of pain, the howling of a wounded animal.

Corstine turned and could see the wounded creature with a brightly colored arrow sticking out of its side. It tried to pull the arrow out with its paws, but it was no use. The arrow snapped in two, allowing the broken shaft to fall to the ground, while the arrow itself still remained burrowed deeply within its victim's body.

The creature again howled in pain as it dug its oversized talons into the ground, digging and scratching as if that would offer some sort of pain relief. Next Corstine heard footsteps, the sound of footsteps coming down the grand staircase. He turned just as the next arrow pierced the air.

The shot was an accurate one and hit the juvenile smack dab in its stomach region. Corstine swiveled his head back towards the footsteps, and once again another arrow pierced through the neck of the juvenile. There was no fight, no struggle, as the creature keeled over to its side with a thud.

The figure continued to race towards the gas-powered Jeep, and before Corstine could even process any of this, there stood his son, Jeremiah Corstine. Jeremiah had a large grin on his face, and for a brief moment, the two said nothing to one another, their eyes speaking what their lips would not.

Jeremiah sprung forward into action, first slinging the bow over his shoulder and then sprinting towards the Jeep as Corstine opened the door. Corstine's feet touched down on the dirt, and the two embraced in a big long and drawn out hug, still not a word being said as they remained suspended in silence.

"Come on," Jeremiah prompted, grabbing hold of his father's shaking hands.

He hurried and pushed his father forward, but Corstine headed off a few steps, then turned right back around towards the Jeep. His pistol it must have dropped out in all the excitement. Frantically Corstine opened the Jeep door and quickly scanned the area with his eyes. It wasn't in the side paneling of the door nor on the seat. Then Corstine saw it, wedged between the floor and the accelerator. Carefully, he reached in with his hand and extracted the weapon. He turned and faced Jeremiah, gave his son another all engulfing hug, and the two began to make their way towards the staircase. Corstine went first, doing his best to sprint, though it was more of a half ass jog with Jeremiah taking up the rear.

When they were about forty yards away from the Jeep, Jeremiah stopped and turned around, the bow ready to fire at anything that caught his attention as he did a quick sweep of the area. There was the Jeep, and there was the dead creature at the back of the vehicle. Nothing caught his eye so he turned and began sprinting in pursuit of his father.

Corstine's feet had reached the grand staircase that opened up to greet would-be guests to his boardwalk creation. Quickly and doing his best, Corstine began to ascend the stairs towards where he hoped both he and Jeremiah could assume safety in his offices. Jeremiah, meanwhile, was in an all-out sprint now, covering huge amounts of ground with his broad and powerful runner legs. In no time he reached the bottom of the staircase and began taking three steps at a time with great huge bounds, the bow still clinging tightly to his side.

He could see his father up ahead, slowing and struggling to keep up the pace that he had set. The sounds and grunts of carnage assaulted Jeremiah's ears as the creatures were most likely ripping into one of their own back at the Jeep, but he didn't bother to turn. Rather, he focused all his efforts on continuing to leap three stairs at a time. It wasn't until the sounds of scuttling and footsteps rang out from the bottom of the staircase that Jeremiah finally forced himself to have a look back.

The creatures had finally reached the bottom of the grand staircase as Jeremiah and Corstine continued to scramble their way up it.

CHAPTER SIXTY-FOUR

J amison and Downs moved about in stone cold silence as the two of them fanned out to the farthest reaches of the nest. The ground beneath them was surprisingly firm, seeming to be built for more than just the weight of two humans.

Downs slowly began taking in what his eyes had originally not. On the ground and seemingly everywhere was what appeared to be all that the jungle had to offer up. There were scattered leaves of every shape and size, vines, thorns, and insects, some crawling and moving about while others were dead. Only their exo-skeletons remained as a subtle reminder of their once existence. The entire nest was a tightly wrapped and wound ball, weaving in and out of the towering tualang trees.

As Downs moved further out and away from Jamison, he could see bits and pieces of dead butterflies, bats, and what looked like the wings of several types of tropical birds, the likes of which he could not identify. Then Downs began to see teeth, small teeth everywhere. He felt a shiver come over him. They were human.

Downs looked back towards Jamison who was busy crouching down in order to examine something. He watched the big man for a second.

What the hell's he doing? Downs thought to himself.

Jamison was holding something, and he appeared to be examining it, but his large and broad back prohibited Downs from getting a better view. Turning his attention away from Jamison, Downs continued to move out to one of the far corners of the nest. He suddenly stopped dead in his tracks, just in time to witness a butterfly as it gently landed on his right shoe. His eyes scanned down for a moment and then back up towards what had originally stopped him in the first place.

Swatting aggressively at his face, Downs managed to shake the flies that had been buzzing in and around his head. They were rogue flies, possibly scouts from the huge black swarm that was up ahead. As he moved closer and closer, the overwhelming smell of dead and decaying flesh stung his nostrils. Eventually the black mass of swarming flies thinned just enough for him to peer inside that over which they had been swarming.

Eyes, hollowed-out eyes, stared lifelessly back at him from inside the buzzing darkened cloud of flies. Downs recoiled and almost choked on his own spit, the sight at what he was looking almost too much to take in.

He must have caused a slight disturbance because he could hear Jamison moving about behind him. He didn't bother to look back, rather he just kept his eyes transfixed on the gruesome and mutilated corpse of Nat Kingsworth, her hollowed-out eyes staring back at him as if they were calling out for help.

Jamison's large hands touched the back of Downs. Jamison did not move from behind him and stood deathly still, whispering in his ear.

"Nothing we can do for her now, bro," Jamison said.

The cold emotion of his statement hit Downs hard, and it was in that moment that he knew damn well that Jamison didn't give a toss about the others. He only cared for himself and his own well being. Downs' gut instinct had originally told him that when they were all assembled at the start of the boardwalk tour. Now it was cemented as he heard first hand and up close Jamison's lack of sympathy and compassion for another fellow human being. Despite this Downs decided it strategically best not to show any ill will towards Jamison.

"I have a plan," Jamison whispered. "And by the way, we have company."

CHAPTER SIXTY-FIVE

Corstine found the visitor center's glass door and the area that had been serving as their makeshift offices completely wide open, as if someone or something had left it so. Once inside he moved about those first few steps with supreme caution, the pistol raised and in front of him as if he were a NYPD police officer. Corstine knew how to handle the deadly weapon in his hands. That wasn't the part that he questioned.

What Corstine questioned was the ability to kill. Did he have it in him? As he continued to put one foot in front of the other, this thought swirled and then settled in his head. Noise back at the glass door caused Corstine to pivot on a dime, and before he knew it Jeremiah stood there panting, and staring down the barrel of his pistol.

"Hurry inside, my boy," Corstine said.

Corstine slid past Jeremiah and closed the glass door. The thing appeared to be jammed. He fumbled nervously with the door until finally it closed, and he latched the lock down.

Taking a deep breath and forcing himself to swallow inside his parched throat, he turned and faced his son, standing there in all his glory. Jeremiah stood just above six feet in height with broad, powerful shoulders and a strong chest that screamed of someone spending ample time pushing weights in the gym. He sported a light black goatee with short cropped black hair. Jeremiah Corstine was thirty-five years of age to be exact.

Corstine's eyes stared into his son's. The words did not come to the tip of his tongue, despite the fleet of thoughts growing inside his head, but nothing escaped his mouth. Jeremiah cracked a smile, and at that moment Corstine saw the young child who used to run around their lavish house in his underwear, raising hell and causing an all out ruckus.

Jeremiah smiled once more and let out a long, drawn out sigh. "Perhaps now isn't the best time for a teary eyed reunion Dad. Let's first get the hell out of here."

Corstine finally broke his silence. "How'd you get here?"

Jeremiah flashed a grin and more teeth. "Got my resources. You know I learned from the best."

The pitter patter of feet on the roof stressed the need for immediate action. They paused in silence as the sounds spread out everywhere over the surface of the roof.

"Quick, my boy. Follow me," Corstine whispered.

The two made their way down the hall and towards Corstine's office, essentially his home away from home. Jeremiah followed closely behind his hobbling father, the sounds atop the roof still evident and bristling with life.

Finally, the two arrived at Corstine's office. Upon entering, Corstine insisted on closing the door, despite the fact that if the creatures in fact got in the building, the measly door would provide little to no protection. Jeremiah had a good look around the place, finally taking in the settings and scenery that he had only seen via Facebook and the occasional Christmas or birthday card.

Jeremiah felt an odd sensation being there, and it was even stranger to be so close to his father. He watched as his father fumbled through his desk drawer for something before finally retrieving a small object. Jeremiah watched as Corstine slid his prized Turkish rug aside, the rug they had happily purchased at Istanbul's Grand Bazaar, on one of their many family trips when he was just a little kid.

For a moment Jeremiah's brain was walking down memory lane, thinking of all the good times he had with his dad on their numerous family trips and world travels, before finally reality took him back to the office. Corstine got down on one knee and carefully took hold of the prized rug, pulling it ever so gently several feet across the floor. Watching with his eye, he kept pulling until the far end of it crossed a certain point on the ground. Corstine then got up to his feet and made his way around the rug. Meanwhile, Jeremiah was watching and found this to be particularly odd.

Corstine once again got down on one knee and removed a small object from his pocket.

A key, Jeremiah thought to himself, now having a full and unobstructed view of the object that Corstine had retrieved out of his desk drawer only moments prior.

Then Jeremiah saw it, the small key hole located on the ground in a secret area that had been completely covered by the Turkish rug. He watched as his father inserted the key into the floor and turned it, the ground making a slight clicking sound.

Corstine smiled. "There it is. Glad this thing still works."

Corstine fielded the key back into his pocket and turned to look at his son. "Really great to see you. Excellent. It really is, and, my boy, I'm terribly sorry it has been so long and under such dreadful conditions."

Jeremiah shook his head and shrugged it off, though his emotional strings were being tugged as well. The emotionally rock solid and stable part of his brain had already determined now was not the time to get all teary-eyed.

"Now," Corstine said with a slight smile. "Now's the tricky part of this."

Jeremiah watched as his father once again put the key back into the small keyhole. Jeremiah realized that his father must have made an error the first time, but he decided it best not to say anything.

"The trick," Corstine continued, "is to just get the door propped open enough to grab hold."

Jeremiah watched as the key went into place. Corstine managed to wedge the trap door high enough to barely grab hold on the side and fully open the surprisingly heavy door.

Corstine let out a personal sigh of contentment as he peered down into the tight and dark space. Jeremiah chuckled a bit. "Don't tell me this is where you store the rest of your rugs from our family vacations?" The comment managed to grab a big laugh out of Corstine himself, but the jubilation came to an abrupt end. The sound of shattering glass rang out, breaking their sanctity and alerting them that something was now inside and roaming free.

"Quick," Corstine commanded. "Hop in."

Like an obedient son, Jeremiah did as he was told and lowered himself down and into the tight and darkened crawl space. Once inside he scooted himself to the far corner, knowing full well that with both he and his father inside, things would be quite crowded. He wanted to give them as much room as possible.

Corstine quickly took one last look around his office before he lowered himself into the crawl space. Once inside he extended his arm back out and managed to maneuver the Turkish rug, until it covered a good portion of the trap door once again. With that Corstine let the trap door down ever so gently, plunging both of them into absolute darkness as all hell broke loose just outside in the hallway.

CHAPTER SIXTY-SIX

A powerful forearm overpowered and overwhelmed Downs as Jamison forced him backwards in a contorted manner. Before Downs even fully knew what was going on, Jamison had violently pulled both of them back behind the rotting eyeless corpse of Nat Kingsworth. Big bulbous green flies continue to buzz in and around them.

Jamison let go of Downs and grabbed hold of Nat's neck, using his huge forearm to prop her body up straight. There she sat fully upright, the two men crouched down behind her as the first intruder dropped down and into the nest, not in the least bit a threatening manner.

The little creature came forward, stumbled a few steps, and then sniffed at the air. The whole scene pointed towards the fact that the little predator looked to be getting its feet wet by walking, meaning it was a newborn, and most likely the mother wouldn't be too far behind.

Jamison held his grip tight on Nat's body as both of them remained crouched down behind her, watching the scene play out before them.

The small creature made its way in several feet, paused, sniffed at the air once more, and swatted with its three-toed front limb a few times at the flies that were still buzzing. Like a curious youngster it seemed to be not only preoccupied by the buzzing flies, but downright fascinated by them. It swiped several more times, missing each time but still giving 110% with each try.

Jamison grabbed hold of a small branch that lay directly to his left and began swaying it back and forth, just in front of where Nat's forearms lay. Downs lowered his head and closed his eyes for a moment, still having a hard time coming to terms with her ultimate demise. He just kept telling himself that she deserved better than that, she deserved better than the way she was taken and overpowered. Over and over the thought repeated itself in his head.

Get a grip, Downs forced the thought upon himself.

Meanwhile Jamison continued waving the branch back and forth like a piece of a meat on the end of a string. He appeared to be taunting the small creature, egging it on. The tactic was working as the small thing took notice of the branch and moved forward towards them.

Jamison continued to work his magic, waving the branch back and forth as the small creature kept moving forward. He let out a low whistle with his mouth, repeating the process several times. As he continued to shake the branch, the whole shebang was now drawing the creature in now at a quicker pace. As the little predator lowered its head to the ground like a hunting dog tracking its prey, it kept moving forward.

Meanwhile, Downs could feel Jamison's breath on his neck, still not fully certain what the big man had planned.

CHAPTER SIXTY-SEVEN

Noise poured in from above as Corstine and Jeremiah huddled close together in the darkness of the crawl space that sat just beneath the office floor. Corstine adjusted himself ever so slightly and could only wonder what was transpiring above. The only separation between them and all out carnage was a slight trap door and a prized Turkish rug. They remained seated with the trap door not more than a few inches from the tops of their heads. Standing was not an option in the dark tight quarters.

Grunts, snorts, shrieks, and loud bellows of every kind imaginable indicated that Corstine's entire office had been officially overtaken and flooded by the creatures. They were uprooting everything. Then Corstine and Jeremiah heard what they had feared all along. They heard it loud and clear from the darkness of their holding cell.

The original noise above them had been soft feet, like the pitter patter of reindeer hooves atop a roof, but that soft pitter patter had sharply transitioned into deep, vibrating, pounding steps.

"Dear God," Corstine breathed softly.

The floor above them rumbled with life, indicating sheer tonnage and weight, pure weight now walking freely down the hallway. It appeared to be coming straight for Corstine's office. One of the adults was in the building.

Corstine fumbled for it but managed to grab Jeremiah's hand and held it. "I'm sorry for getting you into this mess, son."

Jeremiah let out a sigh, deciding to let his dad sweat it out for a second before finally responding. "You might not be here right now if I hadn't gotten myself into this."

Corstine squeezed tighter on his son's hand. "And for that I'm eternally grateful. When we get out of this, I will make it up to you. Promise."

Jeremiah didn't know how he felt about his father's promise. He had heard the same verbage before, perhaps a few hundred times as a youngster, his father always gone on business and constantly letting him down in nearly every facet of his life. Jeremiah did not despise his father though, but he was constantly weary of him breaking his promises. This was something he vowed never to do to his own children. He simply refused to repeat the cycle, but he figured he would take his father's word at face value given the circumstances.

"Good," Jeremiah replied. "When we get out I'll take you up on that offer. Perhaps a round of golf followed by a nice dinner. Your treat."

"Done." Corstine smiled in the darkness, though Jeremiah could not see it, and he squeezed tightly on his son's hand before finally letting go. The two sat there in pitch black for a few seconds, before both of their heads, as if on cue, shot upwards towards the floor of Corstine's office.

They did not have to strain their hearing or tune into what their surroundings were telling them, as it remained fairly obvious what was happening above them as the floorboards creaked and groaned under the stress of sheer weight. The creaking, the groaning, and the stress on the floor came to a stop, several feet from where Corstine and Jeremiah remained hidden.

It was clear as daylight that almost directly above them stood one of the full grown adult creatures. They could hear it breathing in and out, wheezing with big lumbering breaths. Corstine shuddered just thinking about such a beast, and once again he reached over to grab hold of his son's hand. He squeezed down tightly on that hand for all it was worth.

CHAPTER SIXTY-EIGHT

Downs felt his arm being twisted up and in from behind. He felt immense pain before it could even register in his brain. A mottled scream of terror escaped his mouth, followed by a ridiculously powerful kick to his stomach, striking him, undoubtedly bruising several of his ribs in the process.

As he tried to right himself, another powerful blow struck him square in the face. Blood began streaming almost immediately from an open gash somewhere above his eye. He had blacked out momentarily, but as he regained himself and finally came to, he saw Jamison's powerful strides carrying him away as he made a dash for it, towards where Downs had initially fallen into the nest.

Jamison's huge long strides took him out and away from the scene of the crime. In one swoop of a movement Jamison grabbed the young creature, snapping its neck like a chicken, sending its body cracking down over his knee, breaking vertebrae, and essentially delivering a paralyzing blow to the little predator.

Downs had managed to crawl up and out from where he had been left to bleed out and could see Jamison's backside. He could see that the former NBA basketball player had begun to scamper his way up the base of a tree and back towards the boardwalk. Downs stumbled again, crawled and tripped his way towards where the dying and crippled little creature lay whimpering and barely breathing. As he reached the poor thing, Jamison called down to him from a distance above.

Downs craned his neck up to where the big man was, and by the looks of it he had made his way up the tree a considerable distance.

"It's not murder, brotha," Jamison shouted from high above. "I like to call it selective survival. Coined a new term if I don't say so myself. It's letting nature do its thing while weeding out those that don't deserve to find their way out and weaken the gene pool. It's always been about survival of the fittest, and don't think for one second it ever hasn't."

Downs mumbled a few responses back, but the words would not come out. It all seemed to be pure gibberish.

"Oh, and one more thing, brotha," Jamison shouted. "I'll tell them that you didn't make it and that you gave your regards. If you had a trophy wife like I do, which we both know that you don't, I would have passed the message on that you loved her. I would have done that for you, brother."

Jamison let out a loud booming laugh. "Since you don't there's nothin' left to do but sign off and say "Adios, muchacho."

And with that Jamison pushed himself up a little further, grabbed hold of the railing to the boardwalk and hoisted himself up and over. With labored breathing and pain radiating from multiple places, Downs was now within an arm's reach of the crippled creature. Its breathing too was labored, and it struggled as well. Downs leaned closer to examine.

Is it dead?

Downs was glad that the thought had come to him, proving that his brain was still functioning. Yet he was in bad shape and in need of medical attention. He knew Jamison was gone and would not return and found very little comfort in the strange little crippled predator that lay almost all but dead at his feet.

Without warning darkness took him once again as he stumbled and fell backwards.

CHAPTER SIXTY-NINE

John Corstine's stomach and insides felt as if they were being re-arranged and redistributed to various spots beneath his skin. His body rumbled and shook, a sensation he had only experienced once before in his entire lifetime, back nearly a decade ago when he and a buddy visited the National Hot Rod Association drag races in Pomona, California, just south of Los Angeles. Corstine and his close friend had been seated in the front row of the start line, a spot that he had never occupied at the handful of drag races that he had attended prior.

The seats were so close that when the dragsters fired up and went screeching down the raceway, it felt as though one's insides were literally being rearranged. It was a sensation that he had experienced a long time ago, but, nonetheless, had not left his memory. Now as Corstine sat in absolute darkness with his only son, that same odd sensation of movement within his internal organs struck him as the creature roared mightily above them.

The creature above was roaring for all it was worth, the sheer tone and ferocity of it seeming to vibrate even the tight crawl space below.

It must have gone up on its hind legs for a moment as an enormous boom rang out from above.

"What in god's name is going on up there?" Corstine breathed.

"Not god," Jeremiah countered, "Evolution. What in the name of evolution is going on up there?"

Corstine managed to breathe a sigh of frustration despite the unreal terror that was gripping him inside and out. "Let's not start that debate again."

"It's not a debate Dad," Jeremiah countered again. "It's merely a product of evolution, Dad."

Corstine elevated his voice slightly. "And without the good Lord son, there would be no evolution for that matter. Tell me, do you believe in God?"

Jeremiah took a moment to respond. "I believe in the geologic timeline, more importantly the concept called "geologic connectivity." I believe we are all tied to the geologic timeline of life on Earth, meaning I am no greater or lesser than a primitive organism that lived hundreds, even billions of years ago. We are both on and part of the geologic timeline. There's no getting off that train. That's a fact that cannot be disputed."

Corstine wanted to combat his son immediately but instead decided to let him finish his thought pattern, for once in his life.

"We are all currently traveling this geologic timeline of life on Earth, and no one can leave it. We are on it, plain and simple. Whereas a man or a woman can denounce their faith, political opinions, sexual orientation, or a host of other topics, no one can denounce the geologic timeline. We are all connected to it and vice versa. There's no way off this rollercoaster."

Corstine himself was a bit taken aback by his son's wise and yet still ambitious argument. For one of the few times in his life he was speechless, absolutely speechless with no grand argument to counter. Silence would have prevailed had it not been for the situation above them.

The sound of the adult creature breathing heavily above stymied all other activity, as Corstine and Jeremiah continued to sit mired in silence. Corstine's eyes gravitated towards a slight opening. Actually it was a crack in the boards that made up the trap door. A thin almost barely visible ray of light beamed in, and Corstine was surprised he hadn't seen it before. As his eyes continued to gaze upward, they started to take in something, something that was clear, gooey, and see-through.

What the hell is that? Corstine thought in silence, as he watched the substance mold and shape its way through the crack, adapting to what its surroundings were giving it. It hung or at least must have been hanging atop on the ground floor of the office before gravity finally began pulling it through the opening and towards where Corstine and Jeremiah remained hidden in silence.

"Saliva, dear God, it's saliva," Corstine breathed.

Both of them scooted aside as far as their tight quarters would allow for and gave way to the falling substance, watching as the liquid continued to fall before finally touching down on the floor, no more than a foot or so from Corstine's right shoe. It appeared to be ridiculously well put together, and finally at long last it had broken apart. Corstine once again looked back up towards the cracked opening and the minuscule amount of light that was allowed to filter through. This was the only reassurance that there, in fact, was an outside world beyond their dark and forbidden hiding hole.

Corstine squinted his eyes back towards the light, as more saliva poured through the opening at a slow but steady rate. He let out a deep breath, no words needed between the two of them as the saliva continued to pour down towards them while more big lumbering breaths were taken above them. Corstine could only hope, if the worst suddenly struck them and there was no way out, that death would come quickly and without much time to process it all. The thought of rotting and starving in the pitch black, he did not fancy that one bit.

A loud ear splitting roar once again cut through both of their bodies. All they could do was sit and hope, but more importantly pray.

CHAPTER SEVENTY

Downs' eyes flickered several times as filtered light from the rainforest slowly began flooding his pupils, the light coming in bits and pieces like images being projected onto an old movie screen that were finally taking shape and materializing into a complete shot. Groggily he sat up, shocked that he even had to sit up in the first place, shocked that he had been lying down. Based on the amount of still available light, Downs estimated he had only been unconscious for a few mere seconds, but every second now was precious.

A carcass, an already ripe and rotting corpse, was within an arms length from him as he breathed in another huge lungful of death-encrusted air. The stench had already started to fester and the memory of William Jamison grabbing the small predator mid air and snapping the life out of it came flooding back to him.

An onslaught of pain came rushing forward from multiple locations. Downs winced and bit down on his lip, knowing full well that his ribs had been severely bruised and injured. He dabbed gingerly at his jaw, wondering if it was possibly broken. However, that was the least of his worries as his thoughts gravitated back to the pain in his ribs, but more importantly toward William Jamison.

Downs moved his feet, testing them, making damn sure that he still had two functioning legs to accompany the wiggling feet. All good to go there. With that he moved on up to the next area of concern, the arms. The little test quickly proved that both of them were fine as well. Downs began formulating thoughts and doing his best to push aside the pain from his ribs and jaw.

A high pitched cry, like that of a dolphin under water, rang out from the forest canopy. Downs ceased the full body examination, forcing his ears to listen. Again the high pitched cry pierced the air, the oppressive heat still bearing down on him.

Downs moved several feet away from the deceased little predator, as a third high pitched cry rang out again. His body stiffened and tightened up, but there was nothing he could do. He was in the nest of the creatures, a worse and more vulnerable place than he could have ever or would have ever wanted to imagine. This was far worse than wading into one of the many crocodile infested rivers and canals of the world and swimming with great white sharks just off the coast of South Africa-both of which he had done and conquered.

But this was different, this was vastly different, and his senses knew it. High atop the forest floor lay an Indonesian ecosystem virtually unknown to science, with an ancient species of predator that had somehow managed to go undiscovered. His mind tried to take that all in for a second in one great swath. How could it be? How could it be that no one had managed to document this new species, managed to get a sneak peak at it and post it to the likes of Facebook, Twitter, or YouTube for the entire world to see? It perplexed him and was almost as beyond comprehension as the idea of the species existing in the first place.

A fourth high pitched cry rang out, signaling the end of Downs' scientific questioning regarding the mysteries of the universe, and once again bringing shooting pain back to his ribs. He looked down at the now festering carcass, as a host of unruly flies had taken notice and were seemingly going to town on it, buzzing in and out every which way. As Downs continued to stare at the small predator, knowing what it was in its former life, he knew damn well what it would turn into in its much, much larger adult version. It was the process of evolution, nothing more, nothing less, evolution at its wildest and craziest. Downs wondered if these things had persisted since the time of the dinosaurs? Could they have even in some small way accounted for the extinction and ultimate demise of the dinosaurs?

Downs shook his head; he didn't know. In fact as far as he was concerned, it was impossible to draw upon and make sense of such conclusions. The fossil record for dinosaurs and other ancient organisms was minimal, at best, and relatively unknown in this part of the world, more specifically Indonesia to be exact. Recently he had gotten wind of a fish eating dinosaur discovered in Malayasia, but after that it was a big fat blank. He knew from his childhood fascination with dinosaurs and other ancient organisms that the continents of the world used to be connected. Downs wondered if the species they were dealing with had migrated and proliferated to the other parts of the world as well, or had it always been confined geographically to this part of the world. Had it simply persisted or was it due to climatic and environmental changes that it was able to survive this long in Indonesia, if it was in fact as old as he hypothesized it to be.

The cloud of flies seemed to be growing and growing around the carcass, turning itself into an almost unstoppable moving and buzzing black mass. It was there in that moment that geology, paleontology, cryptozoology, and the field of science were screaming full bore at him, as if trying desperately to send one last message to his still functioning brain. In that moment Downs heard it, heard it loudly and clearly above the drone of the flies. The message was this in its most simple and outright form: figure a way out of this jungle, or face the fate of being eaten, digested, and put right back into the cycle of the rainforest.

CHAPTER SEVENTY-ONE

William Jamison's legs had been pumping and working hard for quite some time as he continued to make his way along the boardwalk and towards where the guided tour's intended route should have gone in the first place. His legs, as well as his body, had been trained, honed, and cultivated over the course of his life, taking him up and down the hardwood of the NBA floors season after season. Now they were doing something similar to that in a far flung remote corner of the world.

Jamison brought himself to a halt, hardly even breathing while feeling as though he had already recovered in the few seconds he had been standing idle.

I could still play ball if I had to, he thought to himself with a smile, knowing full well that the statement was mostly false but still held some nuggets of truth to it.

At fifty years of age, he was in far superior shape than people half his age. Hell-if it was any consolation to what he had seen in his nephew's eighth grade physical education class, where a class of thirty students were forced to run a mile, and the best time was fourteen minutes and five seconds, he was in far better shape than nearly every human being on the planet. He smiled again with that thought in mind.

Jamison reached into his backpack, pulling out the copy of the aerial photo of the boardwalk that had been given to him. He quickly scanned the image, running his finger across all that seemed to be pertinent. To Jamison it looked like they had been placed smack dab in the middle of nowhere, with green comprising nearly the entire image, and only a tiny sliver of a figure snaking its way through that dense and lush vegetation, representing Corstine's boardwalk.

Corstine. Jamison thought to himself, wondering if the old fool was even still alive. He laughed. *Cut down the whole forest for all I care.*

Jamison brought his attention back to the aerial photo and continued tracing his finger along what he believed to be his intended route, the route that would allow him to escape and get back to the states. More importantly, this escape route would bring him back to his multi-millionaire lifestyle that he had been enjoying for what seemed like an eternity. He thought back quickly to his sophomore year of college, struggling merely to string together a few extra dollars at the end of the week to go see a movie or even to go and grab a drink at the local tavern.

By the time Jamison had officially completed his first three years at Ohio State, the lure of the NBA and all that money was too much to resist. He decided to forego his senior year of collegiate play and made the jump into the pros, making him instantly a millionaire and cementing what would be a lifetime of money-making opportunities.

Early on and for the first few years of his career, Jamison focused entirely on basketball. His off seasons were spent doing rigorous training, working out in the gym, and running in the hills behind his home, but most importantly getting physically as well as mentally prepared for the next season. Jamison learned early on that despite the massive sums of money that professional athletes were paid, the day-to-day grind still took its physical toll on the human body. Whether one was flying on private jets or commercial airliners, flying was still flying, and it took its toll. Each season he made sure he was in tip-top shape and ready for that physical toll.

Jamison's body was still in supreme shape, seeming to defy gravity and age in the same light, with not one inch of him showing signs of sagging in the least bit. For the third and final time, Jamison scanned his finger along the thin sliver of an image on the aerial photo. By his calculations, actually it was more like eyeing it and relying on sheer raw gut instinct. He figured he had approximately three miles to what the others earlier had simply referred to as the "rendezvous point."

Jamison looked out and into the surrounding vegetation, noticing for the first time since coming to a stop just how thin and spread out the foliage was at this part of the boardwalk. He was liking what he was seeing. He moved forward a few feet and quickly stowed the aerial photo away into his backpack, continuing to look out and into the foliage. Since the vegetation was so spread out and interspersed, it meant that the threat of attack was that much less, at least that was what Jamison had convinced himself.

As he moved around and completed a three hundred sixty degree turn, it seemed highly unlikely that something, certainly something huge, could sneak up on him from the hidden shadows that only the dense rainforest could provide. That thought, along with what his eyes were telling him, made him feel more at ease, but Jamison knew better than to let his guard down, touching the string of the bow that was still slung over his right shoulder. "Only if needed," he muttered to himself. His feelings had changed, and he pondered hard for a moment about the urge to take one of the creatures down. It wasn't that the urge had dissipated and left him. It was just that he valued his multi-millionaire lifestyle more than taking the risk at being killed himself. He wanted off Corstine's floating nightmare in the sky, and he would do whatever it took to achieve just that.

Johnny Depp's famous line from "Pirates of the Carribbean" rang out in his head. "All that matters now is what a man can do and what a man can't do."

Jamison re-emphasized the phrase to himself once more as he zipped up his backpack, tightened his shoelaces, and glanced down at his watch. By his own estimate, he had about twenty two minutes, and as the second hand moved again he now had twenty one minutes. Three six minute miles should do the trick just nicely.

He took a few more precious seconds to stretch out the back of his hamstrings, and then he quickly popped back up to set his watch. Jamison took one last look around him and then hit the start button on the watch. With that he took off at a blistering pace towards, hopefully, his safe evacuation at the "rendezvous point."

CHAPTER SEVENTY-TWO

The rainforest cycle, Downs thought to himself, his mind processing images of insects, earthworms, and other forest floor dwellers munching on the remains of him as his body lay there reduced to nothing more than animal feces. He then pictured a bird managing somehow to get part of his newly formed shape, flying high up into the rainforest canopy, pooping and redistributing him to another part of this dense and steamy ecosystem.

The realism of being redistributed back into the rainforest cycle gave him the chills as he thought about the possibility of being consumed and traveling through the digestive track of one of the creatures, only to come out the other end. A sharp and intense pain from his ribs cut in over his thoughts, bringing him once again to his knees, and reminding him not only of the injuries he had sustained, but more importantly of William Jamison.

The very thought of Jamison brought Downs back up to his feet, and he forced himself to overcome the pain in an all out mind-over-matter battle. As he fully raised himself as best he could, he felt a new and growing sense of purpose coursing through his body, purpose to not only overcome, but, more importantly, to survive. The thought of Josiah and Max popped into his head. Were they okay? He hoped like hell that they had already been rescued or found safety at the very least, until he could make his way back up to them. The alternative to them finding safety was simply inconceivable. What had happened to Nat was again beyond comprehension.

He nodded to himself and mouthed the word "Yep."

"Yep," he said aloud, placing great emphasis on the word. "Today is not the day that I die. Today is not that day."

Downs knew he wasn't going to go out like this. This could not be the end of him. He had to get back and find his way to the others, if they were in fact still amongst the living. The urge was strong but the pain down in his ribcage was still resonating even stronger.

He inhaled a big breath of air and tried to push the pain aside to the deepest and furthest regions of his brain. He turned around quickly, as something suddenly and without warning stirred from behind.

Nothing but the entrance to the nest itself, the area in which he had fallen down, greeted him. Was he hearing things as he staggered forward?

This time though noise came from behind him, and quickly he shot around. Something was glistening back at him in the last bit of available sunlight the jungle had to offer up, as if someone were reflecting the sun off a mirror and shining it his way.

Downs squinted, yet he managed to still stumble forward as the image started to take shape. A smile crept across his face as he moved closer and closer towards it, and within a few more steps an even bigger smile spanned the width of his face. He knew instantly what it was.

"Jamison's kukri knife," he muttered, half not believing it was there lying before him.

He bent down and picked it up, his brain as downright stunned as his hands were to be feeling the deadly weapon. Jamison must have dropped it in his maniacal pursuit to escape the nest and leave him here to die.

Leaving me here to die. The thought hit Downs hard as he tightened his grip on the weapon.

Jamison had done his best to disassemble Downs and leave him to fend for himself, to find out if he really deserved to survive, or as he already so eloquently phrased it, to have the right to pass on his genes to his offspring. Downs gripped the weapon even tighter as he could feel a fury coming over him, anger to both survive and prosper.

He looked down at the tip of the kukri knife. Blood still coated the edges of it. Downs took a quick look around and was just about to stow the knife at his side, when he quickly realized it was pointless. There would be no point in stowing the weapon at his side. It was plain and simple. He had to use it. He had to kill.

Kill or end up back in the rainforest cycle.

CHAPTER SEVENTY-THREE

John Corstine and Jeremiah listened and waited with baited breath, all while watching the last of the saliva drip and drop to the floor. A few seconds of uncomfortable silence passed before all out carnage and chaos picked back up. Corstine listened in silence as he knew his office was being torn to shreds and uprooted like vegetables in a garden. Loud clattering and clunks abounded above. A heavy and fully loaded file cabinet must have toppled to the ground, spilling everything inside and, thereby, exposing a boatload of confidential files that Corstine had accumulated since work began on the board-walk years ago. Corstine had been meticulous in his record keeping, so much that one could have construed it as hoarding.

"Shit," Corstine cursed to himself.

"Much bigger problems on hand, Dad," Jeremiah replied as he repositioned himself just beneath the door.

"What are you doing?" Corstine demanded, but it was too late as Jeremiah pushed the door up and open, leaving just enough room for him to peak his head out.

Now with a full view, Jeremiah could see the battle that was being waged in his father's office, an office that had served as the breeding ground to the very idea of the boardwalk itself, an office which was near and dear to his father's heart. Tables and bookshelves had been upended, splintered, and battered into broken pieces, along with three large filing cabinets and all their contents. Everything spilled out onto the floor and was being trampled like there was no tomorrow.

The physical damage to the office paled in comparison to what else Jeremiah's eyes were processing. The entire scene represented one of both cannibalism and all out savagery. Everything was eating everything in what seemed like an effort to end each other with little thought or reason behind it, except that of relentless carnage. Jeremiah saw quite vividly several little gatherings or clusters where the very young were rolling around on the ground, while the others around them would repeatedly dive bomb their fallen family members, ripping off pieces of flesh, limbs, tails, and even gouging eyes out with their oversized talons.

Quickly Jeremiah searched the ground floor with his eyes. Then he saw it. The massive adult was resting on all fours in full glory. The creature though did not see the small puny human peering at him from just beneath ground level as it sent its prehensile tail plunging into the side of one of the office walls. The crushing impact vibrated the office, and Jeremiah looked back down at his father while still holding the door slightly ajar.

"We need to get out of here, and quickly. They're tearing everything to pieces as well as each other," Jeremiah said, turning his full attention back to the slaughter on the office floor.

The adult again bashed its tail into the wall almost in an act of defiance, sending another vibrating wave that rippled through the building. Jeremiah's eyes frantically searched the ground floor for a possible solution to their dilemma. Noise, tearing, gouging, screaming, and clawing all soaked up his senses before movement out of the corner of his eye finally came into clearer focus, materializing into the image of a body that was moving fast. Not even giving a second thought, Jeremiah snatched the opportunity by the back two legs, the little predator making slashing attempts at any part of open skin.

Jeremiah flung the creature with all his might. He opened the door fully upright now, waiting for his intended outcome, as the creature slammed into the far office wall and fell straight down to the floor. The entire room immediately took notice of the newly dropped piece of meat.

"Come on," Jeremiah shouted down to his father, offering him a hand in the process.

With some grunting and struggle, he managed to pull his father up and onto the surface. Father and son wasted little time as they made a beeline towards the hallway from which they had entered. The wall to which Jeremiah had flung the small creature now reflected a ball of carnage as several youngsters rolled end-over-end in their pursuit to overtake and overwhelm the small individual. The fierce onslaught of aggression had grabbed the attention of the adult, as it let out a loud piercing roar and bounded towards the action.

Corstine and Jeremiah had managed to make their way back out to the hallway and were just about to officially exit the building, but not before Corstine paused momentarily to pull a red lever directly adjacent to the door. With that they opened the door that led back out to the boardwalk.

CHAPTER SEVENTY-FOUR

Thirty-six year old Gajaraja Conly sat in his small yet surprisingly well-organized air conditioned office in a high rise building in Jakarta, Indonesia, more specifically the Jabodetabek region of the city, considered to be the official metropolitan area. Gajaraja's office was located at the end of the hallway on the 43rd floor of the building. The door simply read JC VENTURES, which stood for none other than John Corstine Ventures.

No one had ever questioned him or questioned the very existence of JC Ventures in the first place. Gajaraja had read about how fake companies existed merely as an office door and nothing more.

He wouldn't have gone so far as to call what he was operating for Corstine as a fake company. Essentially he was a call center for Corstine, but from time to time he felt it to be a scam. He didn't question it though, wouldn't dare question the hand that fed him. Gajaraja was being paid nearly $40,000 American dollars per year, enough to make him quite well off by his own standards.

Gajaraja was just about to sip some strongly brewed coffee when an alert started to go off back at his computer. Quietly he made his way to his desk and sat down.

That's odd, he thought to himself, as he toggled a few buttons on the keyboard, opening up several different browser windows on the screen.

In the two years that he had been on the job, he had been running a call center that fielded zero calls day in and day out. Gajaraja had had interactions with John Corstine himself via email, Skype, and the occasional phone call, but now it was something different. An alert was going off on his computer. He reached over and put on his glasses as he scooted his chair in to have a better look at the screen.

The alert was at the bottom of the screen. Gajaraja clicked on the alert and up came the message. It read:

EMERGENCY LEVER HAS BEEN ACTIVATED IN QUADRANT ONE OF THE BOARDWALK. EMERGENCY RESPONSE NEEDED IMMEDIATELY. PLEASE SUMMON A FULLY LOADED HELICOPTER AND BEGIN CIRCLING ALL QUADRANTS AT ONCE. REPEAT. EMERGENCY LEVER HAS BEEN ACTIVATED IN QUADRANT ONE. PLEASE SUMMON A HELICOPTER AND BEGIN CIRCLING ALL QUADRANTS IMMEDIATELY.

Gajaraja felt his pulse quicken, and the hairs on the back of his neck began to stand on end. He suddenly felt warm and clammy all over, the overwhelming rush of excitement taking him by storm like a cold that had come out of nowhere.

"Breathe," he muttered to himself. "You must breathe, Gajaraja."

He took a deep breath and let the air fill his lungs, then paused for a moment while closing his eyes. He opened them slowly, readjusted his glasses, and moved his chair back a few inches from the desk.

Now let's focus.

He quickly reread the warning prompt message once more, scanning to see if he missed anything. He began straining his mind for the next step. At first he drew a big fat blank, but then he remembered that the answer to the warning message lay within his emails. Now that he thought about it, that email was two years old, essentially the length of time he had been on the job.

Rather than go through each page of his email account one by one at a painstakingly slow pace, he quickly typed in the name John Corstine into the filter box of his Gmail account. He hit the button and the search produced ninety seven emails from Corstine himself. Gajaraja quickly began paging back to the very first emails he ever received from Corstine.

It wasn't in the first email from Corstine, but in the third. It held the desired information that he was after. He clicked on it and quickly began scanning the contents of the email. Knowing that he had successfully found the correct email, he allowed himself to breathe a slight sigh of relief, but a slight one at that, knowing full well that he still needed to execute Corstine's orders.

The email read:

GAJARAJA, WELCOME ABOARD AND GLAD TO HAVE YOU AS MY FIRST IN COMMAND FOR THIS CERTAIN PROJECT IN THIS TANGENT OF THE WORLD. BEING THAT THIS IS WHAT I CONSIDER TO BE MY MY FIRST REAL TRANSMISSION TO YOU, I ASK THAT YOU PLEASE ABIDE BY THE FOLLOWING REQUEST. IN THE ADVENT OF AN EMERGENCY DURING THE CONSTRUCTION PHASE OF THE PROJECT OR DURING ANY HOURS BOTH NOW AND AFTER, PLEASE SUMMON THE APPROPRIATE HELP SHOULD THE WARNING BEACON GO OFF.

YOUR IMMEDIATE CONTACT PERSON IN CASE OF AN EMERGENCY IS COPPER LEVINGSTON. I HAVE SENT YOU ANOTHER EMAIL SIMPLY WITH THE EMERGENCY NUMBER TO COPPER. IF YOU CALL IT YOU WILL NOT RECEIVE AN ANSWER. THE NUMBER IS NEVER TO BE USED EXCEPT IN THE EVENT OF AN EMERGENCY. COPPER HAS BEEN BRIEFED

AS WELL ON THIS VERY DETAIL. HE IS EMPLOYED BY ME AND PAID TO BE ON CALL 24/7. ONCE AGAIN, PLEASE FIND HIS CONTACT INFORMATION IN THE NEXT EMAIL. GOOD TO HAVE YOU ON BOARD, AND WE SHALL SPEAK VIA SKYPE VERY SOON.

CORDIALLY,

JOHN CORSTINE

Without hesitation Gajaraja opened up Corstine's next email and immediately began dialing the number that Corstine had provided. The phone immediately went to an automated voice and spoke to him.

THANK YOU FOR CALLING. YOUR REQUEST HAS BEEN PROCESSED AND THE NECESSARY MEASURES HAVE BEEN PUT INTO PLACE. GOODBYE.

Gajaraja took a moment to catch his breath before finally ending the call. He let out a sigh of relief, staring up at the ceiling and praying that he had executed and placed the appropriate courses of action into play.

CHAPTER SEVENTY-FIVE

William Jamison came to a complete stop, shook his head, and then began to start running again. He decided to stop once more after only a few feet. It had been the third time in just a few short minutes that he had forced himself to come to a halt, but he couldn't shake the feeling that he was being watched, couldn't get rid of the overwhelming impulse that he was being eyed from an unseen location. Jamison looked around, feeling as though he had a good vantage point of the surrounding area to field any oncoming attacks, but his senses were now firing on all synapses, screaming at him as his finger gently strummed the string of the bow.

He wiped at a layer of sweat that had been building and building for quite some time atop his forehead. His throat was dry and parched, and he reached behind to unzip his Klean Kanteen from its holding place inside his backpack.

He knew the water would not be cold, but he was already anticipating the feeling of it trickling down the back of his throat as he threw his head back and prepared to drink. The sound of breaking branches caught him completely off guard, sending the Klean Kanteen dropping to the ground.

Jamison saw a blurred movement perform several acrobatic moves through the treetops. Then he saw what the blur was, in all its glory fully using its prehensile tale to swing itself from limb to limb, performing moves that seemed not possible for a creature of its size. Jamison followed the creature, his eyes going wide with horror as it swung itself off of the last huge branch, propelling its body up and into the air like a gymnast, before crashing down on all fours onto the boardwalk.

Jamison stood a mere forty feet from the beast as it breathed heavily and stared down at him, its teeth reddened with blood. Its mouth reeked of rotting and decaying meat.

Jamison stood as still as a statue for a moment with his arms at his side, the two locked in a deep and intense staring contest. He knew full well that the creature before him was thinking and reasoning things out as it tilted its head ever so slightly to the side, a movement one might expect to see from a modern day bird.

Without giving too much away and as silently as he could, Jamison slowly began to bring his hand around towards the sheath that housed his kukri knife, placing his right hand down around where he knew the tip of the handle would be. The entire time he continued to maintain eye contact with the creature, never letting his eyes waver for a second. He thought by now he would have had the knife unsheathed and firmly in his grip. Somewhat confused by the fact that his hand wasn't making contact with the top of the weapon yet, he let go of eye contact with the creature for just a moment and looked down and towards where he had been aimlessly patting. His eyes widened in disbelief. The kukri knife was gone.

With his head spinning in confusion, Jamison flung himself around wildly, doing a quick and sloppy sweep of the area, scanning every place he could muster with his eyes for the weapon. When the effort turned up empty, the creature lurched forward and attacked with talons poised and ready to inflict fatal results with its mouth wide open as it screamed.

The thing let out a cry as if it were flying up and out of the very bowels of hell itself. Jamison had little time to react against the rushing onslaught, and he did the only thing of which he believed he was capable. He charged the creature with his own roaring battle cry while raising his right fist high into the air.

The act of bravery by the formidable yet significantly smaller human must have shocked the creature somewhat, as it flinched but still managed to keep its forward momentum going. The two combatants locked on a crash collision with one another. The creature roared as it propelled itself up and into the air, but just at the last minute Jamison changed his direction and lifted himself up and into the air as well, but not as high up as he had originally intended. It was too late for the creature, with its forward and potential energy set in one place. It could not react and change its intended direction.

Close to one thousand pounds of muscle and mass flew slightly above Jamison as he launched his attack from just below the creature, delivering several swift punches to the massive stomach region, the impact rattling his hands to the core as they connected with a seemingly impenetrable wall of muscle.

At the last second Jamison managed to divert his body further to the right as the creature's tail took a lashing swipe at him. As Jamison's feet touched down on the boardwalk, he quickly turned to watch as the creature clumsily landed and then fell. Its legs collapsed beneath sheer weight, and it slid a bit before finally coming to a stop. Jamison looked on at the creature, expecting it to rise to its feet, but, surprisingly, it remained motionless.

Jamison knew better than to believe the thing was hurt. Was it merely toying with him? The thought struck him as odd and fascinating all in one. He was well aware that his options were dwindling and

Jamison knew from his punches and the stinging pain that was still radiating from his hand that his arrows would have a difficult time puncturing and inflicting any damage at all on such a massively well put together beast. He cursed to himself momentarily, now realizing the full scope of his actions. It had indeed not been the wisest of decisions to abandon weaponry and firearms in the act to take these creatures down by bow and arrow. Yet now here he stood with such primitive weaponry.

Jamison watched as the creature unfurled a long and lathery forked tongue from its mouth, seeming to be over a foot in length, and began licking a wound that had formed on its rear hind leg. The creature licked itself for a few more moments as the great William Jamison stood still as a statue with his arms dangling at his side. Something was trickling ever so gently down his neck and onto his shirt, and as he reached up he discovered he was bleeding from the neck.

Jamison realized the terrifying reality that he had taken both his eyes and attention off the creature, even if it had just been for a split second. It was a split second too long in his book. Jamison looked up and got an eyeful of the back of the creature's throat as it charged, this time like it wanted to swallow him whole, a feat that seemed entirely possible given the size and dimensions of its jaw.

But Jamison had already learned something about the creature, something that he was about to use to his advantage as the thing continued charging straight for him. Jamison held on until he felt he couldn't hold on any longer, and then at the last minute he catapulted himself out of the way as the huge creature lunged for him.

CHAPTER SEVENTY-SIX

The rhythmic sound of tribal drums beat loudly in Downs' head as he stood there and fought hard to straighten himself upright. He tucked the blinding pain away that shot out from his chest as he listened to those drums. They were the drums his father used to play to him when he was a young child, the beating sound helping him to concentrate and fight the attention deficit disorder that he struggled with all through adolescence and even into adulthood. He appreciated those drums for their relenting sound, their relenting ability to never let up or quit, and that was something that Downs had carried with him his entire life. And now as he stood there, the sound of those tribal drums inside his head beat louder than ever. He had managed to do it though, despite the excruciating pain, as if his standing there fully upright was a small victory in its own right, announcing to all that his weary yet existing presence had been fully resurrected.

In his right hand he clutched Jamison's kukri knife for all it was worth. The weapon was his only form of protection against a canopy ecosystem brimming with a voracious species of treetop predator. Downs wondered to himself for a split second what had stopped or what would stop such a species from taking over and simply out-competing all other forms of life? The thought was a short lived one as the usual audible sounds of the rainforest brought him back, a reality that with each passing second was becoming more and more serious.

Get moving Bick, a voice said from somewhere deep within. *You need to get moving immediately.*

It was essential that he get back to the boardwalk, where at least he ran the remote chance of being rescued. Downs had completely lost all sense of time, where the days seemed to mold into the nights and vice versa in a chaotic non linear pattern. Some time ago Nat had told him that the "rendezvous point" was not the end, and that the helicopter would be doing one last final sweep of the entire boardwalk, hovering as low as the treetop canopy would allow while making sure everyone and everything had been accounted for.

Downs paused again, still standing there, kukri knife and all, wondering why Corstine would have scheduled one final sweep of the entire boardwalk in the first place? Did he think the entire group wouldn't make it, that individuals would be scattered and displaced when it came time for pickup? Or did he know of the existence of the creatures all along? Downs shook his head in anger, wanting nothing more than to ring Corstine's neck, believing full well that the real estate tycoon knew all along what they would encounter and potentially be up against at the very top of the rainforest.

Come on, Bick, time is ticking, the voice shouted at him again. *You're wasting precious time. Precious time is ticking. You need to get moving. Act quickly. Act swiftly. Time is ticking. Tick. Tick. Tick.*

Downs nodded in agreement with himself, and although it seemed odd to be doing so, he still did it anyway, further solidifying what he already knew. It was time to start making preparations for what needed to be done. He needed to lure as many of them as he could to the nest for an all out feeding frenzy, a WWE Wrestlemania spectacular. A royal rumble, carnage that would simply implore more carnage until finally everything had wiped everything else from existence.

As Downs took steps away from the buzzing and rotting little creature, he could already see the entire scene playing out in spectacular cinematic detail in his head. There would be biting, scratching, clawing, tearing, gouging, gorging, disemboweling, and a host of other unspeakable acts of cannibalism, all while hopefully allowing him just enough of a window of opportunity to climb his way back up to the boardwalk. Then it would be up to him entirely what he did once he was up there.

Downs made his way carefully out to the far corner of the nest, towards where he had entered and where a gathering of twigs and branches lay in a pile. When he got there, he craned his neck and looked up towards the boardwalk, towards where Jamison had shimmied his way up one of the trees. He wondered if Jamison had made it, and then stopped wondering all together, realizing full well that Jamison was a survivor and would do whatever it took to get off the boardwalk alive.

Downs looked up once more and realized he must have been some forty feet from getting back up and onto the boardwalk. He debated for a second whether he should just shimmy his way up, although his bruised ribs would be having a say as well. They still hurt like hell, but if he wanted to, he believed he could, right there and then, he could have done just as Jamison had done. Downs had learned over the years though to trust his sheer gut instinct. It had led him to correct decisions time and time again. He knew that he'd be a sitting duck if he tried to climb his way up and out right now, and with his bruised ribs he'd be less than 100% all while hanging in a precariously vulnerable position. He needed to give himself the gift of time, but more importantly the gift of distraction.

Downs backed away and had a look at the pile of limbs and small branches, trying to find anything and everything that could be used. The minute he threw back the first of the small branches, several large spiders and beetles were flushed from their hiding places and sent scurrying madly in all directions.

He continued to dig through the pile, and the further down he dug, he could see that things were becoming progressively bigger. Downs pulled out a branch that must have been seven feet long by his own estimates, and he stowed it at his feet. Shooting pain gripped him all of a sudden, and he had to take a moment before continuing on, hunching over as he winced in pain.

He continued rummaging and was just about down to the bottom of the pile, having removed a branch that must have been damn near ten feet in length, far too large and awkward for him to use, but he figured he'd pull it out anyway. With great pain he lifted the branch and managed to let it drop towards where the other one lay. Practically at the bottom of the pile now he continued on, removing vines, branches, fronds, leaves, and nuts that had most likely been scattered and redistributed by the local bird inhabitants. Then at the bottom he saw them, something which took him rather swiftly by surprise.

CHAPTER SEVENTY-SEVEN

Jamison dove hard to his side and rolled end-over-end, scrambling upright and quickly to his feet, and immediately sprinting for the opposite side as the body of the massive creature slammed hard into the railing. The creature managed to hold itself upright just enough to prevent from falling and toppling over the side of the boardwalk as it roared in anger.

Meanwhile Jamison had arrived safely on the other end. Quickly he butted himself up tight to the railing and looked back. The vegetation behind where the creature stood was sparse, with no overhanging limbs or branches and no trees in close proximity, giving it a quite open and airy feeling, a far cry from the thick vegetative growth that they had encountered earlier on the boardwalk. It was the perfect place for what he knew needed to be done.

The creature stared down at him with its mouth agape for a moment, giving Jamison a brief second to see that several planks making up the railing behind the creature had been loosened by the jarring impact. His eyes widened. Quickly he reached back, knowing full well it would be a useless effort, but he did so anyway while releasing an arrow that cut through the air. He had hoped the arrow would pierce the tough almost crocodilian-like hide of the creature, but it bounced off the shoulder blade and ricocheted over the edge.

The shot had done nothing as the creature roared. Instead of firing another useless arrow, Jamison knew he had one chance, and once chance only to execute the opportunity currently presenting itself. He could see that the creature was mounting its second charge as it roared again and lunged itself in his direction. Jamison took up the challenge, vocalizing his own battle cry of a roar as he raced towards the beast screaming like a madman, or a man who was staring into the oversized bulbous eyes of death itself.

With his athletic skills and physical prowess on full display, Jamison faked as if he was going to go airborne. The creature seeing this, responded immediately, and propelled itself up and into the air roaring. At the last second Jamison stopped his body from leaving the ground, ducking low as the huge beast sailed over him.

Jamison made a beeline straight for the broken planks of the railing that he had spotted moments earlier. Wasting no time he let go of the bow and dropped his large hands down onto part of the broken plank and heaved with all his might. When the damn thing did not budge and pull apart as he had predicted, he began to panic as this time he heard the creature come landing down successfully on its four manhole-sized feet.

"Shit," he breathed, knowing full well that he had his back to the creature and lay completely exposed.

Then with one great final exertion of effort, the planks gave way, leaving him with one the size of a fully grown man. Jamison immediately swiveled to face the creature, gripping it like a baseball bat and acting as if he were a lion tamer about to tame the great wild beast as he raised the plank in defiance above his head.

The creature let out another roar from where it stood, but Jamison's attention was on the area just beyond the huge beast, the railing area from which he had come. Jamison felt the powerful muscles in his arms and legs twinge with anticipation. Part of him was terrified while the other half pulsed with adrenaline.

The creature wasted little time as it charged straight for him. Jamison managed to kick the bow out of the way as he gave up pursuit as well, wielding the large plank now as if it were an axe. He bounded with big and commanding steps towards the creature; his speed mixed with the huge plank seeming like his aim was to decapitate the creature with one swing.

The creature went airborne and so did Jamison this time, but just as the two were about to meet mid-air, Jamison managed to go out and to the side of the beast. With everything he had, he brought the plank cracking down upon the creature's massive head, using every last ounce of his almost superhuman-like strength. The encounter had happened in a blur of a second, and Jamison lost control of the plank as both he and it crashed back down to the boardwalk.

In a stunned and dazed sense of confusion, Jamison tried to retrieve the plank while behind him the creature continued to roar. He found it odd that he had dropped the large plank in the first place, but as he swiveled to his side, the bottom part of his left eye caught the horror of why he had dropped the plank in the first place. In a strange out-of-body experience, his eyes widened with both terror and disbelief at what he was seeing. His left arm was gone, taken just beneath the shoulder blade.

Feeling no pain though, bleeding, and in absolute shock, Jamison gripped down on the plank with his right hand and hoisted the thing above his head. He turned and faced the creature, just in time to watch as the thing threw its head back. Jamison caught the tail end of his left index finger as it went down the creature's throat along with the rest of his arm. Then with another roar, the creature's eyes locked onto what remained of William Jamison.

The large man still possessed an incredible amount of strength as he maintained the plank above his head using only his right arm. Jamison was running out of both options and time. Realizing he needed to get into position on the opposite side of the board-walk, this time it was he who took the aggressive route. Blasting a roar as loud as his vocal chords would allow, he charged the creature.

The creature, taken aback for a split second at the bravado and courage shown by the human, sprung into action as well. It bounded towards Jamison. This time though Jamison did not propel himself up and into the air. Like a boxer entering the ring looking for the knockout punch, Jamison came out swinging.

He wielded the plank with impressive power as he attempted to send it smashing down onto the head of the creature once more. As man and beast met in spectacular fashion in the middle of the board-walk, Jamison struck the creature square in the head with the plank, and was just about to pivot and head for his intended positioning when he felt a deep penetrating slash. His brain screamed for him to get to where he deemed he needed to be. It was his only option, to try and fake the creature out into jumping off the boardwalk, into an area where there was no vegetation and it would plummet to its death.

Jamison let the plank drop to the ground, pushed off of the massive beast with his right arm, and immediately began sprinting towards the area where he had broken the plank free earlier. It wasn't until he had taken half a dozen steps or so that he came to the horrifying realization that he was not sprinting at all, rather he was hobbling at best. He stopped for a moment of stark confusion. Bleeding, delirious, and limbless he had lost sight of the creature momentarily, but he could still smell it. Jamison punched and shouted at the air with his right arm as he thought he saw the huge creature take a swipe at him. When he realized it was nothing but his own imagination, he forced himself to keep backing up until he had reached the broken railing.

He could now feel the partially broken railing at his backside. Then his eyes locked in on the creature as his brain registered seeing the backside of it. Like a lion circling its kill, the creature made a wide turn before finally coming around and focusing its eyes back on its intended victim.

Jamison managed to crane his neck to the side. He could see the openness of the area and knew there were no trees or limbs for quite some distance. Beyond the railing it was a sharp drop all the way down to the forest floor. His mind was failing him fast, but it still believed he could fake the creature out one last time and send it plummeting to its untimely death.

Jamison muttered quietly to himself as he spat blood. "Wait. Wait. Wait."

Just before Jamison saw the creature mounting another attack, he started to lose it. With his right hand he frantically tried to remove a large reddish pink snake that was coming straight for his stomach. Jamison grabbed at the thing, but as he did so, the snake fell away from him and plopped down onto the ground. Horror embraced him as he looked down and saw that his stomach had been ripped wide open, and the snake was actually his small intestine that had spilled forth onto the boardwalk.

Jamison had lost track of time as the seconds warped into minutes, and the minutes themselves seemed as long as a mini life age. His mind was reeling, absolutely reeling and spinning with sheer delusion as he took in the sight of his intestines hanging out of him and lying at his feet. He felt dizzy, couldn't tell left from right, up from down, real from what was not real. William Jamison looked up just in time to see a great shadowy figure materialize into a mouthful of oversized teeth as the creature's jaws came plunging down over him, sending him forever into eternal darkness.

CHAPTER SEVENTY-EIGHT

J ohn Corstine and his son Jeremiah had been been running for
about a quarter of a mile, when Corstine saw up ahead on the
far right what he knew would be there all along. Rising up from the
boardwalk was by anyone's estimations a lookout tower, potentially
for an armed guard to stand watch. Corstine had liked the design
feature of such a structure rising thirty feet or so above the boardwalk, with the intended plan of resurrecting another eleven or so
over the entire length of the boardwalk at a later time and date. He
knew damn well though that they would most likely never hold an
armed guard. He had once joked to the early investors that instead of
guards atop the towers, he would line and decorate them with potted
plants and flowers. A statement, that caused quite a bit of commotion amongst investors at the time, citing potential mismanagement
of funds.

Corstine ran to the base of the narrow tower, knowing that the
door which led inside should have been locked. That would be no
problem though because he had made a thin duplicate copy of the
key some time ago and slid it neatly into his wallet. As he got closer

though, he realized that the key would not be necessary; the door had been left slightly ajar.

He slowed himself a bit, emphasizing every bit the word "caution." Jeremiah was now at his back, and quickly the young and athletic son switched his positions, pushing himself in front of his father and scooting Corstine behind him as both of them slowly approached the door to the tower.

The smell of raw feces and blood immediately assaulted their nostrils as Jeremiah paused at the door, which was no more than a few inches open. Although Corstine still had his pistol, he cursed quietly to himself for not taking Collin Fairbanks up on his offer to stock each tower with a fully loaded assault rifle, which would be locked away securely of course. Corstine wondered for a moment where in the hell his bloody assistant was, although the thought was quickly washed away by the foul odor which was getting worse by the second.

Quietly and unassumingly Jeremiah nudged the door open ever so gently, waiting a few extra seconds after it had fully come to a stop before peering his head around. The smell of feces and blood was far worse now that Jeremiah's head and neck were in the tightly confined area, just slightly bigger than a typical elevator. Slowly Jeremiah brought the rest of his body around and was now standing with two feet firmly planted in the tower, the only light shining in from the open door.

"Scoot over son," Corstine said, as he moved in.

Blood stains streaked the four walls that surrounded them, each wall no more than an arm's length away from where they both stood huddled together. Corstine's eyes looked upwards, taking in more of the blood strewn scene. He could tell there appeared to have been a great struggle.

Jeremiah crept a few inches closer towards the wall when suddenly his father let out a deep and resounding gasp. Jeremiah's own gaze shot up to where his father's attention had gone. Jeremiah held his father with one arm as he stared upward.

Up at the top of the landing to the spiral staircase, the part that led out to the small observation deck just outside, hung a fully grown dead Komodo dragon. Jeremiah shook his head, still maintaining his father in his grasp as he appeared to still be lightheaded. He wondered how in the hell what they were both staring at was even possible. Upon first glance Jeremiah noticed deep gouging lacerations to the side of the animal.

The face of the Komodo dragon had been beaten and smashed in, almost beyond recognition. There were also deep gouging lacerations around the thick and muscular neck as well, capped off finally by the fact that a huge chunk had been bitten and taken from its stomach region, as if a shark had chomped right through it. All in all it looked very much like the once fearsome land predator had been put through the meat grinder and spit back out again.

"Dad, you good?" Jeremiah asked, turning his father round and looking him square in the eyes.

For the first time ever, or at least the first time that Jeremiah could ever recall, his father was scared shitless. By the glazed-over look that was now in his father's eyes, Jeremiah could tell that he was completely and utterly terrified.

"Dad," Jeremiah said, shaking him once more.

Corstine slowly came to, but his words, barely audible at that, were no more than a mumble.

"I'm sorry," Corstine said, as he let go of his son's embrace. Sliding down to the ground, he began to sob hysterically. "I'm so, so sorry."

Jeremiah took one last look at the hanging monster above before bending down to his father's level. Corstine was doing his best to wipe away the tears but they just kept coming forward, spewing forth like a small trickling stream.

"I should have known better," Corstine sobbed. "I knew there was something out here, something up here, but I ignored the warnings of the locals. I should have heeded their warnings."

Jeremiah looked up at the Komodo dragon once more, his eyes intensely focused on the huge chunk that was missing, knowing full well what did it, and also knowing full well the seriousness of the situation in which they found themselves.

"Dad, you can't hold yourself entirely responsible. This is something almost beyond the realm of modern day science as a whole, almost other worldly. I'm no scientist, but I think it's fair to say nothing like this has existed for quite some time. This is a remnant, a super predator, a freak of evolution," Jeremiah said while gripping his father by the shoulders.

Corstine looked up at him, his eyes reddened by the tears. "But I knew, or at least I had a damn good idea, and still I proceeded on. Still I proceeded on."

Jeremiah's gaze fell to the ground. "Everyone knew the risks signing onto this project. You said it yourself, that working at these heights during the construction phase would indeed be difficult and dangerous."

Corstine had finally stopped crying, doing his best damage control to compose himself. "But the tour that was organized this weekend, I didn't know with certainty, but I had a good guess that something was lurking in wait in this canopy ecosystem. Yet still I proceeded on, hoping like heck that whatever it was would not rear its ugly head."

"Progress never sleeps," Jeremiah muttered to himself as he continued to stare down at the ground.

"What?" Corstine asked.

Jeremiah looked up at his father. "That saying, I remember it from my earliest memories of you. You would always say progress never sleeps. It seemed to be the theme of all your businesses, all your successes."

Corstine smiled and nodded affectionately. "And my failures as well."

"Huh," Jeremiah replied, not certain where his father was going with the comment.

Corstine's eyes met with Jeremiah's for a powerful embrace. "My failure to both you and your mother, God rest her soul. When I was away on my business ventures, I left the two of you to fend for yourselves time and time again."

"We always had the credit card," Jeremiah joked.

Corstine smiled. "But in all seriousness, behind an overwhelming number of successful parents, you will find a messed-up kid and home life. Thanks to your mother, she did an unbelievable job, and you turned out far better than I could have ever hoped for."

A piercing, screeching cry suddenly rang out.

"We have to act quickly," Jeremiah ordered. "I want to get the hell out of here. Dad, sorry to say it, but you may have to officially scrap this project."

Corstine stood to his feet and brushed himself off. "I'm afraid you may be right, son. I'm afraid you may be right."

As if getting struck by a bolt of lightening, Corstine spun in the direction of the corner behind the spiral staircase. Jeremiah saw this and was on it immediately. He opened the small box mounted on the wall and looked back to his father who nodded in approval. And with that Jeremiah pulled the green lever down.

CHAPTER SEVENTY-NINE

Thirteen human skulls greeted Down's eyes as he recoiled, almost tripping over his feet and stumbling backwards. Moving forward he counted them once again. Thirteen skulls stared blankly back up at him, as if reminding him of their once physical existence on Earth. The empty hollowed-out eye sockets were what really got to him, along with the fact that each of them most likely had met their end at the hands of the creatures. He took a deep breath.

Downs suddenly looked up at the sky. It had started out faintly, almost distant and other worldly. He had practically missed it the first time round, but as he strained his ears, there it was again. This time it became louder and more pronounced. A beeping, warning sound was going off. It was coming in thirty second intervals. Downs quickly turned his attention back to the skulls.

It was all the wake up call he needed. Act now or end up as just another skull at the bottom of the pile. Quickly Downs got started on what needed to be done. He worked surprisingly efficiently with Jamison's kukri knife as he began to transform, mold, and fashion two of the branches he had acquired from the pile into something useful.

Sometime later, although he didn't know exactly how much later, he set down the two things he had been transforming and peeled off his t-shirt, which by now was soaking wet with perspiration. His entire chest glistened with beads of sweat. For a brief moment he thought about toweling the sweat off his chest with the shirt, but he decided to simply shuck the thing. On second thought, he bent down to pick up the shirt, quickly toweled the sweat from his head and tied the shirt round his forehead as if it were a bandana.

Downs stood with his arms across his sweat-laden chest and admired what he had created. Out of the larger of the branches he had acquired, he had made what resembled a very primitive looking spear ending in a sharp tip. It looked like something with which early man might have hunted or speared fish with. He could only hope that it would offer him some sort of defense.

Downs picked it up, noting the sharpness of the tip, despite the robust nature of the rest of it. Like a dancer rehearsing and practicing a choreographed routine; he performed a short array of moves with it. He smiled to himself and placed it down. Next was what he considered to be his dagger, made for close and intimate combat. The wooden dagger was just a few inches shy of two feet in length and was essentially the same as the spear in terms of appearance, just on a much smaller and less robust scale.

Downs looked up at the sky. The alarm was still sounding in thirty second intervals. Once again the tribal drums entered his head, the same drums that he had heard time and time again throughout his life and which had always, in some small way, aided him in his efforts. He heard them loudly and clearly now as he picked up the hand-crafted dagger and stuffed it between his skin and his belt. Now with the dagger placed firmly at his side for backup and with his shirt acting as a bandana, Downs picked up the kukri knife in his right hand and the spear in his left. He knew what needed to be done, and as soon as he began, he was startled by the very act itself. Dragging the knife across his bare and exposed chest, Downs began to cut himself.

CHAPTER EIGHTY

The main warning system to the boardwalk had been sounding loudly and clearly for about forty-five minutes or so, still ringing in thirty second intervals, and ringing out to whomever or whatever might be listening high atop the Indonesian rainforest canopy. Call it good fortune, fate, or the incredible wave of luck that John Corstine had seemed to be riding and receiving his entire lifetime, but shortly after he and Jeremiah had climbed to the top of the small tower, the pilot manning the Bell 407 helicopter had seen them both waving their hands back and forth frantically, like two people stranded on a deserted island up high in the sky.

It had been a little more difficult than he had planned, but the pilot of the Bell 407 had hovered as low as he could without risking hitting the tops of the trees. Eventually a small dangling ladder was lowered, and John Corstine was first to grab hold and climb up, while Jeremiah guided him up from the back as best he could. Jeremiah had quickly and powerfully pulled himself up and into the chopper as it continued to blow the treetops back and forth in its powerful wake.

That had been several minutes ago, and they were now flying, the green rainforest below, stretched out in all directions as far as the eye could see.

Corstine managed a smile and nodded at his son, and then looked back to the pilot. Corstine had to shout over the loud hum of the chopper. "We're going to make one final sweep of the entire boardwalk."

The pilot cocked his head slightly to the side while nodding in compliance, still maintaining vision of the open air space out in front of them. "Will do, Sir."

Corstine stared down momentarily towards the boardwalk, admiring the thing as it snaked its way back and forth through the greenery like a great serpent.

Corstine shouted once again back up to the pilot. "And thank you."

CHAPTER EIGHTY-ONE

Downs brought the blade to a halt just below the corner of his left breast. He was now bleeding as blood trickled down and over his chest, leaving the blade of the kukri knife red. Downs had cut himself at a slight angle across his broad chest, a gash that now spanned some seven inches in length. With powerful breaths his chest heaved in and out as he felt the adrenaline coursing through him like a river. He felt no pain though, could only hear the rhythmic beating of his own heart, mimicking those tribal drums that his father used to play for him. With eyes transfixed like that of a mad man, he watched with baited breath towards the entrance to the nest.

Sucking in several deep and commanding breaths, he prepped himself. Quickly he glanced down and made visual contact with the primitive dagger, spear, and the knife. He took one more deep and fulfilling breath, and then he let it out for all it was worth, the scream to end all screams, something that even he didn't know he was fully capable of blasting from his lungs. The high-pitched scream gave way and melded into that of a monstrous roar as every last ounce of air was expelled from his lungs, announcing to all both his presence and arrival. Several terrifyingly long minutes passed by as his heart pounded away, pounding like there was no tomorrow, before the forest around him finally crackled to life. The noise came from behind him, his brain shouting at him to spin around instantly. As he did just that, several small objects fell out and into the nest, as if the dense vegetation itself had just birthed them.

The two small shapes immediately screamed to life as they edged themselves forward. One of the juveniles bit down hard on the back neck of the other, quickly retracting its teeth and racing out towards Downs with its bloody maw agape. Surprisingly though, the thing stopped itself some twenty feet out from where it had originally taken off.

In an act that most certainly surprised the small predator, this time it was Downs himself who charged with an aggressive roar. The creature sprung to life as well, but it was too late as Downs plunged both the kukri knife and the makeshift wooden dagger into the neck of the creature. Still with the upper hand, he took the creature up high into the air before sending it down hard onto the nest floor, retracting the weapons, and leaving the youngster to die.

More shapes spilled out from the vegetation above, dropping like raindrops from the sky. A gaping roar followed by an overwhelming stench heralded the arrival of one of the adults. Downs suspected it to be the larger female. Quickly he stuffed the bloodied makeshift dagger and knife into the side of his belt and went immediately for the robust spear that he had handcrafted.

The massive creature let itself down and into the nest via its long prehensile tail, surprisingly hanging upside down for a few moments before finally letting go and dropping itself. Downs stood there, eyeing the huge beast, which stared down at him from around a height of some nine feet as it rested on all fours. It was as impressive a creature as one could hope to still find roaming the planet, and Downs felt the same type of awe-inspired terror deep in the back of his throat that one would expect to experience if they had happily stumbled across a tyrannosaurus rex roaming Central Park in New York City.

The creature opened its jaw ever so slightly while letting out a low resonating rumble of a growl. It revealed an impressive arsenal of razor sharp teeth. The whole creature looked like a horrific science experiment gone wrong, with its forest green reptilian skin providing a base. It had several large red and brown swirls of color on its back and sides, and it sported a thin yet spiky row of hair which ran atop its back and up and onto the neck and head, giving it a Mohawk type of appearance. Its skin was beady and reptilian, talons that hinted towards a lineage from the raptor family, and a plush prehensile tale that screamed primate in nature. It was every bit the melding of many different species into one.

Several of the youngsters had gathered beneath the girth of the massive female, appearing as if they were hungry, or chomping at the bit to suckle, though Downs did not know if either was true.

Downs stood still as a statue, still until his body couldn't take anymore. In a moment that screamed to him to take action, he quickly saw that the huge female was paying no attention to him whatsoever, rather she just kept brushing and pushing her youngsters to the side. Like hungry children they just kept coming and coming, continuing to fall out of the vegetation surrounding the nest, and attempting to congregate beneath her.

Downs saw his opportunity, and like primitive man hunting wooly mammoths on the tundra tens of thousands of years ago, he charged straight for the beast with his handcrafted spear, ready to pierce. He catapulted himself off of his left leg. Soaring through the air, he drove the six foot spear into the front left limb of the creature, plunging it until it wouldn't go any further, quickly yanking the weapon back out as gravity pulled him down.

The creature let out an ungodly cry. Downs retracted momentarily, wasting no time as he now went for the handcrafted dagger. Just like that he sped in for another swift and speedy attack, this time targeting the back right limb of the huge creature as it attempted to snap him up in its jaws, threatening to literally swallow him whole as it turned around. Savagely Downs plunged the wooden dagger deep in on the far side of the limb, realizing that the limbs of the creature were as wide as small tree trunks or pillars, and getting a very up close and personal view of the true size and scale of it.

The wooden dagger had gone in several inches, and all of a sudden would not come out. Downs simply left it where it was stuck, as he pushed himself back off of the pillar like limb, hoping he had inflicted some damage and pain at the bare minimum.

The creature was bleeding, this was clear, but what was unclear was whether or not Downs had actually inflicted any damage upon it. As it roared, either out of pain or anger, pushing everything out of its way and coming straight for him, it was clear that he had more than likely angered and agitated it.

Quickly Downs was forced to react as the creature lunged at him with its two front forelimbs, talons erect and outstretched, trying to disembowel and pull him apart. Downs was quick though and darted to his right just at the last second, and as the huge creature went whizzing by him, he had somehow forced himself to slash and assault one of the back limbs with the knife.

The creature slammed hard on the brakes though, managing to bring itself to a stop, the nest itself almost not big enough to accommodate such large and commanding movements. It turned and faced him immediately, like an enraged bull that had just missed the matador by inches. It was fuming mad, almost foaming at the mouth, wanting to end the human who seemed to be systematically picking it apart, with a slash here and a hack there.

Downs faked moving forward with his body once, twice, catching the creature off guard and then pulling himself back. On the third attempt he faked a throw with the wooden spear. By now the creature was on to him and on the move again as it propelled itself up and into the air via its powerful back legs.

Downs, at the last minute, held off throwing the wooden spear and managed to redirect it, releasing it at just the right time, the weapon fashioned out of a tree branch barely managing to penetrate through the light greenish colored underbelly of the creature as the monster went sailing over him. The underbelly itself surprisingly resembling what a crocodile or alligator looks like when turned over. Downs ducked as the long prehensile tail took one last fleeted attempt at a swipe, before the creature crashed to the ground, the booming impact rattling the entire nest.

Downs saw the creature which appeared to be momentarily down and out. The spear had managed to partially impale it. Downs was rapidly approaching, but the huge female twitched her body in a way signaling she was about to right itself, again ready for combat. Then something happened, something that Downs had hoped would happen, but even as he saw the seeds of it beginning, he still could not believe it, a reversal of power.

Downs could see blurs and shapes of varying sizes continuing to drop from the overhanging vegetation above. As soon as his eyes could make out everything that was raining down from above, the little creatures turned on one of their own. Like ants tackling something hundreds of times their size, the youngsters swarmed the massive female as she again tried to right herself and stand. Downs could see that a few larger juveniles were thrown into the mix as well, simply larger versions of the smaller young, but still nothing in comparison to the massive size she possessed.

They swarmed her, jumping onto her back like there was no tomorrow. Several of the speedy youngsters ran around to her side and instantly began digging in with their talons and already voracious mouths. With a commanding and powerful flick of her tail, she most definitely had crushed and fatally wounded a handful of her offspring. More and more poured out of the trees, jumping on top of her back and isolating her in their feeding frenzy attack.

Downs was stunned at the turn of events. It had all happened so quickly, the small but growing army overtaking the huge female. He could see that the feasting ball had grown, as the large female roared loudly in defiance several times, shaking herself to try to deter her offspring. Most remained, gripping down and digging into her backside with sharp curved talons.

Downs turned his back momentarily on the scene, and he looked up to where Jamison had climbed up and out. This was it, this was his chance screaming at him loud and clear. Pain from his ribs shot through him, but this was it if he was to truly get back to the boardwalk. He stood though and straightened himself up, once again hearing the tribal drums beating loudly over his thoughts.

Looking back to the growing and swarming ball of cannibalism, Downs knew it was now or never. In true swashbuckling form, he bit down on the backside of the knife and decided it was time to up and oust himself from the nest.

CHAPTER EIGHTY-TWO

Fighting off the inherent and shooting pain, Downs had managed to work his way up the same tree that had led William Jamison back to the boardwalk. He paused to catch his breath while coping for another moment with the pain from his ribs which was coming in spurts. There, hanging precariously some twenty feet above the nest, he could see down to the scene of cannibalism, the massive female still moving her limbs helplessly back and forth, completely overwhelmed and at the mercy of her own hungry and opportunistic offspring.

Downs could now see that the huge creature had been torn into on both sides as hungry mouths burrowed in wherever they could. He hung there, awed at the raw power of the collective greater good of the offspring. His mind went to the fact that ants have been known to lift ten, twenty, even fifty times their own weight. Perhaps such amazing strength was at work here as well.

A growing and feverish mass was writhing and convulsing atop her back as if the very force of all of them combined was in fact a creature all to its own, something that had the unstoppable urge to feed.

The entire scene was surreal as Downs shook his head and pushed with his legs and continued up towards the boardwalk. He was more than halfway there when he paused again, the sounds of the ravenous pack below rang out as they snarled, grunted, and continued to eat away at their own mother.

Suddenly Downs had noticed that one of the small creatures had made its way out and away from the gorging feast and stared up at him. He took one last look at the small thing and watched as it let out a loud yapping cry. Downs turned around and continued to make his way hastily towards the boardwalk. The boardwalk was now no more than fifteen feet away.

Downs took another short break and removed the knife from his mouth. His jaw muscles ached, but the fact that things with hungry mouths could come popping out at any time from the nearby limbs and vegetation put him on edge. He would need both hands for the ascent to the top as he bit down on the backside of the knife once again.

A quick glance back down towards the nest revealed that there were now five young creatures staring hungrily back up at him, each with bits and pieces of meat dangling from their mouths. That was all it took. Downs had seen enough, and with that he pushed off with his legs, not wanting to stay and find the entire cannibalistic clan looking back up towards him with their hungry, voracious mouths agape.

CHAPTER EIGHTY-THREE

With one final push of exertion, Downs lifted himself up and over the railing to the boardwalk and crashed down hard onto terra firma, the only terra firma he had known since agreeing to come on John Corstine's little weekend excursion. He sucked in several wet and humid breaths, the pain from his bruised ribs evident, but he had made it, and for that he felt a mixture of both incredible luck and relief. The relief was short lived though as piercing cries rang out from below.

Downs quickly stood to his feet and brushed himself off. The alarm was still ringing for all to hear. It was now coming in fifteen second intervals. Downs did a quick 360 degree sweep, trying to figure from where the sound was coming, but the noise was all engulfing, coming and resonating from every which direction. He knew that it must have been some type of warning signal, but a warning signal to what? Was the entire boardwalk going to collapse and implode? Had something been detonated? Questions circled in his head. The sound. The others. Where had they gone?

Were they even still alive? It all was circling oh so very fast deep in his mind.

A new sound suddenly caught his ears by surprise. He strained hard to listen. At first it started as a distant hum, something in the background behind all the usual sounds of the rainforest, but as Downs continued to listen, the hum soon turned into that of a monstrous roar.

He stumbled forward a bit, surprisingly in the direction of this new sound, which was growing in intensity by the second. The roar materialized and gave way as a full-sized helicopter made its way out from behind a large patch of green vegetation that had been keeping it concealed.

Downs could see the pilot up above wearing his dark aviator sunglasses while manning the aircraft. Next he saw John Corstine pop partially out of the open hatch, waving his hands and shouting out something that was incoherent next to the deafening roar. All that could be detected was an expression of fear mixed with the mouthing of words.

Suddenly Downs saw Corstine's gaze go from making eye contact with him to somewhere just beyond him. Corstine's eyes went stone cold. The real estate tycoon had spotted something. Downs' blood went icy cold also as he felt the tingling vibrations in the boardwalk.

In an almost slow motion movie reel effect, Downs saw Corstine waving frantically with his hands as the pilot edged the chopper forward towards him. Time itself stood still as Downs turned and was greeted with a rushing wave of creatures that were propelling themselves towards him. Like a deer caught in the headlights, he stood there awe-inspired for a split second at the tidal wave of energy coming his way, the sheer power and raw savagery of it all, before the roar of the helicopter above broke him from his trance.

Quickly and with no time to spare, he saw the chopper fly over him and then make a wide turn as it began to make its way back. Downs knew what they were doing or at least he hoped he did. The rumbling was growing more intense as the rushing onslaught of creatures drew nearer, with the remaining big male bringing up the rear.

Downs took one last look back towards the chopper, and just as he did so, a head popped out of the open hatch, a face that was completely foreign to him. With that, he turned and began sprinting in the same direction as the chopper was heading.

With the kukri knife still firmly in his left hand he made a dash for it across the boardwalk, as the vegetation around him on both sides began passing by quickly now. Then as Downs stepped it up into another gear, the vegetation faded into the background. He was running hard, damn hard, but the growing mass behind him was closing the distance gap as everything around and beneath him continued to shake and vibrate.

The roar of the helicopter above was almost upon him when he felt an immense pain explode from his back right calf muscle. He managed to turn while slowing himself just a bit, and he was greeted with the sight of one of the small creatures as it tore away at his pant leg. More importantly, it peeled off to the left with a piece of his skin dangling from its mouth.

Downs let out a shriek of pain, still looking back and watched as the small creature was completely overrun the minute it stopped itself in an attempt to swallow down the torn piece of skin. Downs let out another scream of pain, but it was muffled by the cries of the dying creature as a feeding frenzy ensued around it. The other creatures ripped the little thief to shreds.

"I want off this place," Downs roared defiantly, in an attempt to push himself on, fighting off the blistering and burning pain from the back of his now exposed calf. As chaos ensued behind him, the bulk of the mass was now no more than twenty yards from him. It felt as though the entire rainforest itself had turned against him, as well as the odds. Downs' ears registered that another creature must have gone down somewhere behind him, and like a person getting trampled at a soccer match in a large stadium gathering, the sound of breaking bones and the tearing of body parts signaled the taking of another life.

Downs continued on but he didn't dare look back. His ears told him what was practically on his heels now. The snapping of branches rang out from the nearby foliage to his left. The minute he turned his head to have a quick peak, four or five speedy blurs raced out in front of him, low to the ground, and with unrivaled acceleration. As soon as Downs took his attention off of the vegetation and brought it back to the route in front of him, he could see five of the small creatures were gathered up ahead in an attempt to quarden him off.

Still running, Downs was assaulted with excruciating pain again as he felt talons latch onto his back and then puncture through his skin as something bore into him. He now had one of the small creatures acting as if it were a backpack of gripping pain bearing down upon him.

His mind was panicking as the blaze of the helicopter above once again reminded him of its presence. A rope ladder dropped without warning from the sky out in front of him. It did not hit the deck as Downs hoped it would, rather it dangled back and forth some ten feet off the ground. Beyond the rope ladder lay the snarling youngsters who had formed a ring acting as a perimeter of sorts. They appeared poised to strike, and hell bent on trapping him in.

Downs kept up his speed. This was his chance. It was now or never as the young creature continued to dig in deeply with its curved talons at his back. Surprisingly though it had just attached itself to his back and wasn't attacking with its mouth. Downs took the opportunity and with that leaped off of his left foot, the same foot that had allowed him many times over the course of his life to dunk a basketball on a regulation ten foot hoop. As he lifted himself off the ground and into the air, he realized at the last second that Jamison's kukri knife was still in his left hand. Two hands would be needed, but it was too late to make a last second change. As he soared through the air, he braced his right hand for what was to come. Downs' right hand found purchase on the bottom rung of the ladder, and immediately he felt the enormous and awkward tug at his right shoulder blade, as his weight caused the ladder to push out and sway.

His brain screamed for him to hold on, hold on with every last ounce of strength he possessed. Downs managed to look down as the ladder swayed. Then everything below and around him began to happen at light speed. He saw out of the corner of his eye the giant male emerge from the green growth and lunge straight for him. Its huge jaws were wide open, and its talons were ready to inflict damage. The ladder was still in mid-motion as the huge creature went whizzing by and closed its mouth down on nothing more than thin air. Next Downs could see several of the small youngsters that had launched themselves up towards him and the ladder, only to be batted down by one of the creatures the size of a modern day cheetah. The minute the two small shapes hit the ground, the others turned on them again and another small yet fiery ball of carnage ensued.

Downs looked back up towards the open door into the helicopter, and again he saw a young face that was foreign to him, motioning for him to climb up. The knife was still in his left hand as the rope continued to sway.

Sheer pain from his back rang out as the little creature sank its talons further into him. It reminded him that it was still there. Downs instinctively stabbed back at the thing with the kukri knife, the creature letting out a loud hiss of pain as the knife penetrated deep. Downs retracted, and continued his attack, stabbing the thing repeatedly like a man possessed. In and out the blade went, until finally the talons released and the creature fell towards the carnage below. It was immediately engulfed.

Pain radiated from many sources, but he tucked that aside as he bit down once again on the backside of the knife and began to climb the ladder with two free hands. A little less than halfway up into his climb, he felt several tugs from below. A quick look down and he could see two of the youngsters dangling by their mouths from the end of the rope, like dogs that had grabbed hold of a chew toy and would not let go.

Downs was ascending the ladder faster now as he could see the opening. He saw the face he did not recognize as well as that of John Corstine encouraging him to climb quicker. Another hungry mouth had joined the party below at the bottom of the ladder, bringing the total to three, as they climbed and scrambled over one another in their pursuit to get to him.

Downs had focused on the youngsters below, and he failed to see the massive adult male until it was too late. The creature catapulted itself once again from an unseen vantage point and was now lunging straight for him like a great white shark emerging from the dark depths on an unsuspecting gathering of seals. Downs' eyes, along with his mouth, went wide with terror as he saw in the all engulfing blackness that which was the huge beast's mouth. In one continuous motion, the kukri knife spilled out of his mouth and fell to the boardwalk. At the last second Downs let go of the ladder with his right hand and swung his body as far to the left as he could. The massive creature side-swiped and flew by him, but Downs held on with only his left hand and left foot firmly on the ladder. He watched as the huge creature crashed back down to the boardwalk, crushing half a dozen or so youngsters in the process.

The three youngsters at the bottom of the rope had reached Downs and were now beginning to climb up his left pant leg as if it were a tree. One had just pulled itself up to his crotch when he reached down and punched the thing square in the jaw. The impact was powerful enough to send the creature flailing back and off of him, but not before it reached out with its talons and grabbed one of the others, sending them both plummeting down to the boardwalk. The final and remaining creature tore through Downs' legs with its talons as it raced up his chest towards his face. Downs was now no more than seven or eight feet from the entrance to the helicopter when he knew something needed to be done.

In the blink of an eye, it came to him. He visualized a killing claw, and then a downward slash delivered by that killing claw. Like an infusion of knowledge, Downs remembered just what he had, what he had always carried with him since his childhood days. Quickly he reached into his back pocket and extracted the adult velociraptor killing claw, slashing at the oncoming attacker from the jugular up, delivering a penetrating upward ripping blow to the little predator. The claw did just what nature had intended it to do, creating a serious gash several inches in length, and tearing the little creature open. With blood splattered across his neck, chin, and chest, Downs knew that now was not the time to let up. As the creature was just about to retaliate with a slash from one of its own talons, Downs brought the claw down hard and fast across its face, ripping a gash just under its left bulbous eye. The creature howled in pain, momentarily loosening its grip on Downs, and giving him just enough of an edge to shove it free of him.

Downs watched as the screaming creature fell like a bomb towards the madness on the boardwalk below. Quickly, he turned and climbed the remaining rungs of the ladder as four hands greeted him and pulled him through the opening and into the chopper. He managed to belly crawl his way towards the middle and somehow look up. Although he was on the verge of passing out, Downs first saw Corstine who immediately spoke to him.

"Ah, my boy," Corstine said. "We are ecstatic you made it. Our prayers have truly been answered."

Downs did not reply. Rather he managed a slight smile through gritted teeth.

Corstine quickly turned his attention to the opposite side where two gentlemen sat. "I trust you know these young fellas."

Downs looked up and saw Josiah and Max staring back at him with big yet thankful grins on their faces. Downs smiled back at them, shook his head and lowered it to the ground, before mustering the strength to bring it up once more.

"Found them scampering for their lives across my boardwalk," Corstine added. "Allow me to also introduce my son to you. Jeremiah Corstine."

Jeremiah nodded and raised a hand in the gesture of a handshake. Downs managed to nod and do the same back to him.

"Now," Corstine said, still shouting over the roar of the helicopter. "We need to get you cleaned up, Mr. Downs. Both you and I have some very important things that need to be discussed. Pilot, if you will."

The man nodded. "Will do, Sir."

And with that the pilot took the helicopter out and over towards the green tree-lined horizon.

The End of
PREHISTORIC
Bick Downs will return in
KAIJUS

Printed in Great Britain
by Amazon.co.uk, Ltd.,
Marston Gate.